THE ART OF DYING

Partners in Crime 4

JOSH LANYON
JORDAN CASTILLO PRICE

mlrpress

Published by
MLR Press, LLC
3052 Gaines Waterport Rd.
Albion, NY 14411

Visit ManLoveRomance Press, LLC on the Internet:
www.mlrpress.com

Edited by Judith David
Cover Art by Deana Jamroz
Printed in the United States of America.

ISBN# 978-1-934531-25-9

First Edition 2009

MLR Press Authors

Featuring a roll call of some of the best writers of gay erotica and mysteries today!

Maura Anderson
Victor J. Banis
Jeanne Barrack
Laura Baumbach
Alex Beecroft
Sarah Black
Ally Blue
J.P. Bowie
P.A. Brown
James Buchanan
Jordan Castillo Price
Kirby Crow
Dick D.
Jason Edding
Angela Fiddler
Dakota Flint
Kimberly Gardner
Storm Grant
Amber Green
LB Gregg
Drewey Wayne Gunn

Samantha Kane
Kiernan Kelly
JL Langley
Josh Lanyon
Clare London
William Maltese
Gary Martine
ZA Maxfield
Jet Mykles
L. Picaro
Neil Plakcy
Luisa Prieto
Rick R. Reed
AM Riley
George Seaton
Jardonn Smith
Caro Soles
Richard Stevenson
Claire Thompson
Kit Zheng

Check out titles, both available and forthcoming, at
www.mlrpress.com

LOVERS
AND OTHER
STRANGERS

JOSH LANYON

CHAPTER ONE

If he had been painting the scene before him, he would have used only four colors: Permanent Rose alkyd for the pink streaks in the fading sunset and the reflections in the water; Dioxazine Purple alkyd for the shadows lengthening on the creamy sand, the crevices of the rocks, the glint and gleam of water, the edges of the pier; Cadmium Yellow alkyd to blaze from windows, for the dimples in the sand, to limn the rocks, to gild the tips of scrubby, windblown grass, more reflections in the water; Indigo oil for the tumbling waves, for the indistinct forms of the buildings beyond, for the swift coming night.

For the first time in weeks, Finn felt the desire to take a palette knife and mix color, to pick up a brush and try to capture what he saw. For the first time in weeks, he felt a flicker of something close to interest, to emotion.

Maybe it was the salt air, maybe it was the cold — the briny wind whipping off the ocean stung his face — maybe it was the smell of wood smoke with all the warm memories it conjured. Or the cries of the gulls, the slap of the waves, the mingled fragrance of pipe smoke and car exhaust as he waited in the old station wagon for Hiram to carry his bags from the dock. Maybe it was all these things.

But it was the color he felt most intensely. Luminous color seeping into his consciousness, the hues and values, the shadows and lights, the dull tones, the vibrant — he was waking up. It was not a comfortable process, and Finn huddled deeper into his leather jacket.

Hiram strode to the car and threw Finn's bags in the back. Coming around to the front, he climbed in behind the wheel. Starting the engine, he glanced briefly at Finn as he backed the car, narrowly missing a leaning tower of stacked lobster traps.

"Guess it looks pretty different after all this time?"

Seal Island didn't look different at all in the purple dusk, but Finn said, "Three years is a long time."

"Ay-yup," Hiram said. "Your uncle Thomas is going to be happy as a clam at high tide to see you."

Finn's smile twisted. Everyone was being very kind. Especially considering what a pain in the ass he was to show up with almost no warning.

The station wagon crunched its way slowly over sand and shale, past the shadowy buildings and boats, the faded, peeling signs.

"'Course Thomas is in France right now. Some art show or another."

Finn murmured something. He didn't need to say anything. Hiram was happy to fill in all the blanks. There were a lot of blanks after so long.

"Martha's arthritis is giving her heck. Well, we're all gettin' older. Mr. Peabody's gone now. Pneumonia. Last month. Miz Landy took over the general store."

The car reached the surfaced road that ran around the island — smoother in some places than others. By now the amethyst dusk was falling back before the onslaught of night. Finn felt tension growing inside, his stomach knotting up with his fists. It was irrational. Irritating. Fear of the dark? At his age? It was cold, though — bitingly. After a short battle with himself, he reached for the rough plaid car blanket that smelled of a million journeys and spread it over his left leg, which had started aching.

"Not used to the cold anymore," he muttered, but Hiram took no notice, still palavering about people and things Finn had stopped caring about — tried to stop caring about — a long time ago. Ay-yup, what a pleasant surprise — shock, translated Finn — it had been to hear from Finn. Martha had been in a twitter ever since she got his message. And what a surprise Thomas had waiting for him when he got home. What a surprise it was going to be for everyone.

Finn almost asked then. But it was too much effort, and he wasn't sure even now he could take the answer, so he smiled politely and stared out the window as though he had newly arrived from another planet, which was pretty much how it felt.

Stands of pine trees stood stark and sharp against the dusk as the car climbed slowly, winding up through the rolling hills. The pines looked black against the lowering sky, but that was an illusion. He'd start with a sketch, using a No. 0 watercolor brush. For the sky and water, he'd use a blend of Cadmium Yellow Medium, Cadmium Red Light, and Titanium White. For the upper sky, he'd choose French Ultramarine, Dioxazine Purple and more Titanium White...

White. He had a sudden recollection of blazing white walls and the sun bouncing off pale sand — too much light, and a brightness that hurt the eyes. The white beneath a silent gull's wingspan, the white of the craggy clouds, the white of the tiny wildflowers growing beside the white speckled stone walls.

The lighthouse was on the other side of the island. No need to see it at all if he didn't choose to — and why the hell would he ever want to see it again?

Hiram was saying, "Miz Estelle won first prize at Union Fair for her wild blueberry sour cream cake."

Finn felt an unexpected twinge of hunger. "I still remember those cinnamon-sugar biscuits she used to make."

The old man nodded in heartfelt agreement.

The car turned off the main road and ground its way up the steep last stretch. The house was called The Birches. One of those charming turn-of-the-century, ten-bedroom "cottages," it stood in a grove of white birches overlooking Otter Cove. Green lawns swept down to the rocks at the water's edge, ancient, gently tilting pines framed sunsets so beautiful they made the heart ache. In the failing light, the house looked eerily untouched by time.

Hiram pulled up in front of the long front porch. Lights shone welcomingly from several downstairs windows.

"Ain't no place like home," he said, and Finn made a sound in his throat that was supposed to be humor but wasn't.

Hiram got out of the car. The front door of the house flew open, and Martha came bustling down the shell-strewn path as Finn climbed carefully out of the station wagon. Tears glittered on Martha's wrinkled cheeks, and she hugged him tight, pulling him to her ample bosom like he was a child again.

"Look at you, you young rascal!"

Finn didn't have to do much more than smile and permit himself to be hugged again; Martha was doing all the talking — although afterward he had no idea of anything she'd said. He was literally overwhelmed with memories and unwelcome emotion.

Hiram went to get the bags, and Finn was being urged inside the house to warmth and comfort — the prodigal returned. By then he was exhausted. He should have brought the cane; he was hobbling badly, not used to walking any distance yet, and the plane flight and boat ride not helping any. Maybe he was more crocked up than he wanted to admit — he was certainly in more pain.

The house smelled familiar. It smelled of baking and wood fire — and the invariable ghostly hint of oil paint, although it had been decades since anyone in the house painted with oils. It smelled like his childhood: safe and warm and loved. He stared curiously as he was hustled past a familiar painted chest, wing chairs upholstered in pale gray roses, white bookcases, well-remembered paintings. It felt odd to see these things again — like he was visiting a museum.

Ushered into the kitchen, he was ensconced in the old rocker and ordered to stay put near the enormous gas stove where Martha had cooked breakfast, lunch, and dinner for the Barrets for the past thirty years. That suited him fine. Gave him a chance to catch his breath and get control of himself.

Martha and Hiram conferred outside briefly — he could imagine how *that* went — and then Martha was inside the kitchen and chattering a mile a minute, banging pots and pans around to relieve her feelings.

Finn eyed her curiously from the perspective of his years away. She was in her late sixties now, a small, very plump woman with silky white hair — it had been white since her early thirties — and soft dark eyes. Something about her had always reminded him of a dove, though doves were fairly stupid birds and Martha was a far-from-stupid woman.

"Now that you've been living in New York, I suppose you won't be happy with fiddleheads and potatoes anymore? It'll be fancy curries and nouveau cuisine you're used to, I reckon."

Finn laughed — he lived on peanut butter sandwiches half the time — and said, "I haven't had a decent bowl of chowdah since I left here."

She stopped chattering then, coming to him, putting her hands on either side of his head. She turned his face to the light, examining him closely. The only damage that showed was the one scar — still healing — on his temple. What didn't show was the horrific long gash from his hip to the middle of his calf. Torn muscles, damaged nerves, but oddly no broken bones. He had been left with one hell of an ugly seam down his leg, but he knew how lucky he had been. And aside from the scars, he was going to be as good as new eventually. That was why he had to stop dwelling on the might-have-beens. The close call didn't matter, because he was going to be all right — as soon as the headaches stopped.

Martha was staring into his eyes as though trying to read his mind. He blinked up at her, and her eyes filled with tears again. She kissed him — something he couldn't remember her doing since he had been very small. She was clearly horrified at herself. Not as horrified as he was, though — not that she had kissed him, but that he had been so moved, his throat closed and he had to look away.

It was only for an instant. Nothing more than the aftermath of the accident — and probably his meds. It did something to you, nearly dying. And dying sometimes felt like the least of it.

"Your uncle Thomas will be here tonight," she said.

That snapped him out of his self-consciousness. "Uncle Tom? I thought…"

"Why, I phoned him the minute I heard from you," Martha said a little defiantly — because Finn had expressly told her not to bother Thomas. "Of course he'd want to know! Of course he's coming home. And while I'm thinking of it, that friend of yours phoned up. Mr. Ryder. He's coming day after tomorrow."

The funny thing about the spell the island cast, the silken weave of childhood memories, was that he'd already forgotten he'd asked Paul to come along and lend moral support. Now he wondered why. Paul was going to be a fish out of water here, and Finn was going to have to expend energy he didn't have in trying to keep him amused. Paul took a lot of amusing.

He brooded over this while Martha rattled cheerfully on, finally surfacing to hear her say, "…Barnaby Purdon retired from school teaching."

"Do he and Uncle Tom still get together to play checkers once a week?"

"Every Wednesday when your uncle is here. What else? Oh, Miss Minton took first place at Union Fair for her wild blueberry sour cream cake."

"I heard that. Is she still taking painting lessons from Uncle Tom?"

"No. No, she gave up on that idea. Your uncle Tom doesn't teach anymore, you know. Too busy judging art shows and writing his books."

She brought him a mug of coffee. Finn took the yellow cup, sipping cautiously. It was boiling hot, but creamy and sweet — the way he had liked it when he was a kid. Creamy and sweet — and spiked with something.

"What's in this?" he asked. "I'm on pain pills, you know." In fact, he urgently needed medicating. His back was beginning to ache — his leg never quite stopped — and his head was starting up again despite the muted light and warmth.

"A little something to warm your bones," Martha told him. "It won't do you any harm. Might put a little color in your face."

Finn raised his brows but kept drinking. It was good. Martha's version of an Irish coffee perhaps. All at once he was so tired he thought he might fall asleep at the fireside wrapped like an ancient granny in these cedar-scented blankets. Martha chattered comfortably on about this and that person, the changes he would soon see in the island — and of course, in Martha's view, none of the changes were for the better.

He smiled to himself and sipped his coffee.

His smiled faded as she said, "Mr. Carlyle has a new book coming out."

She was not looking at him, which was just as well, since he couldn't think of anything to say.

"He's not here now. He was in England for the six months doing research for the one he's writing now. It's supposed to be a murder mystery about the princes in the Tower. And then he went on a book tour for the last one. It's hard to keep 'em all straight. I don't expect we'll see him back till next month sometime."

That was a relief. More than he wanted to concede. "I'll be long gone by then." His voice came out flat.

Martha still didn't look at him. "Well…that's all right so long as you don't take three years to visit again."

She spoke cheerfully, but he could hear the strain and knew that he had to make the effort. For his own sake, if nothing else. Had to prove that he could say it and not…well, what? That he had moved past it. That it was over and done with, chapter closed. Not forgiven, not forgotten…but old history. Con should appreciate that.

So he said, "How's Fitch?"

And after a funny little pause, Martha said, as though the name were unfamiliar to her, "Fitch?"

"Is he…?" He tried to make his voice light, but he was never good at that kind of thing. Fitch was the old pro at games and deceiving. "Are he and Con… Did they… Are they still together?"

"Fitch and…Mr. Carlyle?" She said it almost wonderingly.

Finn remembered belatedly that this was a small island, a backwoods sort of place really, and that while a romantic relationship between two men might be silently tolerated and civilly ignored, it was never going to be openly acknowledged and condoned. But his nerves were on edge, he was tired and much more raw than he had realized; he simply blurted out, "Or did he split?"

Martha said, "Didn't Fitch come to you in New York?"

"Come to me?" That made him blink. What a funny idea — but maybe not so funny, because Fitch wouldn't see what he had done wrong, would he? He would expect to be forgiven as he always was by his — his words — *better half.*

"Didn't Fitch follow you to New York?" asked Martha again, and she was staring at him hard now, as though only realizing that something was very wrong. But Fitch had always been her favorite. Fitch was everyone's favorite for all he shocked and appalled people with his outrageous — but God, yes, funny — antics. The things he did and said. It was impossible not to love Fitch.

Even when you hated him.

Finn said, "He didn't follow me to New York."

Had that been Fitch's intention? Had better sense prevailed? It must have hurt Fitch too; he must have felt the same persistent ache that was almost physical pain, the pain of being cut off from your other half. A phantom pain, like losing a limb. It had never happened to them before: a break so deep, so wide, there was no bridging it. Oh, they had fought, fallen out — what brothers didn't quarrel? Finn had always forgiven Fitch, because…he loved him. And he couldn't do without him. Until he could.

Until Con.

Because there was no forgiving that. Con had been different.

Not that Con wasn't every bit as much to blame.

But then Finn hadn't forgiven Con either. Never would.

Anyway, it was a long time ago. He was never going to see Con again. So what did it matter? As for seeing Fitch…he had always accepted that Fitch knew how seriously he had transgressed, because he hadn't followed his twin to New York.

And that was just as well, because as lonely as he had been, there was no forgiveness in Finn.

Not then. Maybe not ever. Something had died in Finn that summer. That last day of summer.

But now he sat in the kitchen of the house he had grown up in, the home he had shared for twenty-three years with his twin. Slowly, he worked it out, tried to absorb what it meant. He said, "Fitch isn't here?"

And Martha shook her head slowly, her bright, birdlike eyes wide.

Reading her expression, Finn smiled reassurance, because it seemed ridiculous — like they were talking at cross purposes and they would soon realize what the other actually meant. In a moment they would laugh as the misunderstanding was straightened out. "You mean no one's seen him since...?"

"No."

"No?" He took it in slowly, absorbing it much like the heat soaking into his chilled body or the alcohol wending its way through his bloodstream — a gradual realization that he was warm and tipsy and...alone in the world.

He said carefully, "No one has seen or spoken to Fitch in three years?"

"No." And Martha looked...frightened. It was her fear that woke Finn to the belated realization that his twin brother was missing.

"Come here, Huckleberry," Con murmured. His pale hair was wet and dripping from their swim, his bare brown skin shining in the sun. His dark eyes laughed into Finn's, and his mouth — covering Finn's — was sweet with the taste of the berries. His skin smelled like the sun and clean sweat and deep water.

From overhead came a burst of laughter —

A hand on Finn's shoulder woke him. He jerked, opened his eyes, and his uncle Thomas was gazing down him. Uncle Tom was smiling, but his eyes were grave.

"Welcome home, Finn."

"Hi," Finn said. It was probably a little anticlimactic after three years, but he was fogged from sleep, disoriented to suddenly find himself in the kitchen at The Birches. He straightened, wiped his eyes with the heel of his hand. "I must have fallen asleep."

Martha chuckled, although her voice had that strained note again. "Sleep is exactly what you need!"

"Sounds good to me," Uncle Thomas said, sounding and looking weary. He was tall and very thin with the bony features and red-brown hair that distinguished the Barrets from the rest of the small population of Seal Island. Now in his sixties, he was going silver at the temples, which perfectly suited his image as an esteemed art critic.

"I didn't intend for you to be dragged home from Paris," Finn apologized.

His uncle was looking at him as though he were speaking a foreign language. Translation having failed, Uncle Thomas said, "Martha told me about your accident. Said you insisted you didn't want anyone there at the hospital. You're all right?"

"A few bumps and bruises."

"Well, you're staying here till you're back on your feet."

Finn chuckled. "I'm on my feet now." Or he would be if he could unfold from this rocker without landing on his face.

"You know what I mean." Uncle Thomas said it firmly; that was the polite fiction they had all played. That Uncle Thomas was actually in charge. He had been, at best, an absentminded guardian, but he was fond of them in his own way, and Finn and Fitch had certainly never lacked for anything growing up. Well, possibly attention. But then they had always had each other, so nothing else really mattered.

"Yes," Finn said. "Thank you."

"This is your home," Martha said sharply. Both men looked at her, having forgotten for a second that she was in the room, and she blushed. But she said stubbornly, "It's not right, you and Fitch gone all these years and never coming back for so much as a visit."

"Now, Martha," Uncle Thomas said in his easy way. "He's here now." To Finn he said, "It's too late for talk tonight. We'll catch up in the morning. Did you need some help getting to bed?"

"I'm okay. Is it really that late?" Finn looked automatically for the old wall clock, shaped like a ship's wheel, but it was gone, replaced by an efficient and modern titanium square.

"Nearly midnight," Uncle Thomas said. "I meant to be here much earlier, but my flight was delayed."

Nearly midnight? Could that be right? Could he really have been sleeping for over six hours? "Hell. You really shouldn't have dropped everything to come home for this." Finn was growing more awkward by the minute. "I didn't mean to disrupt everyone's life. I just…"

Just needed time to rest and recover. Time to come to terms with how close he had been to dying. To losing everything. Time to regain his strength and natural optimism; he was still astonishingly, aggravatingly *weak*. In fact, as he forced himself up out of the comfortable rocker, he was made painfully aware of how feeble he still was.

"Nonsense," Uncle Thomas and Martha both said — and then looked at each other.

Martha said, "But you've neither of you had any supper."

"I ate on the flight," Uncle Thomas said, which happily distracted her while Finn stood swaying, biting his lip against the myriad aches and pangs and throbs.

Uncle Thomas said with unexpected determination, "I think I'll give you a hand upstairs anyway."

Finn nodded. No point pretending he didn't need it. Uncle Thomas wrapped a strong arm around his waist, and Finn hung on to him as Martha bade them good night.

"I'm stiff from sitting so long." Finn explained as they passed slowly through the hall with its lilac sprig wallpaper. "I really am fine now."

"Of course you are. You'll be working again in no time."

Ah. Of course. In this house, the work was paramount. Well, it was to Finn too.

They crossed the dining room with the long formal table and harp-backed chairs where they had all eaten dinner when his grandfather was alive, across the back hallway, and then up the narrow staircase with the gleaming banisters Finn recalled sliding down as a child. Or was it Fitch who had slid down the banisters and Finn who watched? Sometimes it was hard to separate Fitch's adventures from his own memories.

Uncle Thomas's voice jarred him out of his preoccupation. "Martha said your friend was killed in the accident."

Finn nodded tightly.

"Was he...was your friend...?"

Uncle Thomas floundered awkwardly, and Finn said, "He was a friend, that's all. A good friend. He yanked the wheel at the last minute so that his side of the car took the worst of it."

The stairs seemed to take forever. Finn could have cried in gratitude by the time they reached the upper landing — then the final leg to his old room, the room that had been his since his teens. Fitch's room was on the other side of the adjoining black-and-white checked bath.

There was no sign of Finn's bags, but his pajama bottoms and robe were lain across the foot of the dark wood sleigh bed. He bit back a tired smile. Martha would have unpacked while he slept downstairs. There was no privacy in this house. Lucky thing Finn had no secrets. Not anymore.

Uncle Thomas helped him undress. It was embarrassing, but Finn really was exhausted beyond action now. With his uncle's help, he pulled on knit sleep pants — and though the older man said nothing, Finn saw his face tighten up at the terrifying scar down the left side of Finn's body. One inch more, and Finn would have died with Tristan.

"You won't be warm enough like that," Uncle Thomas said. "You've forgotten how cold the winters are here. I'll get you one of my pajama tops."

He was gone down the hallway, and Finn sat looking around the room. Once again he had that weird sensation of looking at an exhibit in a museum. Books and model ships... He stared at the framed photographs on the bookshelves: pictures of himself and Fitch sailing and climbing and fishing and swimming. A skinny eleven-year-old Fitch's arm looped around his neck in a friendly choke hold, himself giving the eighteen-year-old Fitch an impromptu piggyback. People said they couldn't be told apart, but Finn never had to wonder who was who in the pictures — not even in the earliest photographs of them.

Uncle Thomas returned with a striped flannel pajama shirt, and Finn shrugged into it, did up the buttons.

"Is it true Fitch left the island when I did?" he asked, eyes on the buttonholes.

"Yes."

"And no one's heard of him since?"

"I don't think that's so surprising," Uncle Thomas said grimly. Finn wasn't exactly sure what he meant. Surely no one knew the full story of what had happened that day? But he was too tired to question.

He crawled into bed, rediscovering the pleasure of clean flannel sheets that smelled faintly of the crisp ocean breeze. Stretching out gingerly, his spine seemed to unkink like a Slinky. He was astonished when his uncle shook the folds out of the quilt at the foot of the bed and spread it over him.

"Good night," he said politely, wondering if he was about to be tucked in and kissed.

He was spared that much. The bedside lamp went out, and his uncle said quietly, "Good night, Finn. I'm glad you've come home." He went out. The door closed silently behind him, shutting Finn into the darkness.

His heart began to pound, turning over sickly in his chest. Finn waited, sweat breaking out along his hairline as he listened.

Through the dormer windows, he could see the mutable darkness that was the sea; stars glittered on the waves, pinpoints of light.

No need for panic. There was plenty of light. Moonlight, starlight, reflected light...

His uncle's footsteps died away down the hallway. Finn sat up and turned on the lamp.

He relaxed, let out a long breath. In the mellow glow, the books and toys of his childhood looked very old, very fragile.

He stared at the photos of his cheekily grinning twin and whispered, "Where are you, Fitch?"

They had grown up on the island; the Barret Boys, people called them. Their grandfather was Holloway Barret, the famous artist. His lush illustrations, reminiscent of an earlier period, livened up all kinds of dry history tomes and sappy children's stories. Their mother was Pamela Barret, whose elegant watercolors hung in galleries and private collections all around the world. But here on Seal Island off the coast of Maine, they were simply the Barrets, and Finn and Fitch were the Barret Boys. Sometimes Those Damned Barret Boys. But they were good kids mostly, and it was a tightly knit community, and they had grown up safe and sheltered.

For a time it looked as though the Barret drive for success had skipped a generation. Fitch had been expelled from college after one too many pranks, and Finn had flunked out. In Finn's case, it was homesickness as much as anything else. That, and desperation to paint — really paint — not spend his life talking about painting or studying how others did it. At twenty, he had returned to the island in disgrace, for the first time experiencing what it felt like to disappoint the people you love. A feeling Fitch was well acquainted with and had learned, mostly, to laugh off.

He had certainly laughed off Finn's guilt. Finn had done exactly what he wanted, why feel guilty? And if he felt truly bad about it, he could always go to Grandy, who would pull a few strings and get Finn admitted to another brand-name college where he could excel at listening politely to people who had never painted a real dab in their lives tell the people with talent what to do. Well, Finn didn't feel *that* bad about it, and Fitch had laughed at him again.

Grandy had been less amused. Finishing university was about discipline and learning your craft and respect — it was nothing to do with talent. It was already obvious Finn was the keeper of the flame for his generation of Barrets. Even when he had been quite young, messing around in his mother's studio, he had heard the adults quietly appraising him and agreeing; Finn had "the gift." No, Finn had failed by leaving school, and Fitch was equally to blame for encouraging him.

The fact that Grandy had never gone to college was irrelevant.

And how the hell dare Fitch disparage art critics and art teachers when his uncle Thomas was one of the same, and a damned fine one!

Never mind that Fitch had been practically quoting Grandy verbatim.

That had led to one of Fitch and Grandy's famous blowups, which ended with Fitch leaving the island yet again. He was gone for nine months that time — only returning when their mother lay dying.

Finn, quietly accepting that he was in disgrace, returned to his painting and blissfully lost himself in the work. He politely ignored everyone's disappointment and disapproval — it only lasted a week or two had he even been aware of it. He was pretty much unaware of everyone and everything but the work. That was the summer he had finally given himself over to painting.

He had missed Fitch, of course, but he had missed Fitch in college too, and Fitch did periodically disappear when he and Grandy butted heads. No one antagonized Grandy like Fitch, and yet the old man adored him — when he wasn't calling for his head on a palette. But then everyone adored Fitch. Finn did. Their mother had postponed her painful dying that long summer in order to spend as much time as possible with her eldest.

But that first spring — the spring after Finn had bailed out of college — was the happiest of his life. He felt that he had at last come into his own; he was consumed with painting, with "making up for lost time," which (had he known it) amused the adults around him no end. He ate, drank, and slept painting. It was all he thought about, all he wanted.

For years it was all he wanted. And then Conlan Carlyle came home.

Conlan Carlyle, the writer — the writer of dry and dusty histories that, as Fitch had once said, could have used Grandy's illustrations to perk them up. Con Carlyle was by way of being a neighbor although his folks were "summer folk," wealthy New Yorkers who summered in their elegant and enormous "cottage" on the island. Con hadn't any time for the Barret Boys, being so much older and busy with his own friends — female and otherwise...

So many recollections; it could have been memory lane down which Finn was making his painstaking way rather than the path that led from The Birches to Gull Point. It was the morning after his arrival on Seal Island. He had borrowed his grandfather's old walking stick, a maple cane with a nickel-silver wolf-head handle, and he was suffering the fresh air and sunshine so beloved by physicians everywhere. The fact that it was fucking *freezing* skipped everyone's notice. There were thin layers of ice over the puddles in the path as he hobbled slowly past the black fir spinneys and meadows turning gold and red in the late autumn.

Automatically, his eye began isolating colors into the paints he would use...Raw Sienna, Old Holland Yellow, Indian Red, Burnt Umber, Burnt Sienna, Cadmium Orange...

He didn't want to remember how things used to be, but it was impossible here with the salt scent of the ocean, the chill spice of pines, the taint of wood smoke — funny how fragrance brought it all back.

He passed Estelle Minton's house. Yellow shingles and red brick, red roses behind a white picket fence. The roses Estelle had been in the process of planting three years ago were now tall — if wind-tattered. At this time of year, her beloved garden was not at its best. Smoke rose cozily from the chimney. Finn half expected Estelle to wave him down — rarely did anyone slip past her front window without being spotted — but if she saw him, she did not come out to say hello, and Finn walked on, dogged by memory.

"You're Finn," Con had said. "The Barret boy." As though there were only one Barret boy.

He was twenty-three that spring, and he had met Con — literally bumped into him — walking into the Curtis Memorial Library. He had gone to the mainland to pick up art supplies and a couple of Ross MacDonald mysteries for Grandy. His thoughts had been a million miles away; he'd spent days trying to paint the fishing fleet's sunset return but couldn't get it right — and he had walked right into the tall man coming out the west entrance.

At the time he had thought the collision was his own fault, but now he realized Con had been nearly as distracted as he was. It was Con who had reached out to steady him, hands warm on Finn's arms.

"Whoa! All right?" he'd said, and he was smiling, a cynical twist of his lips as though this was exactly the kind of behavior he expected from the natives. And then his brown-black gaze had seemed to sharpen. "You're...Finn. The Barret boy."

Finn recognized him immediately, although it had been at least two years since he'd seen Con Carlyle. All the same, he was genuinely surprised. People — strangers — had trouble telling them apart, and when had Con Carlyle been anything but a stranger, for all that they'd summered on the same island for twenty-three years?

"Yeah. How did you know?" he'd asked.

Con had smiled again — and the smile was a revelation. Finn had never seen Conlan genuinely smile. Oh, maybe a polite grimace when someone — often Fitch — was acting more like an idiot than usual; Fitch had always had a little bit of a thing about Con Carlyle.

Con had grinned that devastatingly attractive grin and raised his elegant eyebrows. "How could I *not* know you? You've been stealing my blueberries and swimming in my cove for the last twenty years."

"Twenty-three, but who's counting?"

He was so very attractive — pale hair, a lean, ascetic face, sable eyes lighting with unexpected laughter. It was like one of those paintings of old saints suddenly coming to life, suddenly animated and vivid.

"But maybe I'm Fitch," Finn had suggested.

And Con said, "You're not Fitch."

The funny part was that at the time Finn had imagined it was a compliment.

But he didn't want to remember these things. What was the point of sinking down into quaggy, regretful thoughts? If he was going to dredge all that up, better to focus on the hurt, the anger, the betrayal. But why think of it at all? It was a long time ago, and he had more important things to worry about.

Like…the fact that he had walked too far from the house. That was his impatience getting the better of him, but to hell with "not rushing things." What did that mean? You could only rest for so long. And what on earth did peace and quiet have to do with anything? It wasn't as though he lived in a box beneath a freeway underpass. This whole idea of being sent away to recover his health was so fucking Victorian.

Even more irritating was the fact that the only place he had been able to think of going to recuperate was Seal Island. What had he been thinking? But at the time — or perhaps it was due to too much pain medication — he had yearned for home like the homesick college kid he had once been. And of course the doctors thought Seal Island was a terrific idea. The fresh salt air, the sunshine, the long, quiet nights — everyone cheerfully ignorant of how goddamned cold it was, and how…painful and tiring to face the memories you had been running from for so long.

At least he didn't have to face anything more than the ghosts. Con was safely on his book tour, and Fitch…

That was strange about Fitch.

All these months…years without word. That wasn't like Fitch. Even when he had clashed with Grandy the last time, he had stayed in touch with Finn. Granted, he couldn't very well stay in touch with Finn this time.

Still…

The spark of uneasiness Finn had felt on initially hearing that Fitch was missing had kindled into quiet worry. Three years was a very long time to disappear without a word. And Fitch had never been one to hold a grudge — nor had Fitch any reason to hold a grudge, since he had come out the winner that time.

Finn became aware that with his thoughts running elsewhere, his feet had followed the familiar path to the cottage by Bell Woods. The cottage was on the edge of the old Carlyle estate; Con worked there most days, safely out of reach of his devoted family. There was no phone at the cottage — or at least there had not been a phone three years ago.

For a time Finn stood, leaning on Grandy's cane, studying the white shingles and black shutters, the brick chimney and neglected garden. He felt surprisingly little. It was only a building, after all, and the memories existed independently of the architecture.

Lost in these thoughts, he noticed too late the door to the cottage swinging open. Con stepped outside. "Finn," he said.

There was an alarming moment when Finn thought his mind had snapped, that he was rolling and sliding off the edge of sanity, and then he realized that he was not imagining things. Con was striding down the path toward him.

Too late to flee even if could manage it without looking like the loser in a three-legged race. So he held his ground, clenching his grandfather's walking stick, as Con reached him.

"Finn," Con said again, and he sounded out of breath.

He had not changed much in three years. Tall and lithe, his hair was still ash-blond, straight, and fine as silk, but he wore it a little longer now. His eyes were a shade of brown-black that Finn had never managed to determine; he remembered reading in one of the books his grandfather had illustrated about a pirate with "sparkling black cherry eyes," and he'd always thought that perfectly described Con's eyes — although the wicked laughing eyes were at odds with a face as elegantly and distantly beautiful as the saint in a Renaissance painting. But there were faint little lines now around Con's mouth and eyes, a tightness to his features. He looked tired like he'd run too long and too far and had still not found what he was looking for.

Idiotically, the only thing Finn could think to say was, "I didn't know you were back."

"I got back last night."

Good Lord. They should have held out for a group rate given the amount of traffic to the island yesterday.

"Oh. Well…nice to see you." Finn turned to go, leaning heavily on the cane.

"Wait." Con jerked out, "Can you…come inside for a minute?"

"Not today." Finn kept moving, crablike, trying to escape. "I've got to get back."

"Finn —" Con came alongside him.

In his slow-motion panic, his foot turned on a stone, and Con reached out to steady him. Every nerve in Finn's body flinched away from his touch. He'd thought he was over it, but the feel of Con's hand — the warm weight through his sweater — warned him otherwise. Bewilderingly, it was as though no time had passed at all, all his emotions were boiling right there at the surface.

"Jesus, Finn, you're white to your lips. You should never have walked so far. Come in out of the cold for a few minutes." Con looked — Finn didn't think it was an expression he could capture on canvas. It surely wasn't an expression he remembered ever seeing before on Con's face.

"Please," Con said.

It was something in the way he said "please." Not a word Con had ever used a lot. Certainly not with Finn. As he stared at him, Finn was suddenly and utterly exhausted — light-headed with it. It was borne in on him how very far he had walked — and what a bad idea that had been. His head began that slow, ominous pound. He allowed himself to be led inside the cottage.

It was blessedly dim and warm inside. A fire crackled welcomingly in the fireplace, classical music was playing softly, the wooden blinds stirred in the draft, finding a way through the window casement. A stack of printed pages sat neatly beside a desktop and printer. It hadn't changed.

Finn dropped down on the long leather sofa, put a hand over his eyes. Con hovered.

"I can't believe you're here,"

Finn looked at him and failed to think of anything intelligent to say. He agreed, though. Quite fucking unbelievable that he was here.

"Can I get you anything?"

"Ouch. No." Finn shifted gingerly. Dropped the cane.

Con retrieved the cane and propped it within Finn's reach. Con straightened, and Finn realized he was staring at the bones of Finn's knees poking at his Levi's, at his wrists, which still looked too thin for the rolled cuffs of his sweater.

"I heard about your accident," Con said. "Are you... You're all right now?"

"I'm fine." He looked away.

"Relax, Finn. You look like you're going to fly up the chimney any second."

Finn's mouth curled. He didn't fly so well these days.

"Sit back," Con was urging, and Finn cautiously lifted his leg onto the sofa. Easing back, he sighed relief. Yeah, whatever made Con doubt he was in great shape?

He became aware that Con still hovered over him. He looked up warily. Con asked, "Do you have anything you can take?"

"Huh?"

"For the pain."

"Oh." Finn grimaced. "This isn't that bad. Anyway, I don't like taking that crap. It makes me dopey."

"So? I'll run you back. Go ahead and take the stuff." Con strode out of the room. From the kitchen, Finn heard water running, the sound of ice cube trays cracking open.

He closed his eyes, trying not to give in to the hot, throbbing poker of pain jamming into the base of his skull. Overexertion, that's all it was. Maybe there was something to that not-rushing thing.

"Here, Finn."

His eyes flew open. He hadn't heard Con return, but he stood over the couch with a glass of water.

Finn inched up against the cushions, found his pills, palmed two, and reached for the glass.

He handed the water back to Con, who set it aside and pulled up a footstool.

"Finn...I've been waiting three years to talk to you."

Goddamn. If that wasn't just like Con. After three years, it was all about getting off his chest whatever it was he'd forgotten to say the last time.

"Oh, man. Please don't." Finn shut his eyes, leaning back. He really did not have the strength to deal with this now. Why the hell had he walked down this way? Why the hell hadn't someone warned him Con was back?

Con's voice dropped. "I know what you're thinking."

"Yeah?" He grinned faintly at that.

"Please hear me out."

"I can't exactly run away."

Silence.

Finn opened his eyes. Con looked as though he were in more pain than Finn. Meeting Finn's gaze, he said, "I've thought about that day a million times."

A million times? Why, in three years, that would be nine hundred times a day. Impressive. Finn said, "Forget it. Ancient history."

Silence. Anger began to bubble up inside Finn. Why did Con have to start this up again? It was over. Done. Why couldn't they preserve a polite fiction...like neither of them remembered or cared? What the hell did Con want from him?

But Con plowed on. "To this day I don't know why... I don't understand how I let it happen. I didn't want that. I didn't want him." His voice sank so low, Finn hardly recognized it.

He said wearily, "We both know what it was, and it *doesn't matter*. Forget it."

"I *can't* forget it. Not a day goes by that I don't remember what a fool I was."

Finn said irritably, "Well, you need to forget it. It was three years ago. What's the point of bringing this up now? It's over."

"It's not over for me."

Finn stared at him, torn between shock and outrage. His heart was starting to slug his ribs like an angry prizefighter preparing for a match.

"What are you talking about?" He pushed up on an elbow and realized he was already starting to feel the effects of the pills. "You're not going to pretend — This is such bullshit. Do you need me to say I forgive you? Fine. I forgive you, Con. I chalked it up to a learning experience."

Maybe that was a cheap shot. Con swallowed hard. "Finn. God." He scrubbed his face with his hands. "You hate me, don't you?"

"Not at all."

He heard his tone: polite. Con heard it too.

"I was afraid you would feel like this if I didn't —" His jaw worked. "But you were so...adamant. I thought...give him time to cool down. I tried writing..."

Finn had received the letters — he'd tossed them.

The medication was kicking in big-time; the sofa beginning to glide in slow, lazy swoops. Finn dropped back in the cushions. All at once he felt quite relaxed. He felt like being candid. Why not? What did he have to lose? Nothing. "I don't know why it mattered so much, Con. I know how Fitch is, and I always knew it wasn't anything more than a summer romance for you —"

"Finn."

"You made it pretty clear, really." He smiled faintly at unfocused memory. "You were scrupulous about never saying you loved me or anything, so I don't know why I feel the way...the way I did... Maybe I was embarrassed because it meant so much to *me* —"

Con kissed him, his mouth covering Finn's, warm and insistent. Finn was too narcotized to do more than murmur a vague protest. Con released him immediately.

"I'm sorry. Damn it to hell. I'm sorry, Finn."

"Me too," he said woozily. "Love to chat. Have to...sleep now..."

He thought Con answered that, but by then Finn was whirling away into a comfortable blankness.

When he woke, it was to darkness.

Panic gripped him, and he threw out a hand for the lamp beside his bed, but there was only empty space. Instead of sheets, there was a giving stiffness beneath him — leather. At the same instant he realized he was dressed, although his shoes were missing, and that he was tangled in some kind of afghan. Desperately, he struggled up, saying, "Turn on the light!"

Even as Finn absorbed that the room was not in complete darkness — embers burned molten orange in a grate, and platinum moonlight filtered through slats of the blinds — a darker shadow detached itself from the sable nothingness.

A light snapped on.

Bright, inarguable light, golden warmth turning the room from a threatening unknown to a collection of comfortable old furniture and familiar paintings, one of them his own.

Con was crossing to him, saying, "I'm sorry. I thought you would sleep better with it off."

Finn scrabbled to collect himself. Between the dark and Con, it was a rocky awakening. He tried to hide that moment of naked fear, pushing into the corner of the sofa and raking a hand through his hair.

"I didn't know where I was." He tried to say it casually; his heart still racing and bounding like a deer in terror. Given the way Con was looking at him, he wasn't sure how successful he was. "You shouldn't have let me sleep so long."

Con ignored that. "Are you feeling all right?"

"Fine."

"You're quite sure?" Con was frowning, studying him.

"I'm sure." Actually, now that the unreasoning alarm was receding, he realized that he had slept well, and the nap had refreshed him. His head had stopped hurting, and his back was about as pain free as it got these days. Self-consciously, he smothered a yawn under Con's searching gaze. "What time is it?"

"After five."

"Oh hell. Martha is going to think I fell off a cliff." He glanced around the cottage. "You haven't —"

"Installed a phone? No." Con liked being incommunicado when he was working, and that was the purpose of the cottage — although they had used it for other things once upon a time.

Better not to think of that now.

"You still don't carry a cell phone?"

"I'm morally and ethically opposed to cell phones." Con was smiling, but Finn knew he wasn't entirely kidding.

"I left mine in Manhattan." Then, "What?" he asked edgily as Con continued to stare at him.

"You can't know. It's...to see you sitting there again. To hear your voice. You don't know how long I've —"

"Don't."

Con nodded tightly. After an awkward pause, he said, "I'll run you back now if you like."

"I like." He reached for his cane. Con slipped a hand under his elbow, giving him a lift to his feet.

Finn appreciated the no-fuss tact of that, but he resented needing help. Where Con was concerned, he was a mess of contradictory feelings. He freed his arm, not rudely but pointedly enough that Con's face tightened.

Saying nothing, he helped Finn into his jacket again, the juggle of cane and flapping sleeves, and then Finn was doing up his jacket and Con was going to the cottage door.

He walked out of the cottage ahead of Finn, feet crunching on the shell-strewn path, a small, angry sound. It was a relief to Finn to realize that he didn't care that Con was upset. Time had been he would have been racking his brains for what he'd done, how to fix it, whether it was going to end between them. He could even spare a small twisted smile now for that insecure boy.

Con opened the Land Rover door and stood back. This was the tricky part, climbing up into the seat while hanging on to both his cane and dignity. Finn knew Con wouldn't offer help unless he asked for it.

He requested gruffly, "Will you give me a hand up?" and knew Con felt like a bastard for forcing the request.

Con took the cane from Finn's hand, set it aside. Finn turned nervously, not sure what to expect, and then Con slipped one arm around his waist, half lifting him into the seat without any apparent effort. Unnecessary and startling, but certainly efficient. Finn flicked him a quick, uncertain look, but Con's face gave nothing away.

He handed Finn his cane; then Con shut the door and walked around to his side of the vehicle. Finn buckled himself in; his heart was beating fast, and he knew it had something to do with being in Con's arms again for those brief heartbeats.

Con started the engine. Neither of them looked at the other or spoke as the Land Rover bounced over the potholes and rocks. Out of the corner of Finn's eye, he could see Con's profile, grim as the imperial profile on an old coin. Like an emperor of ancient Rome with a rebellious senate on his hands.

They hit a bigger hole in the road, and the truck came down hard. Finn must have caught his breath, because Con glanced his way.

"Sorry. Does it give you a lot of trouble?"

"What's that?" he managed to ask calmly.

"Your leg. What do the doctors say?"

"It's fine. Mostly. I'm supposed to exercise it regularly. Which is why I walked too far today." In case Con thought he had deliberately strolled down memory lane.

Silence.

They passed Gull Point. Across the bay, Finn could see the ghostly white tower of the old lighthouse. He looked away.

Con said slowly, "Or is it driving in general? Is it still difficult getting in a car?"

Funny that Con would understand that. Finn didn't have to answer; one sharp look had confirmed Con's guess. His foot eased off the gas, and Finn relaxed his white-knuckle grip on the armrest as they slowed to a sedate jog.

After another mile or so, Con questioned, "Do you remember anything about the accident?"

"I remember thinking *oh shit* as the truck plowed into us." He added wryly, "Famous last words." Finn glanced at Con and was startled at how green he looked in the lights from the dashboard.

The rest of the short drive to The Birches passed without further discussion, which was a relief to Finn.

Con parked in the shell-shaped drive in front of the long porch and opened his door.

"You don't have to get out," Finn started quickly, but Con ignored him, coming round to his side.

He opened Finn's door, waiting in silence as Finn fumbled the seat belt. Yanking it open at last, Finn reached to steady himself on the hand rest. Con took his other arm, ignoring the exasperated look Finn threw him.

"Can I see you again?" Con asked as Finn clambered awkwardly out of the Land Rover and grabbed for his cane.

"I'm sure we'll run into each other."

"That's not what I meant."

"I know." It was hard to look away from the pain in Con's dark eyes.

"I still care for you, Finn."

Finn's hand was clutching the cane so tightly his fingers hurt.

"I want to make things right."

Finn bent his head. Took a deep breath. "I'm sorry," he said and met Con's gaze. "I don't feel the same."

Con stared at him, then nodded curtly.

Finn waited politely as Con got back into the Rover and reversed in a smooth, neat arc.

That had been easy enough. The only problem was, he thought, watching the taillights as Con drove away — he knew he hadn't told Con the truth.

They had not spoken of Fitch. Not even said his name. Later, sitting at dinner with Uncle Thomas, that seemed strange.

The whole day — the whole trip so far — had a strange dreamlike quality to it. Maybe that wasn't surprising given the meds he was taking and the fact that he'd spent a good part of the afternoon napping on Con's sofa. What had he dreamed there? He had no recollection, but he had slept deeply and well. Better than he could remember sleeping for a very long time.

He'd had to tell Martha, of course — she had been giving him an earful about vanishing without a word, listing in Martha fashion all the terrible things that she had imagined happening to him. He'd stopped her at falling off the ledge at Gull Point.

"I didn't go to the point. I walked down to Con's cottage."

Martha had fallen silent, eyeing him a little doubtfully. "That's too far for you to walk yet," she scolded feebly.

"Con's back," Finn told her. "I spoke to him. In fact…"

She waited, and he could see the worry in the back of her eyes.

He said, "It's not a big deal. I overdid it walking down there, and he let me rest on his sofa. That's what took so long."

"Is…everything all right?"

Finn's smile was rueful. "It's okay. He said his piece. I said mine. We're never going to be pals again."

He was surprised when she turned away from him and began rolling out dough on the lightly floured breadboard. Without turning to face him, she said, "We're not so backward as you might think, Finn. We still get the newspapers and now days we get satellite TV and the Internet. We've heard of gay people all the way out here, and we're not all as close-minded as you might have been telling yourself these three years."

Finn couldn't think of anything to say.

Martha, still not looking at him, said, "It wasn't ever any secret that you and Fitch were a little bit different, and I was glad when it turned out how you felt that young Mr. Carlyle was a little bit that way too."

The rolling pin made a comfortable and familiar thump on the board as she rolled with ferocious energy.

"I know something happened with Fitch to spoil it. I don't know what, but you both left the island — Fitch that very day and you the next. And Mr. Carlyle went around looking like a thundercloud for a few weeks, and then he left too."

Thump. Roll. *Thump.*

"I don't know what happened, and I guess it's none of my business —"

"I didn't think you'd *want* to know," Finn managed, finally.

"I don't! That is, I don't want to know about anyone's personal business like that. But I don't want you feeling like you have to go around pretending or telling me lies. It's your own business who you're...you're sweet on. No one here ever thought any the worse of you or Fitch for that. And if that's why you've been staying away all this time..."

Thump. Roll. *Thump.*

Finn cleared his throat. At last he said, "It wasn't anything to do with that. At least...I don't know. Maybe it was a little. But the main reason was I couldn't be around Fitch or Con anymore. That's all."

Martha stopped rolling. "Do you think that's why Fitch went away?"

Finn said astringently, "Fitch had everything he wanted. I don't know why he went away."

Later, thinking of that conversation while he and Uncle Thomas ate beef pot pie at the long dining room table, he asked, "Did Fitch say anything to anyone when he left that day?"

"What day?" Uncle Thomas asked, preoccupied, glancing over a review of the book he'd written on practical art criticism.

"The summer I went away. Fitch had left the day before."

Uncle Thomas looked into the past and said, "I wasn't here. I'd gone to Portland. I was flying to San Francisco."

"But you came home that evening," Finn said. "I remember your car was parked in the drive when I got back that night."

He remembered because he had been grateful that there was no sign of his uncle when he'd let himself into the house and begun packing.

There had been no sign of anyone.

Mostly he had feared an encounter with Fitch, and when there had been no sign of him — no light beneath his door — Finn had guessed that Fitch was waiting in the cottage for Con. Because despite all Con had said — even if it was all true — Fitch would see things differently.

Fitch always did see things differently.

"I don't remember," Uncle Thomas said. He looked thoughtful now, but not unduly concerned. "I think my flight was canceled. Or maybe... Was I giving a guest lecture? Something happened, I remember, and I didn't need to fly out after all until later in the week."

Finn had not talked to anyone that night. He had packed his things, and he had left the following morning. You couldn't really run away at twenty-three, but that had been what it felt like. He said, "Martha had gone to Harpswell. Her sister was ill."

Uncle Thomas nodded, considering, and then he went back to eating his supper.

Finn ate slowly. The food was good. He mostly didn't think about food, and he was surprised to find he was hungry. But as he swallowed the last bites of golden, flaky pastry, he couldn't help thinking that there was something strangely apathetic in everyone's reaction — lack of reaction — to Fitch's disappearance.

Disappearance.

Because that's what it was. Fitch had disappeared. He had fallen off the face of the earth. And no one had noticed.

Even now no one seemed to be noticing — even when Finn was pointing it out.

"I've been thinking," he began, and Uncle Thomas reluctantly refocused on him. "I think maybe something happened to Fitch."

There. It was out.

"Happened to him?" Uncle Thomas sounded doubtful, eyeing Finn over the tops of his reading glasses.

"When he left the island the last time." That sounded too portentous. "When he left three years ago."

His uncle waited politely.

"It's not only that he never contacted me, he never contacted anyone that I know of. We traveled in the same circles."

"Fitch wasn't an artist." It was said bluntly, dismissingly. Considering that tone, Finn understood that maybe Fitch hadn't been everyone's favorite. Perhaps some of those careless jabs about teachers and critics had found their mark and left their wounds. Or perhaps the jabs had been in retaliation to a perceived rejection?

Finn said, "He wasn't a painter, but he still traveled in art circles. We knew all the same people, shared a lot of the same friends." They went to the same shows, the same bars, knew the same people — the Manhattan art scene was a small one, especially in the rarefied stratosphere the Barrets traveled in.

Uncle Thomas said slowly, clearly treading with the greatest care, "It's possible he'd have tried to stay out of your way."

"More than possible. At first." Finn's smile was crooked. "But Fitch, being Fitch, would have got over it, and he'd have expected me to do the same. He'd have arranged to bump into me at some public gathering I couldn't escape from."

Uncle Thomas looked unconvinced. "Maybe he knew this time was...different."

Finn absorbed the fact that his uncle seemed to be well versed regarding his relationship with Con — including the sordid end of it. Not only was Uncle Thomas aware of it, it didn't appear to have unduly shocked him. Granted, he'd had three years to get over the shock.

"Maybe," Finn agreed. "I never talked to anyone about what happened, yet no one ever mentioned him to me — other than to ask how he was or what he was doing."

Uncle Thomas still didn't seem to get it.

Finn tried to articulate his uneasy instinct. It was difficult, because until he struggled to put it into words, he wasn't sure himself what was bothering him so much. "Fitch couldn't have made it to Manhattan, because no one ever mentioned him again unless it was to ask me how he was doing. Someone would have said something in passing. He wasn't — isn't — somebody you could ignore very easily."

Wasn't? He listened to the echo of that word in something very like alarm. *Wasn't?*

"Perhaps he thought it would be wiser starting over elsewhere."

"I guess that's the way it could have happened," Finn said slowly, unconvinced. "It's just that he was a creature of habit."

"Bad habits," Uncle Thomas said grimly, and that seemed to be the end of that conversation.

◊ ◊ ◊ ◊

Upstairs in his room much later that night, Finn found himself going through his old books looking for something to read, something nonnarcotic to put him asleep, turning to the comfort of vaguely recalled childhood favorites. He was flipping through Verne's *Mysterious Island* — mostly studying his grandfather's illustrations — when a snapshot fell out of the yellowed pages.

Con at age twenty or so. A reluctant smile curved Finn's mouth as he appraised the shy arrogance of the boy staring directly into the camera lens. Bold, dark eyes watched from beneath the soft blond forelock. Elegant bone structure: a hard jaw, a proud nose, but an unexpectedly sensitive mouth. They had called him The Prince. He called them — when he deigned to notice them at all (eleven years was a big gap at that age) the Gruesome Twosome. Which pleased them inordinately.

Finn and Fitch had always pretended to not think much of him, and Fitch had gone out of his way to be frankly offensive on more than one occasion, but the fact was, they both had frightful crushes on Con. Granted, he was very good-looking, like the prince in a fairy tale or a romance novel — a living, breathing embodiment of the kind of man their grandfather had painted into his illustrations. In fact, looking back, Finn realized that Grandy had probably used a few earlier models of Carlyles for inspiration. Well, why not? Those dark and luminous eyes, the noble brows and arrogant noses and stubborn chins — and those mouths…oh those beautiful mouths.

Studying the old photo, it surprised Finn that he had never wanted to paint Con. Or had he wanted to but never dared ask? It was difficult to say. He had been so terrifyingly, overwhelmingly in love with Con. Terrifying because he knew even then it could not possibly last, so he had simply snatched at every day, every moment with Con as though it were his last.

But now, looking at the photographed face, he was sorry he had not painted him. Sorry he had not captured the play of light and shadows on that beautiful young face. Once again he felt the yearning to start work again. When he felt a little stronger. Because, as much as he wanted to tackle the work once more, he was afraid. Afraid because it had nearly been lost to him — and maybe it was supposed to be lost.

Maybe it wasn't coming back.

◇ ◇ ◇

Paul arrived in time for lunch the following day, Tuesday. Finn drove down to the wharf with Hiram, and while the old man piled Paul's suitcases — way too many suitcases for a four-day stay — into the station wagon, Finn trailed uncomfortably after Paul, who wanted to see "the village."

"It's not really a *village* village," Finn tried to explain while Paul tripped along from general store to post office to pub.

"If it has a pub and a post office, it's a village," Paul said, shoving open the green door of Wylie's Tavern. "Let's get a drink. I'm *parched*."

"We should probably get up to the house. Martha will be waiting lunch."

"No *way* am I getting into a car with my tummy feeling the way it feels now," Paul warned, heading for one of the battered wooden booths against the wall.

A couple of fisherman types turned from the bar to give him a long look. Finn felt color rushing to his face and was irritated. Paul was a flamboyant personality, true, but that flamboyance had never bothered Finn in Manhattan. He hadn't thought about it twice. But here on Seal Island...Paul's high, light voice, the white silk scarf, the broad gestures...Paul suddenly seemed like someone in a play. A play debuting on a night Finn would have preferred to stay home.

"There's no waitress," Finn told him. "If you want a drink, you have to get it yourself from the bar."

Paul raised his pale eyebrows and eyed the fishermen who had gone back to nursing their beers. He raised his eyebrows lasciviously, and it was all Finn could do not to groan.

"What'll you have?" Paul asked, and Finn shook his head.

"I'm on pain meds."

"Anything good?" Paul threw over his shoulder before sashaying over to the bar. Finn could hear him ordering from across the room. Paul spoke to the fishermen, who answered politely, looked at each other meaningfully, then glanced back at Finn. They left shortly after, and Paul carried over two bottles of Allagash White, setting one in front of Finn.

"You haven't changed," Finn said. "You're still a lousy listener."

"One drink won't kill you."

"Why does everyone keep trying to pour alcohol down my throat?"

"Because if you were any more uptight...well, actually that's hard to imagine."

"Thanks!"

Paul fastened his mouth daintily over the lip of the bottle and guzzled. Finn watched him, but the exasperation was slowly giving way to affection. He'd stayed with Paul when he first left the island, and they'd become close friends. Not least because Paul, as one of Fitch's ex-lovers, wasn't about to push Finn to reconcile or forgive and forget. The only thing he ever pushed Finn on was letting him handle his work. Paul was an art dealer — a very successful one.

Paul set the bottle on the table. "How's Fitch?" he asked, seeming to read Finn's mind.

"I don't know. He's not here."

Paul arched his eyebrows. He was very tall, very thin, with white blond hair cut in a bob, and a pale, bony, mobile face. "Where is he?"

"That's the funny thing. No one seems to know."

"What's that mean?"

"Simply that. No one knows where he is." Finn added reluctantly, "It seems like he vanished after he left the island the last time."

"Three years ago?"

Finn nodded.

"After you caught him and...what's-his-face in the lighthouse?"

Finn scowled, nodding.

"How...extraordinary."

"I don't know." It was extraordinary, though. And not in a good way.

"Maybe he killed himself out of guilt," Paul said cheerfully. "Chucked himself out of the lighthouse. It would be the first decent thing he did."

"No," Finn said, ignoring 90 percent of that comment. "He left voluntarily. He took his suitcases. As it was, he was only staying for the summer."

Paul watched him with his cool, bright eyes. "Then why did you say he vanished?"

"Because…" Finn hesitated. "Well, let me ask you this. When was the last time *you* saw him? I mean, saw him at all. Even from a distance."

Paul leaned back in the booth, squinting thoughtfully into his memories. "It's been a couple of years, I guess."

"Three years, I bet."

Paul's eyes met his. Neither of them said anything.

Finn said finally, "The only time anyone ever mentions Fitch to me is to ask how he is or what he's been up to. In three years, I can't remember a single person telling me they'd seen or spoken to him."

"Gadzooks."

The door to the tavern opened, and Hiram walked in. "Do you boys want me to come back and get you later, or did you want to come up to the house now?" His gaze rested on Paul without particular pleasure.

"What do you want to do?" Finn asked Paul, resigned.

"Home, James!" Paul rose, gathering up the two beer bottles and sauntering out. Finn sighed, and Hiram glanced his way.

"Don't know what Martha is going to think of *that*," he remarked.

Finn rose, steadying himself with the silver-topped walking stick. His mind was still on the conversation with Paul, and he said, "Hy, three years ago, when Finn left the island…did you give him a ride down to the wharf?"

"Drove himself," Hiram said. "He left the station wagon here and I had to walk down to get it. Don't you remember?"

No. Finn did not remember. He had been preoccupied with his own problems that morning. He had packed the night before and had wanted to leave at first light. In his memory that was what had taken place. Granted both Hiram and Martha were early risers, so Hiram could have hiked down to the wharf at dawn and had the station wagon back at The Birches by the time Finn had appeared, bags in hand.

Hiram was already turning away, and Finn followed him out of the tavern. As they made their way down the boardwalk in Paul's wake, the door to the general store opened and a woman stepped out.

She nodded in passing to Hiram, nodded at Finn, and then her hazel eyes widened. "Finn Barret," she exclaimed. "I'd heard you were coming home."

Coming home. Not how Finn had chosen to think of it, but it was true that when he had been lying in the hospital, Seal Island, not his Manhattan loft, was the place he had longed for. Longed for quite desperately.

"How've you been, Miss Minton?" he asked, shifting his cane to shake hands.

"Miss Minton!" She snorted. "You're very formal these days, Finn."

Estelle Minton was a cousin of the Carlyles. She had their fair coloring and elegant bone structure, although she somehow appeared more rawboned and faded than her relations. But then Miss Minton was both a little older and not as comfortably off as the Carlyles. She supplemented her savings by supplying baked goods to the island general store — and making wedding cakes for mainlanders. Her wedding cakes were quite well-known in Harpswell and beyond.

For a second Finn couldn't think what she meant about being formal, but then he remembered that Fitch had always called her "Minty." Finn had generally tried to avoid the social dilemma by not calling her anything.

Without waiting for his response, Miss Minton went on, "How are you? Still pretty crocked up, I reckon. We heard about your accident."

Miss Minton always spoke in the plural — the "royal we," Uncle Thomas called it. Fitch had joked that Miss Minton had an invisible best friend. Actually an invisible *only* friend was the way Fitch had put it.

"I'm okay," Finn said. "I'm up and around, that's the main thing."

"It's a large part of it," she agreed. She was studying him frankly, and Finn wondered at this unusual attention. Miss Minton had never had much time for either him or Fitch — he was a little surprised to find she even remembered him.

Noticing that Paul, tired of waiting in the car, was coming toward them down the boardwalk, he said hastily, "Nice to see you again! I've got to get off this leg."

Miss Minton followed the direction of his gaze. "*What* is that?" she asked disapprovingly, watching Paul cast his scarf over his shoulder and toss his head.

Finn muttered, "Excuse me."

He hobbled to head off Paul, who greeted him as though he'd been given up for lost, and they made their way to the station wagon parked beside Miss Minton's battered old pickup. Hiram joined them a couple of minutes later.

"Was that the local witch or *what*?" Paul inquired as the car left the marina.

Finn couldn't help the edge that crept into his voice. "No."

"Quaint. Very quaint. It explains a lot, I think."

"What does?"

"This place. You. You and Fitch both. You especially, though. You're sort of…well…a throwback."

To *what*? Finn clipped, "Gee, thanks!"

"It's not an insult. It's not a compliment, I admit, but it's not an insult. So are you working on anything?"

"No."

Paul sighed disapprovingly. "I thought that was the excuse for coming back to Salem's Lot?"

Finn glanced at Hiram, who could have been a cigar store Indian for the interest he showed in their conversation. "I never said that."

"You did. You said you thought it would be good for your painting."

He probably *had* said that, although he hadn't meant it in the way Paul imagined.

Paul thrust his head forward from the backseat. "My, my. You're interestingly pale all at once. Not feeling well?" he suggested.

Finn snapped, "I'm fine. Tired, that's all."

"Your head's hurting again, isn't it? Why don't you take some of those painkillers you've been taunting me with?"

Finn glanced at Hiram, who was chewing the inside of his cheek and seemingly still not paying any mind to either of them. He said, "I don't want to get in the habit."

Paul shook his head. "Now *there's* where you're making a mistake. We are *all* creatures of habit." He rattled cheerfully on, and Finn's headache, which had only been the faintest suggestion, bloomed into full-blown pain.

"...was reading an article about migraines in *Scientific American.* You have to catch them before they really get their claws into you. What you want to do is disrupt the *pattern* — it's like an electrical disturbance in the circuitry of your brain..."

Finn listened without hearing and nodded and told himself that he was really glad that Paul was there to keep babbling so that he couldn't sit and brood in peace, because thinking about the past was getting him nowhere fast. It wasn't healthy.

They reached the house, and Paul enthused about the view and the fresh air and the sea breeze and the architecture, and then they were inside and Martha was bustling up to meet them, wiping her wet hands on her apron.

"Lunch is all ready," she said briskly. "Your uncle is working in his study."

She seemed to be trying to telegraph some warning to Finn. He said, "We won't disturb him then."

Martha nodded, but he had misread her. She said, "And Con Carlyle is waiting for you in the parlor."

"Why do I know that name?" Paul asked into the silence that followed Martha's words.

Instead of replying, Finn asked curtly, "Why is Con here?"

Martha looked uncomfortable. "I…snum he wants to talk to you."

"*Snum*," murmured Paul delightedly.

Finn was less delighted. He opened his mouth, but what was he going to do? Ask Martha or Hiram to throw Con out? Even if it were possible, it wasn't practical. The island was too small and all their lives too intertwined to allow him to really avoid Con.

Anyway, there was always the possibility that Con really did have something of importance to say to him — like oh-by-the-way-I-forgot-to-mention-Fitch-is-now-living-in-Australia So he nodded at Martha, told Paul he'd join him in a couple of minutes, and squared his shoulders, heading for the parlor.

Con was standing at the bookshelves by the bay windows that looked out over the ocean. He was looking through *Treasure Island* — the edition featuring Holloway Barret's illustrations. He looked up at the tap of Finn's cane.

"Martha said you wanted to see me," Finn said with determined aggressiveness.

Con closed the book with a snap, slid it back into place on the bookshelf. "I think I owe you an apology. When I thought it over later, I realized how…"

He didn't *quite* realize it, since he couldn't seem to think of the word.

"Unwelcome?" Finn suggested, and Con's face tightened. "Inappropriate?" Finn offered. "Overbearing?"

"Look," Con said shortly. "Whether you want to hear it or not, the fact is I owe you an apology. Not for yesterday, for what happened three years ago."

The light flooding through the window behind Con was very bright. Finn had to narrow his eyes against it; in fact, it was easier to turn away. Con said, "I treated you badly. Maybe I need to say it more than you need to hear it. Either way, it needs to be said."

"All right, you've said it," Finn said.

"No, I haven't." Con was walking toward him, calm, measured steps, and Finn felt ridiculously at bay — mostly because he couldn't easily walk away. "I hurt you...badly. I know that. There was no excuse for it. I've regretted it every single day since. I'm very sorry. Sorry for what it's cost me, but mostly sorry for hurting you. That was the last thing I ever wanted to do."

Finn made an impatient sound. Con had hurt him all kinds of ways that summer. Betraying him with Fitch was merely the coup de grâce. He kept his face turned, but he couldn't shut off his awareness of the other man. He was very much afraid he was going to start shaking — from tiredness and not feeling well, but Con was liable to read that all wrong.

He came right up to Finn, and his breath was warm against Finn's cheek and hair. He ran a light finger down Finn's forearm as though he didn't dare touch him but couldn't quite stop himself either.

Softly, he said, "I realize after yesterday that you don't feel the same anymore — I guess I didn't really expect that although I'd hoped, obviously, that we might have another chance. That probably wasn't realistic on my part. Both of us have changed."

Finn risked a look, but it was a mistake, because Con was right there, gazing into his eyes, watching him far too closely. He should say something, of course, agree with Con or at least have the grace to accept his apology since there was no reason not to on these terms.

"Maybe...I don't know. Maybe we can one day be friends," Con said. "I'll leave that decision up to you."

Finn managed a grudging nod. Con seemed to be waiting for something more. When nothing was forthcoming, he turned away, moving toward the door.

Finn struggled with himself, cleared his throat, and said, "Con…thanks."

Con paused. He said, "If it had been anyone but Fitch, would there have been a chance of you forgiving me?"

Finn said, "If it had been anyone but Fitch, it would never have happened."

"So that's the famous Con-man," Paul said when Finn sat down at the dining room table. Paul was staring out the window, watching Con, tall, lean, and long-legged, striding down the gravel drive toward the woods.

"That's him," Finn said unemotionally, reaching for his water glass.

"What does he say happened to Fitch?"

Finn knocked back a couple of pain pills. Swallowed. "He hasn't said anything."

"That's a little suspicious, don't you think?"

Finn stared. Paul was joking, but not entirely. For reasons more unfathomable than any murder mystery, he was a big fan of the Margaret Rutherford Miss Marple movies. When they had roomed together, he had coaxed and cajoled Finn into watching all four films several times.

Finn admitted, "Well, in fairness, I haven't asked him."

"You haven't *asked* him? Kind of an oversight, don't you think? I mean, he's probably the last person to see Fitch alive."

"What are you inferring?"

"Isn't that what you were getting at, at ye olde tavern?"

Finn opened his mouth to deny it, but the fact was, once the idea of foul play had infiltrated its way into the back of his brain, he couldn't quite shake it.

"It's your theory," Paul pointed out graciously. "You're the one saying Fitch vanished off the face of the planet, that no one's mentioned seeing him in three years."

"Well, yeah. But that doesn't mean…"

"What *does* it mean?"

Good question. If no one had seen Fitch since he left Seal Island…

Finn sat very still, taking it in. Fitch…*dead?* He realized he was shaking his head, denying it. "I'd…know," he said. "I'd feel it."

"Uh…" Paul's pale brows were meeting his hairline. "You'd *feel* it? When did you develop the psychic powers?"

"We're tw…twins." He actually swallowed on the word, a caught breath as the implications sank home. He'd been so angry for so long, it hadn't ever occurred to him how he'd feel if there was no chance of ever making it up, no chance of ever seeing or talking to Fitch again.

Paul must have seen something in his face, because he said hastily, "True. True enough. I've read plenty of articles on the twin thing. Maybe you *would* know. And maybe he did split for Australia."

That pretty much killed the lunch table conversation.

◊ ◊ ◊ ◊

The light station at Seal Island had been established in 1870, but it hadn't been operational since the 1920s. The eighty-one-foot tower was built of rubble stone and originally painted pristine white. There were two levels to the cast-iron lantern at the top of the tower: a watch room and the actual lantern room above, where once upon a time the whale oil lamp had hung. The small attached keeper's dwelling was built of creamy white brick. Tattered berry bushes grew along the side of it, and the casement windows had been boarded up. The door wasn't quite fastened, though, and he'd pushed it open wide…

It had taken Finn's eyes a few seconds to adjust to the darkness, to make out the two figures tangled in desperate humping need on the tarp on the floor. Recognizing too late what he was looking at, he stood frozen, and they had looked up, shocked at that blaze of sunlight, both their faces briefly lit as though by a flashbulb.

Not one of them had said a word.

Finn had turned and walked out, letting the door swing back on its rusted hinges, letting that broken shriek speak for him. He had not looked back, not faltered or flinched even when Con called out to him. Con had shouted twice...and then...nothing.

That vast nothingness filled only by the waves and the shrill cries of the sandpipers.

He had walked until he had run out of beach, and then he had climbed up to the highest point on the island — Ballard's Rock — and he had sat there motionless and numb while the sun climbed up the sky and then slipped down again. What he most remembered of that time was his amazement that anything could hurt that much and not kill him.

It never occurred to him that Con might have mistaken Fitch for him — and for that he was grateful. Grateful that he didn't try to tell himself any comfortable lies, because that's all it would have been. Con knew them apart, always had. He knew them in bright sunshine and he knew them in the darkness. Funny that it had never occurred to Finn just why that was.

As for Fitch...Finn didn't waste his energy trying to understand. He knew he would never in a million years understand. If he thought about Fitch at all, it was to acknowledge that this really shouldn't come as a surprise. Fitch firmly believed in the old saw about asking forgiveness being easier than asking permission.

Con had found him as he was making his way down the trail that night. Finn had been moving very carefully down the hillside. Moonlight was not enough to guide him, and he was damned if he was going to break his neck and have everyone think it was over Fitch and Con.

He was halfway down the rocky slope when Con materialized out of the shadows ahead of him.

"Where the hell have you been? I've been looking for you everywhere!" He sounded both angry and weary — and there was another note in his voice that Finn couldn't quite place. Worry? Fear?

Finn didn't know and didn't care. He had stepped around Con, and Con had tried to put his arm around him. Finn had shoved him off.

Con had stopped walking. "We have to talk."

"There's nothing to say." It was the first and only thing he said to Con that night.

He kept walking, and when Con realized he wasn't going to stay and chat, he came striding after him.

"I know you're hurt. I'm sorry. I'm truly sorry. I wouldn't hurt you for the world. You know that."

Finn had stared straight ahead, calculating how far to the beach, and then how far from there to the road that cut through Bell Woods.

"It was a mistake. I don't even know why… It was…stupid. I'm very sorry. Sorry you saw it, sorry it ever happened. I haven't been with him since you and I — It's only the one time, and it will never happen again. I swear to you."

And Finn had thought about how weird it was that the stars never changed. Even when something like this happened — you would think it would be raining stars — but the world never missed a beat. Ink blue waves washed gently, rhythmically against the pale sand, and the stars were still and bright and cold.

"You're being childish, Finn. It didn't mean a damn thing. You know it didn't. You know I… Can't you stop for one minute and listen to me? This is crazy." He reached a hand out, but Finn moved his arm away without ever breaking stride, so that it was a ghost touch.

"Finn. *Finneas.*"

Any second now Con was going to call him Huckleberry, and Finn was going to turn around and punch him in the mouth.

But Con didn't. He continued to stride beside Finn, watching him, talking to him all the way down the beach, climbing up to the main road, through the woods and all the long walk back to The Birches. It got a little stream of consciousness by the end with Con telling him how he'd looked for Finn all day, how afraid he had been that Finn might do something rash, how every minute he'd regretted what he'd done, what he'd risked — and for what? For nothing. Fitch meant nothing. Finn was all that mattered.

On and on. Words Finn would have given anything to hear twenty-four hours before, but that now meant nothing. Nothing. Because something had died inside him that morning when he opened that door.

When they reached the drive leading to The Birches, Con's voice was husky with talking so much — he wasn't used to it. Finn was the one who always did all the talking, although Finn was not by any stretch a chatterbox.

Con's footsteps dragged a little as they got closer and closer to the house — reluctant to face Fitch perhaps? Or Thomas. He said huskily, "It's no use talking to you now, I can see that. I'll talk to you tomorrow. I'm not going to let this destroy what we have together."

But he followed Finn right onto the porch. Finn reached the doorstep with a feeling of relief. Sanctuary. He grabbed the handle and slipped inside.

Behind him, Con had said quietly, steadily, "I love you, Finn."

Finn closed the door.

Finn watched the shadows of the sea's reflection moving on the ceiling of his room and let himself remember the things he had refused to consider for three years. He was mildly interested to find that he had been healing during that time, because he could remember without pain.

Or maybe it had something to do with Con's apology. Maybe he had needed to hear it as much as Con needed to say it. He believed Con now. He had not believed him at the time; not that Con lied — far from it — just that he thought Con didn't know what he felt — or was confusing regret at hurting Finn for something more. He knew Con was fond of him, liked him, liked fucking together, but Con had warned him early on to lighten up, to not make too much of it, to not try and turn it into some big romance.

Really, when he looked at it like that, his own shock and hurt seemed childish — exactly what Con had feared at the start.

No, the only real surprise should have been that Fitch hadn't come after him.

Oh, not immediately. Fitch knew better than that. Fitch knew to give his twin time to cool down. But to not come at all? That was the one surprise of the day. Fitch couldn't bear it when they quarreled, couldn't bear to be cut off from Finn — even more than Finn couldn't bear to be cut off from him. Even that day. Even that day, part of what Finn grieved for was the knowledge that Fitch too was lost to him. Lost forever.

Because he wasn't going to be able to forgive him.

Maybe Fitch sensed that. Maybe that was why he never came.

Safe to say he wasn't fleeing out of remorse or guilt, because Fitch had never experienced such emotions. Embarrassment at getting caught, maybe. At least that was what Finn had thought before, when he had allowed himself to think about it all. Now he had to wonder.

Suppose something had happened to Fitch when he reached the mainland? Suppose he had been mugged or hit by a bus? But if either of those things had happened, Uncle Tom would have been notified by the authorities. It was barely possible that Fitch had been ashamed of what he'd done and split for parts unknown, but even if Finn could convince himself of such a scenario, he couldn't believe that Fitch would stay away for three years. It wasn't in his nature.

And it was perfectly obvious Fitch had not returned to their old stomping grounds. Even if he'd taken new lodgings, made new friends, hung out at new places…at some point their paths would have crossed.

So what were the remaining possibilities? Foul play? That was Paul's theory — an appropriately melodramatic one. And yet…what else was there? Amnesia? Kidnapping? Murder?

Murder.

But if someone was going to murder Fitch…wouldn't it be the people he had spent the summer with? His nearest and dearest? It was too hard to believe he'd caught the eye of a roving homicidal maniac. And if someone on Seal Island had wanted Fitch dead, would they have waited to strike until he left the island?

Yes. If they wanted to make it look like an accident. But in order to make it look like an accident, Fitch needed to turn up looking accidentally dead — not vanish into thin air.

Finn studied the row of model ships on his bookcase — collected one by one with loving care through his childhood. It had been rather a long childhood, now that he thought about it. But he wasn't a child anymore, and it was time to face things.

Suppose…Fitch hadn't left the island?

CHAPTER FIVE

"Screw Frank and Joe," Paul growled. "I want to be Nancy!"

Finn gave him a long look, and Paul giggled delightedly.

"No pun intended."

"Would you tone it down?"

Paul raised his eyebrows. "Maybe it's something in the water. You seem to be turning straight."

"I'm not turning straight. I...this is a small town. It's not even a town. It's a...a conservative little backwater."

They were sitting in the station wagon in the marina eyeing the harbor master's office.

"That's their problem," Paul pointed out. "What does it have to do with us?"

"Get real, Paul. We're trying to get information out of people. We need their cooperation. We don't want to put anyone's back up." Paul opened his mouth, and Finn said, "You know what I mean."

"Unfortunately, I think I do." Paul shook his head, his blond hair swinging against his cheek. "Look, Frank, I can't be anyone but who I am. Deal with it." He got out of the car, and Finn slowly followed.

Was he in the wrong here? He wasn't sure.

Despite everything, he had slept well again the night before, and he was starting to feel a little more like his old self. His leg wasn't giving him constant hell, and even his headache had been a no-show nearly twelve hours now.

They went into the harbor master's office, empty on a Wednesday morning, and asked the girl working behind the old walnut desk if there was a way to verify what boats had left for the mainland on the afternoon of August eighteenth, three years previous. They'd got the date from Martha, who had managed to piece together history based on her recollection of family disasters — her own and the Barrets'.

The girl went into a back room. Finn moved to the window and stared out at the wharf and thought about what it would take to capture that dazzle of sunlight on water. If he used a glaze of Ultramarine Blue over both the shore and sea, it would reduce the values... He could paint the ripples into the water using a mix of blues, greens, and Titanium White...then mix the Titanium White with Flake White and a bit of Cadmium Yellow, work it with a bit of Liquin into an impasto paint to catch the glitter of the sun on water. It calmed him to focus on something besides whatever information that girl was going to dig up in her dusty files.

Paul poked around, making uncomplimentary comments on the decor. Finn glanced around. Paul had a point. Gray walls, nautical charts, and a girly calendar from the year before.

The girl returned from the back room. *"The Sea Auk,"* she verified. Her expression was commiserating.

"Is that a problem?"

"The Sea Auk sank last year. I don't think you're going to have much luck tracking down her captain — he's in Florida now — let alone her passengers."

Paul and Finn exchanged long looks and returned to the station wagon.

"That's *awfully* convenient!" Paul said when they had closed the doors against the stiff, salty wind.

Finn laughed. "What, you think someone sank *The Sea Auk* to cover up the fact that Fitch wasn't onboard three years ago?"

"If the flipper fits..."

"I don't think it does. Not that flipper, anyway. Not sabotage."

"Fine. The boat conveniently sank so we don't know for sure if Fitch took it or not. That doesn't mean this is a dead end. It's merely...a cul-de-sac. What I think you should do is start with the person with the strongest motive for getting rid of Fitch, and then work backward."

"That would be me," Finn said.

"Ah. Then…second strongest motive. And that would be Con-man."

Irritably, Finn said, "Don't call him that."

Paul chuckled. "Int-ter-esssting."

"No," Finn said.

"No? What do you mean? Are you telling me you don't have any feelings for him at all? *Hmm?*"

"I'm saying I don't want to talk about it with you. I don't ask you about what happened between you and Fitch."

"That's because you already had Fitch's version."

"That's one side of the story."

"It was probably true. I never knew Fitch to lie. Even when it would have been the smart or kind thing to do."

That was true. Fitch was not a liar. Brutal frankness was his specialty. According to Fitch, he had grown bored with Paul's jealousy and tantrums. But then Fitch always found something to grow bored with.

Paul said, "Well, personally I rule you out. At least for now. Which still leaves Con Carne or whatever his name is. You need to go and ask him the obvious question, which is: what happened after you ran off?"

"I didn't *run* off. I walked off in a slow and dignified manner."

"Whatever. What we want to know is, what did Con and Fitch chat about after you stalked off? Can you imagine being a fly on *that* wall?"

No. He couldn't. Or maybe he didn't want to, because he was sure whatever had been said would have hurt him even more badly. He said, "I still don't see why Con would have a motive for getting rid of Fitch."

"Oh my God. Keep your day job, lambkin! Fitch deliberately seduced him and broke up his relationship with you. Of course he would want to strangle him."

Finn sighed, staring unseeingly at the mountain of lobster traps to the side of the car. "It wasn't like that, though. First of all, Con had told me that he wasn't interested in anything long-term, and that he wasn't going to make promises to be monogamous. Secondly, although I was too stupid to see it at the time, Con had had some kind of relationship with Fitch before I ever came into the picture."

"You're kidding!"

Finn shook his head again.

"And they both kept that from you?"

"Fitch wasn't staying on the island when Con and I started up. He came home later that summer — Con was already getting restless. I knew that. I could see the signs. He kept doing stuff to push me away." Finn's mouth curved bitterly. "I saw it, but I was in love with him."

Paul considered this grimly. "That doesn't mean he didn't resent being manipulated by Fitch."

"What makes you think Fitch manipulated *him?*"

"You forget. I was on the receiving end of Fitch — and I mean that in every possible sense — for nine months. I know exactly how he operated. And it wasn't pretty."

Finn considered Paul. Fitch could be — and frequently was — a bastard, but Paul was the only one of Fitch's ex-lovers — that Finn knew of — who carried a grudge against him. And Paul definitely carried a grudge. He'd taken Fitch to small claims court for three months of back rent and the monetary equivalent of several gifts.

"What kind of temper does Con have?"

"I never thought of him as having a bad temper."

"Maybe he's the type that represses it, and when it blows...*kaboom!*"

Finn said doubtfully, "I just...don't really see that."

"You're not being very helpful." Paul tapped his tooth with a buffed fingernail. "Fine, who else would have had it in for Fitch? Who inherits his share of the family fortune?"

"I don't know…I guess it would be split between me and Uncle Tom. But if money was the motive, why conceal the fact that Fitch is dead?"

"Good point." Paul started the engine. "It's Con. It's got to be. You need to go talk to him."

Finn gave a disbelieving laugh, staring as Paul guided the car across the uneven road. "You think he's a killer and you want me to go talk to him? Thanks!"

"Are you afraid of him?"

"Of course not." He felt a little indignant at the idea, for reasons probably best not to analyze.

"So what's the problem? It was probably an accident."

If it had been an accident, then Fitch's body would have turned up. You didn't accidentally dispose of a body.

Paul said thoughtfully, "*Could* it have been an accident? I mean, could he have fallen into the ocean?"

Finn considered it. "I don't think so. He'd have washed up sooner or later. If not here, then on one of the other islands or the mainland." He shivered, stared unseeingly out the window at the choppy green-blue water.

◊ ◊ ◊ ◊

Martha was beginning to "take against" Paul. Finn knew the signs. It was not so much what she said as what she didn't say, uncharacteristically cryptic as she fed them a late lunch of smoky potato soup with bacon croutons after their return from a hard morning of snooping.

Her dark eyes rested on the back of Paul's head with a certain grimness, and when she caught Finn watching, Martha gave a little disapproving sniff. Paul represented Finn's new life, which was probably reason enough right there for Martha to dislike him.

It was a shame, because Martha was generally a gold mine of information, but her suspicion of Paul made her closemouthed. Granted, she had not been on the island the day Fitch left. She had not been there that entire week. She had been tending to her sick sister on the mainland. By the time Martha returned to the island, it had all been over and both Finn and Fitch were gone — Fitch perhaps forever.

After lunch, pressured by Paul, who had decided sleuthing was the only credible means of entertainment on Seal Island, Finn went up to Uncle Thomas's study to ask if he remembered anything about the day Fitch had disappeared.

Uncle Thomas, up to his elbows in art books, looked up distractedly and frowned. "Disappeared? You mean the day he left? I wasn't here."

"But you came back that evening."

Uncle Thomas frowned. "I don't recall seeing you or Fitch."

"Fitch was already gone by then. We just didn't know it."

"Perhaps he left the following morning."

"No, because *I* left the following morning. Hiram had to walk down to the village to get the car."

"I'm sorry," Uncle Thomas said, a fraction impatiently. "What was the question again?"

That really was the crux of it. What was it that Finn was hoping to learn? And why was he asking the people most unlikely to have reason to want Fitch dead? Was he stalling because he was afraid to face the person to whom he should most obviously be talking?

"If Fitch is dead," he asked finally, "who inherits?"

Uncle Thomas looked taken aback. He answered without having to consider it, "You do. You and Fitch equally inherited your mother's share of this estate. If one of you predeceases the other, the survivor takes all."

Since Finn seemed to have nothing to say to that, Uncle Thomas went back to his research, and Finn went downstairs to find Paul. Hearing him out, Paul seemed unreasonably amused.

"We're building quite a case against *you*," he said.

"I'm laughing so hard."

"It's ironic, don't you think?"

"Mostly irritating."

Paul smirked. "Well, my suggestion is we — meaning *you* — go talk to the only real suspect we have."

Finn rubbed his face in his hands without answering.

"Are you afraid of him?"

"Of course not," he replied, his voice muffled behind his hands.

"You can take my cell phone, and if I don't hear from you in…say, one hour, I'll start yelling my head off."

"I'm not afraid of Con."

Which wasn't exactly true — although he wasn't afraid of Con for the reasons Paul probably imagined.

In the end, he decided to walk down to the cottage. He needed the exercise, and he wanted time to think before he arrived on Con's doorstep. But no sooner did he close the door on The Birches than he seemed to be facing Con's front door, and he could not claim that the walk had done anything to clear his thoughts.

He knocked before he had time to change his mind and beat a retreat.

Con came to the door. He wore jeans and a heather and blue tweed sweater. Reading glasses were pushed back on his forehead, and he held a green and white paperback titled *The Princes in the Tower*, keeping his place with a finger between the pages. He stared at Finn as though he were the last person in the world he expected to see — which was probably about right.

"Are you busy?" Finn asked awkwardly, since it was obvious Con was.

"Not too busy for you." He said it simply and moved aside so that Finn could step inside the cottage.

The last time he had been here, he had been too tired and pained to really look around, but his impression of time unchanged seemed accurate now. It was all as it had been: the same comfortable furniture and rugs, the same pictures on the wall — including Finn's painting of the cave at Otter Cove, the first place they had made love. Well, Finn had made love. For Con it had been fucking, but that was all right. Either way, Finn had good memories of that day.

The computer was a new one, and there were a couple of framed snapshots on the fireplace mantle. Finn noticed because Con had never been one for family photos.

"Did you walk down here?" Con was frowning.

"Yeah." As Con's frown deepened, he said, "I'm supposed to walk. Really. It's good for me."

"It's two miles from The Birches. I doubt if your doctor had that kind of hike in mind."

Finn didn't really register that, because he had realized that while one of the photos on the mantle was of Con and his family at some anniversary celebration, the other one was of Fitch. It gave him a very strange feeling, and he missed the next two things Con said.

Picking up the frame, he studied it. They were standing outside some kind of antique store, and Fitch was smiling. He looked relaxed and happy — and so did Con. He had draped a casual arm around Fitch, who was holding a large handcrafted model of an "Ironsides" yacht.

When the hell had Fitch and Con gone off together...? Finn had the peculiar sensation of missing a step in the dark because...it *wasn't* Fitch in the photo, it was him. He had completely forgotten that trip to Union — less than a week before he'd walked in on Fitch and Con in the lighthouse keeper's cottage.

Ironically, he had started to believe that weekend that Con was falling in love with him.

"Finn, what's the matter?" Con asked for the third time, and by now he sounded alarmed. He put a hesitant hand on Finn's shoulder. "Why don't you sit down?"

That seemed like a good idea, and Finn dropped into the nearest chair, still holding the framed photograph.

"You can't keep doing this," Con said, and if had been anyone besides Con, Finn would have considered him to be fussing. "You can't keep doing these marathons until you're stronger. You could fall, you could faint —"

Finn looked up into his hard, anxious face. "What happened between you and Fitch that day?"

His question cut Con off midsentence. "What do you mean?" He sounded wary.

"After I left the cottage. What happened between you?"

"Nothing."

Finn was abruptly irritated. He put the framed photo on the table next to him with a clatter. "*Nothing?* Something must have happened. You must have had *something* to say to each other. Like…*gosh, this is awkward!*"

"I don't recall what I said to him." Con's expression was bleak. "I think —"

"What?"

After a hesitation, Con said, "I think I hit him."

"You…hit him?"

"He was laughing. I don't even remember what he said, but I…I seem to recall punching him."

Finn closed his eyes for an instant. "Did you kill him?"

"*What?*"

Finn opened his eyes, and Con was staring at him, aghast. "No, I didn't *kill* him. What the hell are you talking about?"

"No one has seen Fitch since that day."

"What are you talking about?"

Finn didn't bother to repeat it. Con's black gaze seemed fixed on his.

"That's not possible. He left the island. Someone had to have seen him go."

"I haven't found anyone so far."

"Wait a minute," Con said, and it was his normal, brisk tone. He sat down in the chair across from Finn's, leaning forward, his expression intent — he could been applying his mind to any academic puzzle. "Let me get this straight. You're saying no one has seen Fitch in three years?"

"Right."

"That's not possible."

"It's not possible if he's still alive."

"You think he's dead?"

Finn said carefully, "As far as I can make out, you were the last person to see him alive."

Con drew back. His expression was startled, but not...particularly guilty. He seemed astonished more than anything.

"I didn't kill him, Finn." Con said it plain and simple, and Finn found that unexpectedly reassuring. "I was angry, but...it was mostly at myself. What I'd done. What I'd...destroyed."

"What happened after you hit him?"

"I didn't wait to see. I went after you. I spent the entire fucking day searching the island for you. I thought you would go to the cove. I waited there. Then I thought you might come here. Then I thought you might go into the village. Then I tried the cove again. Then I tried The Birches. Finally I thought of Ballard's Rock, and that's where I was headed when I found you that night." He swallowed hard. "By then I was...terrified..."

Finn's smile was caustic. "You thought I'd done something dramatic like pitch myself from the cliff?"

Con said quietly, "All I knew was that you loved me and I took that love and shoved it right back in your face. You weren't the most worldly kid."

"I wasn't a kid."

"You were twenty-three, but you'd spent most of your life on this rock in the company of folks who were a lot older than you. People who thought queer only happened to other people. People in big bad cities — like Sodom and Gomorrah."

Finn said defensively, "I had Fitch."

Con said nothing.

"You don't know a damn thing about it," Finn argued hotly. "No, I wasn't *worldly*, but I did get that I was only a passing thing for you. And I wasn't about to kill myself over it."

"I know," Con said. "I realize that now. At the time I was...scared."

Unappeased, Finn said shortly, "So you punched Fitch and left him there, and in all this running around the island, you never ran into him again?"

Con shook his head.

"What about when you went to The Birches?"

"I didn't see him —" Con paused, and his expression changed.

"What? What did you remember?"

"When I was waiting for you outside the cave in Otter Cove, I vaguely remember seeing someone up in the lighthouse tower. My first thought was it was you, but then I remembered your tracks had led away down the beach."

"So who was it?"

"I couldn't tell at that distance, but at the time I think I assumed it was Fitch. If he'd wanted to see where either of us went, the tower would have given him a bird's-eye view of half the island."

"What time was that?"

"Less than half an hour after all hell broke loose." Con studied Finn's face. "Are you serious about this? You honestly believe Fitch is dead?"

"I...don't know."

Con was frowning, watching him. "Then why does everyone believe he left the island that afternoon?"

"Because his things were gone. His suitcases and clothes were gone, and Hiram's station wagon was left at the wharf as though Fitch had driven down there and caught the boat for the mainland. And it made sense given everything that happened."

"Does it? But didn't Martha see him come back and pack? Didn't Hiram drive him? Didn't he say good-bye to Tom?"

"Martha was in Harpswell that entire week. Her sister was sick. Hiram was clearing out poison ivy at the back of the property all that afternoon. Uncle Tom was in Portland stuck at the airport. Everyone assumed Fitch came in, packed, and drove the station wagon down to the village himself."

"He didn't leave a note or anything?"

Finn shook his head. "But that wasn't so unusual. He always came and went as he liked. Anytime he left a note, it was for me. He wouldn't have done that this time…"

"I'm not so sure. I always thought that scene was more about Fitch's jealousy over you, than Fitch's jealousy over me."

"I don't know what that's supposed to mean."

"It means," Con said dryly, "that you were the most important person in Fitch's life, and he didn't like sharing you. Especially with me." Finn opened his mouth to object, but Con was already following another thought. "Someone at the wharf or in the village must have seen him leave that day. There would be a record of a ticket sale, a ship's log — something that would prove either way?"

"Paul and I did some checking earlier. The only ship that Fitch could have sailed on was *The Sea Auk*, which sank last year in that freak storm. No records. As for anyone remembering seeing Fitch…it was the summer. There were all kinds of visitors on the island. If this had happened last week…but three years ago? Nobody remembers anything. Even Martha and Hiram aren't that clear on the details, and they're part of the household."

"But you realize what you're saying?" Con asked quietly. "If Fitch didn't leave the island, you're hypothesizing that someone went into the house, packed up his things, and borrowed the station wagon to make it look like he did. You're saying someone deliberately concealed the fact that Fitch was dead."

Reluctantly, Finn nodded.

Con's voice was very low. "You're suggesting that someone murdered him."

"It could have been an accident."

Con was shaking his head. "If it was an accident, why wouldn't that person come forward? Why go to elaborate lengths to hide the truth?"

"I don't know."

"If what you're suggesting is true, I don't believe it could have been an accident."

Finn's gaze met Con's dark one. "But I don't see why anyone would deliberately... I can't believe that anyone would want Fitch dead."

Con reached out and squeezed his uninjured knee; he withdrew his hand immediately. He said neutrally, "There was a side to Fitch you didn't see — or didn't see it until that day."

"What are you saying?"

"Only that...for one instant in that cottage, when you walked away and Fitch was standing there laughing, I wanted him dead. I'm not the only person who ever felt that way."

Finn straightened, unconsciously bracing himself as Con continued, "Finn had a cruel streak. I don't know why or what made him the way he was, but he enjoyed being rude, he enjoyed seeing people squirm, he enjoyed hurting people."

Finn got up fast — and awkwardly, belatedly steadying himself on the chair, ignoring the pain in his injured leg. "That's not true!"

Con rose too. "It is true. Are you telling me you never heard the way he talked to Thomas? Or Hiram? Or plenty of other people?"

"He was joking."

"He wasn't funny. He was cruel. *You* never talked to anyone that way."

"I…"

"Don't make excuses for him. The reason you never noticed any of that was because you were such a nice, sweet-tempered guy."

"Oh great!" Finn's face twisted in comical disgust. "*Nice.* There's the kiss of death right there."

"I know." Con's smile was crooked. "Awful, isn't it? But you were the nicest guy I've ever known. And I wish to hell I had appreciated it at the time. I mean that as a compliment. Fitch was different with you, and you…didn't see the way he was with others."

"So you're saying he made fun of someone and they killed him?"

"I don't know what happened. I know that Fitch could have said the wrong thing to the wrong person at the wrong time — sometimes that's the way it happens."

That was the historian talking. "But if someone did all those things…packed his clothes, took the car…then it was premeditated."

"Not necessarily."

"If someone hid his body…"

"That's the question, isn't it?" Con said. "It's not that big an island. So where would someone hide Fitch's body?"

Finn sat down again. "I can't believe we're casually talking about this, talking about Fitch being dead. Murdered." He rested his face in his hands. "I can't believe it."

Con came over to him, squatted down next to him, putting an arm around his shoulders. It took all Finn's willpower not to lean into him.

"You might be wrong. I hope you're wrong…but you've made a pretty convincing case. Now I'm wondering. More than wondering. Frankly, I think Fitch probably *is* dead."

Neither said anything for a time. Finally Finn raised his head. He said wearily, "I don't know what to do. Should we call the state police? I haven't even talked to Uncle Tom about the possibility yet. What if I *am* wrong?"

Con's gaze seemed to linger on his mouth, and for an uncomfortable moment Finn thought Con might lean forward and brush his lips against Finn's. Instead, he drew back, rising.

"Let's wait a bit," he said. "Why don't we try this: why don't we go out to the last place we know Fitch was alive?"

Finn stared at him. "The lighthouse?"

Con nodded. "The lighthouse."

"Who is Paul?" Con asked as they took the long, meandering road that wound up to the abandoned lighthouse. "You said you and Paul went down to the marina to check when Fitch might have left the island."

Finn, distracted by any number of unpleasant reflections, dragged his gaze away from the rise and fall of the road ahead. "Paul Ryder. He's a friend."

"Close friend?"

"Close enough." Finn added, "We're not lovers, if that's what you mean. He came because...I needed some company. At least, I thought I did. I wasn't sure what to expect here. Paul's an art dealer — a pretty successful one — so his schedule is, well, he makes his own schedule."

There was nothing to read in Con's voice or profile. He might simply have been making polite conversation. "He must be a pretty good friend to drop everything to keep you company."

"He's a pretty good friend," Finn agreed. "But I think part of the attraction was he wanted to see where Fitch grew up. They had a thing a few years back, and I don't know if Paul ever really got over it. I mean, he's still pretty caustic and sometimes that means there are still feelings there."

"Yes," Con said. "Indifference is the worst."

Finn stared out the window at the trees, the flash of brisk blue water behind the golden wall of autumn leaves. The sun was very bright. He'd forgotten sunglasses, and he put his hand up to shield his eyes.

"All right?"

He hadn't realized that Con was watching him so closely. "I'm okay."

"There's an extra pair of sunglasses in the glove compartment."

Finn shook his head. "I hate them. I won't wear them until I don't have a choice."

Con's brows drew together.

After another mile of silence, Con's voice jerked him out of his reflections again. "The guy who was killed in the car accident that injured you...?"

"Tristan. Another friend," Finn said unemotionally. "He might have been something more. We never got the chance to find out."

After a hesitation, Con said, "I'm sorry."

"Yeah."

They did not talk the rest of the way. It was not a long drive, but the road was a roundabout one snaking through the hills and woods. As the road wound its way, Finn glimpsed the lighthouse through tree branches. He studied Con's profile and thought that Con's expression was peculiar. Remote and yet resolute. As though feeling his gaze, Con glanced at him and then — perhaps misreading Finn — slowed the Land Rover.

Finn *was* increasingly tense as the miles passed, but it was not the fear of another accident. In fact, he couldn't understand his own mounting stress.

It wasn't until the final stretch of road at last uncoiled at the top of a green hillock overlooking the ocean, and Con rolled to a stop in the sandy square beside the keeper's dwelling, that Finn recognized what was disquieting him. He glanced at Con's grim profile, stared at the small white brick building with the boarded windows, and all the while his heart was pounding in hard, hollow slams as though someone were kicking an empty oil drum. Suddenly he was very sure he did not want to take this any further. Very sure that he would be happier not knowing what he was about to find out.

Con opened his door, and Finn said desperately, "Con —"

Leaning back inside, Con said, "What is it?"

"I'm not feeling — Can we do this another time?"

"What's wrong?"

Finn shook his head, but Con was already coming around the front of the Land Rover, opening the door on Finn's side. "What is it? What's wrong?" He slipped his arm around Finn and helped him out on the vehicle, his hands very gentle, his face concerned. "It's your eyes again?"

"Yes. No. I'm okay," Finn said. "Maybe a little —"

"Carsick?" Con asked. "Light-headed?"

Try afraid of you, Finn thought. Because as he stared into Con's buccaneer eyes, he couldn't help reflecting that everything Con had told him that day indicated that Con was the person most likely to have murdered Fitch — if Fitch *were* truly dead and not playing some cruel game.

"Jesus," Con said, sounding alarmed as he eased Finn back against the side of the Rover. "You're as white as the fucking stones. Do you want to — What do you want, sugar? You want to sit down or do you want to walk a little?"

Sugar. Finn could have cried at the old pet name. Why did Con have to do that? Why didn't he call his something stupid, like "Huckleberry"? Why did he have to be so tender and...loving *now*? Why did he have to do any of this?

But it was Finn who had started it, not Con. It was Finn who had made the mistake of coming back here, coming back to Seal Island. He should have let well enough alone. He should have left this place and all its memories to slide into the past and sink to the bottom of his consciousness.

"Rest for a minute. You're pushing yourself too hard." Con was worrying aloud. "These headaches... I keep forgetting you're only a couple of days out of the hospital. This could have waited."

"I just need a...little air," Finn said desperately, because he couldn't think while Con's hands were moving in conscious or unconscious caress on his shoulders, and Con's face was mere inches from his own.

"You want to walk?" Con was watching him intently. "I'll help you. Lean on me."

He tried to slip his arm around Finn's waist, but Finn freed himself clumsily. "In a minute. Why don't you…why don't you go up into the lighthouse and see…if there's anything to see?"

"You don't want to look for yourself?" Con's dark eyes never left his own.

Finn shook his head.

"Are you all right if I leave you for a minute or two?"

Finn nodded tightly.

Con scrutinized him for another few seconds, clearly divided; then he said, "All right. I'll run up and take a quick look around. The place may be locked up for all I know."

Finn licked his dry lips, nodded again.

Con turned away and strode toward the boarded-up dwelling. Finn watched him try the door. It opened with a soprano screech of frozen hinges, and Con disappeared inside.

Finn reached into the Land Rover and grabbed his cane. He hadn't been kidding about needing air. He felt woozy with a combination of dread and confusion. At least part of it was that irrational dread of going into that claustrophobic dark of the keeper's dwelling, but the rest was genuine foreboding that he had started something that couldn't be stopped.

If he forced himself to look at the situation with cold logic, Con had opportunity, means, and motive — by his own admission. And as Paul would no doubt have pointed out, Rutherford's hatchet-faced Miss Marple was always boisterously enthusiastic about such a criminous trifecta. Con had not wanted to call the police. Con had wanted Finn to come out here alone with him. Why? So he could kill Finn too?

But…this was *Con.*

He was the most civilized man Finn knew; he still used the library for God's sake. Con who drank Earl Grey tea and read fantasy and listened to Barber and wrote histories about long-ago injustices in an effort to set the score straight. Con, who had held Ripley in his arms to the very end when the old dog had to be put down. Con, who, despite his determination not to get enmeshed in a relationship, had been the gentlest and most painstaking lover Finn had known. That weekend they had gone to Union, staying at a quaint bed-and-breakfast, going to the Farnsworth Art Museum, Damariscotta Lake, the Antique Toy and Art Museum…that had been the single best weekend of Finn's life.

It wasn't…possible.

But what else made sense? Fitch had his faults, God knew, but the idea that someone had killed him because…because he was rude to them? Because he had been insensitive?

He got Paul's cell phone out and began to dial the house.

"Finn, you're closer to the edge than you realize." A hard hand came down on Finn's shoulder, and he nearly jumped from the rocky cliff all on his own. Lost in his own thoughts, he hadn't heard Con's approach, and there was no hiding his alarm as he turned, dropping the cell phone and knocking the other man's hand away, ready to fight.

"What's the matter with you?" Con's expression was startled.

Finn clutched his cane with both hands, braced for whatever was coming. But it seemed that nothing was coming.

The surprise on Con's face hardened slowly into disbelief, then anger.

"You think *I* killed Fitch?" He didn't wait for an answer. "And then what? Brought you up here to murder you too?"

"What's in the lighthouse?" Finn croaked.

"I don't *know* what's in the fucking lighthouse, because it's too dark to see and I forgot to replace the batteries in my flashlight. What do you think is in the lighthouse? Proof that I killed your brother?"

"Did you?" Finn got out between stiff lips.

"How can you even ask me that?" Con cried, and the anguish in his voice seemed too raw to be faked. "I already told you I didn't. I told you exactly what happened that day."

"And you told me that you punched him and that for a minute you wanted him dead. Maybe when you hit him, he fell and hit his head —"

"If I had accidentally killed Fitch, I'd have gone to the authorities. I wouldn't have tried to hide it." There was contempt in Con's voice. "I wouldn't have spent the afternoon searching for you — which, by the way, I can prove. In part at least."

"All right. Prove it."

"Barnaby Purdon was fishing in Otter Cove most of the time I was waiting there after I left Fitch — alive — here."

"That doesn't prove anything! I only have your word that Fitch was alive when you left him. Besides, you said yourself it was too far away to know for sure who was in the lighthouse tower."

"Well, who else could it have been?"

Finn shook his head stubbornly. "I-I don't know. But it's not proof, Con."

He raked an impatient hand through his pale hair. "All right. Try this on. Estelle Minton was working in her garden when I walked up to The Birches. I think she'll be willing to testify I wasn't carrying a body."

"Don't make fun of it. For God's sake!"

"No. You're right," Con said tightly. "There's nothing funny about this. And there's no point discussing it with you. If you think I killed your fucking brother, then go call the state police. Go do whatever the hell it is you think you need to do, Finn. But stay away from me."

He turned and walked away to the Land Rover. He got in, started the engine, and drove away without looking back.

Finn painfully lowered himself to the ground, picked up the dropped cell phone, and dialed The Birches. He got Martha, who instructed him to invite Con to supper. He told her Con was otherwise engaged and asked for Paul.

Paul's fluting tones answered a couple of seconds later.

"I'm at the lighthouse," Finn told him. "Can you bring the station wagon? And can you borrow a couple of flashlights from Martha. Tell her...I don't know. Something. Tell her I want to paint the tower or the cliffs from above and I need to get into the old building to look around."

"Are you going to paint the tower?" asked the ever-hopeful art dealer.

"No."

"Oh. What did you find out?" Paul demanded. "Did he admit it?"

"No, he didn't admit anything. I don't believe he did kill Fitch." Finn added shortly, "I think Fitch might be playing some cruel game on all of us."

There was a sharp silence. "Are you serious?"

"Yes. Oh, I don't know! It's...very hard to believe that anyone would kill Fitch. And I sure as hell don't believe Con did."

"What did he say that so convinced you?"

"Among other things, he told me to call the cops."

"*Oh.*"

"Can you bring the car?" Finn asked wearily when the empty buzz on the line persisted.

"On my way," Paul said and hung up.

It was about twenty minutes before the station wagon tires crunched onto the sandy shale and parked in front of the lighthouse. By then Finn was chilled through and completely depressed.

He picked himself off the ground as Paul unfolded from the station wagon and waved cheerfully.

Paul loped up, inquiring, "Is Martha a blood relation?"

"Technically she's not any relation at all."

"That's good. So she can't actually send you to bed without supper? Because those were the dire threats she was muttering when I left."

Finn snorted.

Paul studied his face. "What's up? Why so glum?"

Finn shook his head. "Did you bring flashlights?"

Paul held up a cautioning finger and ducked back into the car. He brought out two high-powered flashlights. "I don't know how you're going to get up those stairs, with that leg, though. You probably should leave it to me."

"I'll be fine."

Paul shrugged. "Suit yourself."

They opened the front door of the keeper's cottage, flashlight beams stabbing through the darkness. Faded daylight pried through the boards nailed unevenly across the windows throwing odd bars of light here and there on the stone walls.

Plenty of light...really. Anyway, he couldn't spend the rest of his life afraid of the dark.

"Gadzooks. It's like a cave in here!"

Finn swallowed hard, said conversationally, "I'm amazed the place hasn't been totally trashed."

Paul retorted, "I think you must mean *trashed* in a relative sense."

He had a point. The wooden floor and wall paneling had been pulled up and removed, and there was silver graffiti painted over one wall — a pentagram and some odd symbols — but otherwise the structure was mostly unharmed. It smelled strongly of damp and animal.

Finn's heart was ricocheting around his rib cage in panic. It made him angry. He was not giving into this, not giving into irrational, superstitious fear. He forced his voice to stay steady, unhurried. "It's so far from the village, there's nothing really to tempt anyone out here but hikers and photographers." He shone his flashlight to the black oblong at the end of the room that had once served as a kitchen. "There's the entrance to the tower."

"It looks like the doorway to a tomb." It did too.

"Nice," Finn growled.

"Well, you know. One tries," Paul said breezily, but his voice sounded as nervous as Finn felt. It helped a little knowing he wasn't the only one struggling. Paul added in that strained tone, "This place isn't haunted or anything, is it?"

"It didn't use to be."

"Nice one yourself!"

They moved slowly to the door of the tower and looked upward. Light from a window midway up the turret cast a perfect square on the opposite wall. In the blue light filtered from the windows in the lamp room, the narrow spiral of iron staircase looked like the interior of some exotic conical seashell.

"Do you think it's safe?" Paul inquired, shining his flashlight at the cobwebbed lowest step.

"I think *safe* is another one of those relative terms." Finn directed his own beam around the circular room. "We used to play in here when we were kids. It felt different then. Not so…empty."

"How tall is it?"

"The entire tower is about eighty feet, but that includes the lamp."

Paul shone his light in Finn's direction. "Not that I wouldn't like to see the prices of your work appreciate, but I'd hate them to skyrocket because of a fatal accident. I think you should stay down here while I go up."

No way was he staying down here with only this watery blue light to hold the darkness at bay. "You can go first," Finn said. "I'll take my time."

"I'm not sure what we're looking for at this point."

Finn wasn't sure what to make of this about face. Paul had pushed him to question Con, but now he seemed to be leery of the idea of investigating further. Was he maybe a little freaked inside the creepy old structure? Finn couldn't blame him for that.

"I don't know. That's why we're looking."

Paul started up the staircase. The metal steps rang hollowly beneath his feet. He stopped.

"I'm not sure what the point of this is," he said, a little testily. "It's not like his body is going to be up there." In the silence that followed his words, he said, "I didn't mean it like that. You know what I mean."

"It's all right if you don't want to go up," Finn said. He was moving very slowly, very cautiously up the staircase, holding tight to the metal banister with his free hand and his cane with the other.

"You're going to break your neck, and your housekeeper is going to send *me* to bed without supper."

Finn stopped. "Paul, you don't have to go up, but I do. I don't know why, but I feel like I do. This was the last place anyone saw Fitch alive."

But had it *been* Fitch in the light tower that morning? Con was not sure. Finn shrugged that thought away.

"Oh, fuck!" Paul said and turned, marching up the staircase. It clanged noisily in the wake of his steps.

"Wow!" Finn heard him say after a time.

His own progress was tedious and painful. Soaked in sweat by the time he made it to the top, it wasn't until he was tottering on the last step that he began to consider how difficult the trip down was going to be in the fast-encroaching dusk.

"That doesn't look too promising," Paul said as Finn stepped out onto the circular landing. He nodded out to sea, where the sky was turning an ominous black and green. Witch lights seemed to flash and flicker in the roiling clouds.

"There's a storm moving in," Finn said.

"Duh. I recognize it from the movie. The one with *gorgeous* George Clooney and Marky Mark."

Finn snickered, wiped his perspiring face on his sleeve. It had been a long time since he'd experienced an island gale. He wasn't thrilled at the idea. It usually meant power outages and being completely cut off from the mainland for hours, if not days. "It may pass us by," he said without much hope.

"I have to admit," Paul said after a pause. "It's quite a view."

In accord, they stared down at the gray-green surf churning over the rocks far below them.

Paul said finally, "If...someone fell, he'd have gone straight into the drink."

"It depends on the time of day and year," Finn said. "In the morning, at that time of year, the tide was probably out. He'd hit the rocks."

"Lovely." Paul heaved a heavy sigh. "Well, I don't know what you're thinking, but there's no way Fitch jumped. And there are much easier ways of killing someone than dragging them up seventy-three stairs and pushing them off a balcony.

"He climbed up to look for something that morning — there was something he wanted to see on the island. I'm wondering what it was." Finn slowly traversed the metal platform staring out over water, rocks, hills, treetops, hills, and more rocks and water.

"See anything?" Paul asked when he rejoined him.

Finn shook his head. They stood in silence, watching the storm rolling toward them over the choppy water.

"I think we should go down before that hits," Paul said. "This tower must act like a lightning rod in a storm."

Finn nodded.

Paul pushed away from the side, crossed the platform, and started down the stairs, his feet clanging on the metal rungs. Finn started to turn away, stopped. The railing around the platform was painted a dull brick color. It was weathered and chipped in places. Where Paul had been standing, there were several long, narrow marks where the paint had scraped away. The marks curved over the top of the railing and continued down the other side — dropping away to nothing.

Finn counted the scratches in the paint. There were ten of them.

Wednesday evenings for as long as Finn could remember, Barnaby Purdon came to The Birches for dinner and checkers with Uncle Thomas.

Barnaby had been a teacher on the mainland, and before his retirement he made the trip back and forth from the island every weekday. Finn and Fitch had been homeschooled, but Barnaby had overseen their education as much as anyone could be said to have overseen it, and Finn had always liked the pale, twitchy but enthusiastic young man Barnaby had been. Barnaby had a way of pointing out the gossipy, interesting bits of academia, so Finn and Fitch hadn't only studied geometry, they had learned about Harappan mathematics, and the *I Ching*, and Plato.

No longer young, and no longer twitchy, Barnaby was still enthusiastic, and he greeted Finn warmly that evening. "How's that brother of yours?" he inquired as Uncle Thomas handed whiskey sours — another part of the Wednesday evening tradition — all around.

Barnaby was smiling quizzically. Gazing into his pale face, Finn abruptly remembered that here was another person Fitch had not cared for. He had called Barnaby the White Rabbit and mocked him in secret — and sometimes openly. Finn had always tried to ignore it, tune it out, but Con's words of the afternoon resonated even though Finn had tried to deny them.

"I haven't seen him in three years," Finn answered and took a cocktail glass from the tray.

Barnaby raised his white eyebrows. His blond hair had turned silver now, and that reminded Finn of Miss Minton. That was something he *really* didn't want to remember: the way Fitch had mocked Barnaby about Miss Minton being in love with him.

As little as Finn wanted to admit it, Con had been right. Fitch's sense of humor could be cruel sometimes. He had been cruel about Miss Minton and Barnaby, and if there had been the tentative beginnings of something between them, it had shriveled by being exposed to merciless light too early on.

"Out of the country, is he?" Barnaby asked. "He always did have itchy feet."

"They have powder for that," Paul chimed in. "In Fitch's case, I'd have recommended rat poison."

Barnaby looked surprised, and Uncle Thomas coughed. Paul met Finn's glare innocently.

Finn said, "To tell you the truth, I've been trying to find out what happened to him. No one seems to have seen him since he supposedly left the island three years ago."

"*Supposedly?*" Barnaby repeated.

"Finn," Uncle Thomas said uncomfortably and then stopped.

As though speaking to the at-home viewers, Paul said airily, "He's very stubborn. Once he gets something into his head, it's impossible to shake him loose. He's convinced that Fitch is dead. That he was murdered."

Into the shocked silence that followed Paul's words came the sound of smashing glass from the dining room. They all turned as Martha appeared white-faced in the doorway.

"What are you saying?" she asked. Her eyes were enormous in her stricken face.

"Why did you have to put it like that?" Finn asked Paul, moving to Martha.

"What in God's name is going on?" Uncle Thomas demanded, looking from face to face.

"It's not true," Martha said to Finn, but she sounded like she was begging for reassurance, not really denying it.

"I don't know," Finn said. "I mean, I'm not sure. There's no proof that Fitch ever left the island. And no one ever saw him again after that day."

"What day?" Barnaby asked, sounding bewildered.

"The day Finn found Conway Twitty and Fitch fucking in the lighthouse," Paul said.

"That's about enough of that," Uncle Thomas said in a tone Finn had rarely heard. "I won't have that kind of talk in this house."

Paul laughed. "You do know your nephew is gay, right?"

"That's Finn's business. I'm not going to —"

"This is totally off the track," Finn interrupted. "The point is that Fitch disappeared three years ago and hasn't been seen since. I think something happened to him that day."

"You think he's dead," Paul corrected.

Three horrified faces turned his way. Finn said, "I do. Yes."

Martha faltered, "But if...if there had been some accident..."

"I don't think it was an accident. Someone packed his things to make it look like he left on his own. That couldn't happen accidentally."

"But that's...that's crazy," Uncle Thomas said. Barnaby glanced at him but said nothing.

"I knew it," Martha moaned. "I always felt something was wrong, him leaving like that and Finn the next day. I knew when Finn said he hadn't seen him..."

"No." Uncle Thomas spoke firmly. "*No*. It's impossible. Ridiculous. No one would do such a thing. And if it were true...where are his things? Where is the...the body?"

Martha moaned again. Rain shushed softly against the windows.

"No one's looked for them," Paul said. "No one's looked for *him*. If someone started looking..."

"Have you called the police yet?" Barnaby asked calmly into the stunned silence.

Finn shook his head, gazing at his uncle. "I wanted to talk to you first."

"C-call the police?" Uncle Thomas was practically stuttering. "That's the craziest thing I've heard yet. Call the police based on...on what? This is Fitch we're talking about, is it not? He's just as likely to be deliberately playing some hoax on us."

"For three years?" Martha cried. "He wouldn't. Not for three years."

"Martha's right," Finn said. "I think three years negates the possibility of this being a hoax."

"Although I don't put anything beyond him," Paul said casually, moving to take a layered cream cheese biscuit off the tray on the credenza.

Uncle Thomas put his glass down. "Finn, I don't believe you've thought this all the way through. Do you have any idea how truly unpleasant a police investigation would be? It would be in the papers, you understand? They would ask questions of all of us, and they wouldn't stop until they had all the details of that day — the whole story of what happened between you and Con and Fitch."

Not for the first time, it occurred to Finn to wonder how, if Fitch had never returned to The Birches, everyone at the house seemed to know what had taken place that morning at the lighthouse? He blurted, "How do you know about that?"

Uncle Thomas looked at Martha, and Martha, oddly enough, was the one who answered. "Mr. Carlyle came to the house to find you the next afternoon. It wasn't hard to put together what must have happened. Fitch was... Well, he had his funny ways. No mistake."

"Fitch was jealous of you," Paul said. "He was jealous of you, and he was jealous *of* you, if you get what I mean."

"Huh?"

"He competed with you, competed with you for attention from people like Con. From everyone, I imagine. But he also wanted you all to himself. He was jealous of time and attention you gave others, right?"

Finn stared at them bewilderedly. This was very much what Con had said, but Finn had never seen any of this in his relationship with his twin. He wanted to tell them that they were all wrong, but he was too much of a realist to believe that everyone else could see it the same way and still be mistaken.

Martha said uncomfortably, "Mr. Carlyle was… Well…"

"Con was distraught," Uncle Tom said crisply. "I don't see what's to be gained by digging all this up now."

"I think Tom's right," Barnaby said quietly. "Best to let sleeping dogs lie."

"I don't understand."

Paul said, "They want you to shut up about it. They want you to forget about Fitch."

Finn stared at the ring of faces watching him with varying degrees of wariness. He said to Martha, "You don't believe that, do you? You don't believe we can — we should — just forget this? Forget that Fitch has been murdered?"

"We don't know that for sure," she faltered. "He might have left the island. Just because we can't prove it, doesn't mean he didn't leave of his own free will. And if the police start digging…and the papers…it's going to be…bad. Bad for all of us."

"Murder is bad for all of us," Finn said.

"It's not merely you and your reputation at stake," Uncle Thomas said flatly. "There's my own name and reputation — this family's name and reputation. There's Con's name and reputation. A thing like this could ruin us all."

Finn opened his mouth to make an impatient reply, but Barnaby said, "Have you thought about the fact that you'll be under suspicion as well?"

"Me?"

"If I understand correctly, there was some falling out between you, Fitch, and Conlan Carlyle. That means that you and Carlyle will be the prime suspects."

"Do you have an alibi for that day?" Paul inquired sweetly.

Finn stared at him.

"You're talking about disrupting a lot of lives…and we don't even know for sure that Fitch isn't perfectly well and merrily raising hell in some other corner of the world." Uncle Thomas picked up his drink and sipped it. With an air of having said the final word, he said, "Martha, is dinner about ready?"

Martha made a visible effort to pull herself together. With a guilty look at Finn, she nodded to her employer and left the room.

"I don't believe this," Finn said at last.

Barnaby smiled uncomfortably at him — offering that same sort of silent half apology Martha had — before handing his glass to Thomas for a refill.

Finn opened his mouth. He closed it. Clearly, if he was going to proceed, it was going to be against the will of everyone at The Birches — with the exception of Paul, who moved to his side and said under his breath, "Don't worry. We'll find proof."

Dinner was a strange affair. The food, as always, was excellent. Roast beef and Martha's shrimp-stuffed triple-baked potatoes. Barnaby and Uncle Thomas chatted pleasantly about politics and general island business, directing comments to Finn and Paul, but not pausing long enough for either of the younger men to really join in the conversation — let alone redirect it. On the surface, everything seemed normal. The conversation in the parlor might never have occurred, but as casual as Uncle Thomas and Barnaby seemed, Finn was conscious of being carefully and deliberately corralled.

The discussion regarding Fitch was clearly over.

It was unbelievable, and yet…it was a perfect example of how life on Seal Island had always been…isolated and self-contained. It was as though they none of them realized how unrealistic — otherworldly — their attitude was. In fact, scooping the creamy, steaming-hot filling out of the potato shell, Finn couldn't help wondering if maybe *he* was the one missing the point. Maybe he *should* leave well enough alone.

Not only did he dread the idea of being the focus of a police investigation — what the hell kind of an alibi did *he* have for that day? He'd spent it sitting on top of a mountain staring at the ocean and trying not to think. He was horrified at the idea of dragging Con into the limelight. Nothing could have convinced him of Con's innocence as effectively as his hurt fury at the lighthouse that afternoon.

He remembered only too clearly how fiercely protective of his privacy Con had always been.

In fact, every time he thought of Con, his stomach knotted with anxiety. It had been much easier when he was confident in his unyielding anger and rancor. But Con's remorse, his continued displays of affection and caring, were wearing Finn down. Equally wearing were the times when Con seemed to indicate that he was moving on or losing interest in pursuing anything with Finn. When it came to Con, Finn was a mess of contradictory feelings — the bottom line being that whether he could sort them out yet or not, he did still have feelings for Con. Con was making it hard to ignore those feelings. And now Finn had weakened his own position of utter inviolate righteousness by doing something fairly unforgivable…like accusing Con of murder.

'Cause nothing put a damper on romance like suspicions of homicide.

But Fitch…as angry and hurt and unforgiving as Finn had believed himself…he couldn't bear not knowing what had happened to Fitch. Nor could he bear the idea that someone had killed Fitch and was going to be allowed to get away with it. Perhaps that was ironic, given how certain he had been that he could never forgive his twin — but knowing that now there truly would be no chance for reconciliation had changed everything.

At the same time, he couldn't help being afraid of waking this particular old hound dog. It was a small island, and he was painfully aware that he could rule out the possibility that Fitch had been killed by a passing madman. The odds were, whoever had killed Fitch was someone Finn knew quite well. Maybe loved.

Granted, Fitch had had his secrets — certainly Finn hadn't known about Con and Fitch until the day that he'd discovered them in the lighthouse. Maybe there was someone else on the island who had known another side of Fitch.

Or maybe someone had followed Fitch to the island. Finn glanced across the table, and Paul met his eyes.

No.

No, right? Because if Paul had been going to kill Fitch, it probably would have been when they were still together. Who waited years? And Paul had moved on. Well, he didn't have a steady lover — but neither did Finn. No. But it wouldn't hurt to ask whether Paul had an alibi for that weekend.

When at last the meal was finished, Uncle Tom and Barnaby took their brandies and went off to the study to play checkers.

"Where can we go to talk?" Paul asked in a stage whisper.

Finn shook his head, rising. He led the way upstairs to Fitch's bedroom. A little frisson rippled down his spine as he pushed the door open and turned on the light.

Looking around himself, Paul said, "This was his room?"

Finn nodded. There was an obstruction in his throat that made it difficult to speak.

The room was the twin of his own — same window seat flanked by dormer windows, same funny-sloping ceiling and long bookshelves. The heavy, mismatched furniture was similar — both rooms had been furnished from other rooms within the house. As with his own room, nothing had been moved or changed, although the room was neatly dusted, the bed made.

How weird to stand here in this room again. Finn closed his eyes, trying to remember, trying to…perhaps reach out to Fitch. But all he sensed was a room that hadn't been used for a long time. He opened his eyes. There were photos stuck on the mirror over the dresser: a snapshot of himself crossing his eyes for Fitch's camera, a much older picture of them together swimming, and several shots of people unknown to him. There was a small bowl on the dresser with loose change, a couple of fishing lures, and a pair of dice.

Paul opened the closet door. "His clothes are still here."

Finn joined him, looking inside. There were some odds and ends pushed to the side. A fishing vest, a couple of flannel shirts, a heavy parka. "Those are mostly his older things. Stuff he'd outgrown or only wore here on the island. He took — well, someone took — most of what he'd brought with him that summer. His suitcases are gone."

Paul backed out of the closet and looked around the room. "There's not a lot here."

"He didn't like collecting junk."

Fitch had never been one for acquiring possessions. He had a few books, not nearly the number Finn had — nothing from his childhood. There were no games, no equivalent of Finn's collection of old sailboat models. There was a fishing pole behind the door and a tennis racket in the closet.

"Did he keep a journal?" Paul asked.

Finn shook his head.

Paul went over to the dresser and took the photos down from the mirror, one by one. "I know some of these people."

Finn joined him, glancing at the familiar and unfamiliar faces. "Anyone with a grudge against him?"

Paul snorted. "I have no idea why, but most people thought Fitch was perfectly charming — even when he was screwing them over."

Finn moved to the desk and examined the desktop calendar. It was open to August eighteenth. There was nothing noted for the day. No "betray my brother before breakfast" reminder. He flipped through the back pages, but they were all blank. He said slowly, his thoughts on Uncle Thomas and Barnaby, "I can't decide if they honestly don't believe Fitch is dead, or if they're afraid he really is."

"I think they know he's dead. I think your uncle has suspected it long enough that it's not even a shock."

Finn sighed. "They're right, though. I can't go to the police without something more than this."

"You could file a missing persons report and let it follow its natural course. Let the police decide if there are grounds for a murder investigation."

"Yes, but what they said is true. If I open this can of worms, there's no way of controlling it."

"So?"

"So? So if the police determine that a murder investigation is warranted, Con and I will both be prime suspects."

Paul studied Finn, head tilted to one side. "*Did* you kill him?"

"Ha-ha."

"I wouldn't blame you if you had."

"I didn't kill my brother," Finn said shortly. "If I had, I wouldn't be pointing out to everyone that I thought he'd been murdered."

"You might," Paul said seriously. "If you thought it had been long enough that people were going to start wondering and asking questions."

Finn said wearily, "If I had been going to kill anyone that day, it would have been myself. And I wasn't about to kill myself."

"You still had too many wonderful paintings left to give the world," Paul trilled, waving his arm in a broad gesture toward the room's only painting — one of Finn's early studies of the lighthouse.

"Yeah, actually. You can laugh about it, but as miserable as I was, I still had a strong sense of the work I wanted to do. I knew it wasn't always going to be as bad as it was right then."

"I suppose that makes sense." Paul eyed him speculatively. "And so you fled to me."

"You were the only person I knew in Manhattan."

"Now don't spoil it, because I've always been immensely flattered that you came to me."

Finn spluttered, "I told you that day when I apologized for barging in on you."

"Shhhhh, don't speak...no no no...don't speak," Paul said, seemingly channeling Dianne Wiest in *Bullets Over Broadway.* "Now that I think of it, I wonder why we never got together. We had an obvious natural bond."

Was rage at Fitch an *obvious natural bond?* Finn answered, "Because I was still in love with Con and you were still in love with Fitch."

For a long moment, Paul stared at him. He smiled — he had a surprisingly sweet smile. "I guess that's true." He put a hand on his hip, surveying the room thoughtfully. "All right. So if you were a body, where would *you* hide?"

CHAPTER EIGHT

It was a small island, but there were many places one could hide a body. It could be buried in Bell Woods or in the soft sand of the cave at Otter Cove. It could lie undiscovered beneath the wildflowers in one of the meadows or on a hillside beneath a cairn of stones.

The first challenge would be in transporting a corpse in broad daylight.

If Fitch had died at the lighthouse — and Finn and Paul could not agree on this point, as Paul did not concur that the scratches in the light tower looked like marks left by clawing fingernails. But for the sake of argument, if Fitch *had* died at the lighthouse…the simplest thing would have been to bury him there. The lighthouse was off the beaten track and there was less chance of discovery by a stray hiker's dog. It also eliminated the need to move the body any distance.

"It wouldn't be hard to lift you," Paul commented, examining Finn, who was sitting on Fitch's bed. "Even when you're your normal weight, you're pretty skinny. Maybe one forty, one forty-five? Fitch was more muscular — not a lot a heavier, though."

"A deadweight is different."

"Even so. I could do it. You could do it if you didn't have to carry someone too far."

Finn considered. "We should talk to Miss Minton. I don't know if her memory is as sharp as it used to be, but in the old days, no one traveled the road to The Birches without her seeing them. Con said she saw him that day. She might have seen someone else."

"Is there another way to get to this house besides the main road?"

"There isn't another drive. There's a trail that leads to the back of the property." He remembered that Hiram had been clearing poison ivy out that day along the path.

There was a tap on the door frame, and both Finn and Paul jumped guiltily.

"You boys have been up here awhile," Martha said, bringing a tray into the bedroom and setting it on the desk where Paul sat. "I brought you some hot chocolate and lobster butter cookies."

Paul spluttered and put a hand over his mouth, his gaze finding Finn's.

Martha straightened and eyed Finn sternly. "Mr. Carlyle called a little while ago. He wanted to make sure you got home safely."

Paul laughed outright. Finn ignored him. He said to Martha, "Con and I argued. It's not anything new."

"I don't understand these things," she said. "It seems to me that Mr. Carlyle still has powerful feelings for you. And despite what you say, I think you still have feelings for him. Is that such a bad thing? It's not like there's so much love in the world that people can afford to go turning it away."

Finn tried to imagine what Con must have said to Martha to inspire that little speech.

He opened his mouth, but Paul forestalled him, saying, "Martha, between us, who do you think might have killed Fitch?"

She turned slowly and stared at him. "I loved Fitch," she said. "But I'll tell you right now, sonny, you're meddling in things best left alone. And you're dragging Finn into dangerous waters with you."

"No one's dragging me into anything," Finn said quietly. "If someone killed Fitch, I can't ignore that."

"There are all kinds of things we have to ignore every day," Martha said. "Sometimes it's better for everyone to let certain things go."

"You're talking about turning a blind eye to murder, not spitting on the sidewalk," Paul said shrilly.

"I know exactly what I'm talking about," Martha said grimly. She looked at Finn. "Don't you stay up too late, Finn."

Paul closed the door after her with a suggestion of a bang. Catching Finn's expression, he burst out laughing.

◊ ◊ ◊ ◊

It was still raining on Thursday morning, a steady wash of silver rain that was almost invisible in the gray daylight. Fog shrouded the sea, pierced here and there by a dripping tree. It did not look like a particularly auspicious day for sleuthing.

"You don't think it's going to snow, do you?" Paul asked, meeting Finn on his way down to breakfast.

"It's not cold enough."

"Are you kidding me? I thought the next ice age had come last night."

Finn threw Paul a guilty glance. He'd been perfectly warm; Martha had brought him extra blankets before he'd fallen asleep. Well, perhaps there was a blanket shortage at The Birches these days. Or perhaps not.

Probably not — as Martha still seemed a little stern when they found her in the kitchen. She ordered them to the table and began piling their plates.

It brought back comfortable memories. The kitchen was very warm and smelled deliciously of bacon and coffee and cinnamon rolls. Martha had the radio on low as she listened to the weather report.

"Paul and I are going to borrow the station wagon this morning," Finn told her as she refilled his coffee cup. "Unless you or Hiram need it for something?"

Martha directed a disapproving look at Paul, who was busily eating his haystack eggs — baked eggs on fried potato sticks with cheese and bacon topping.

"Dangerous driving conditions today," she pronounced like a hash-slinging oracle.

"We'll be careful."

Martha hmphed. "I don't need the car today." She didn't say more, though it was clear she wished to. Paul grimaced at his plate without looking up.

Breakfast finished, Finn and Paul climbed into the station wagon — Paul driving — and headed slowly and cautiously down the muddy road to Estelle Minton's.

"So your uncle and the ex-school teacher... Are they...?" Paul peered over the steering wheel at the lazy whorl of fog before them.

"Are they — Huh?" Finn stared at him and did a double take. "Uncle Thomas and Barnaby? God no. They've been friends forever."

"So?"

"You better get your gaydar recalibrated. Neither of them is a member of the sisterhood. I think Barnaby used to have a thing for Miss Minton, and Uncle Thomas was once engaged to a lady from the mainland."

"What happened to the lady from the mainland?"

"The story is she declined to live on an island, and Uncle Tom couldn't picture living anywhere else."

"Uncle Tom is a little set in his ways, isn't he?"

"Here it is," Finn interrupted. "You can pull to the side of the road, but don't get stuck in the mud."

Most days Miss Minton could be found working out in her yard, but today there was no sign of her, although the battered pickup in the drive indicated she was home. White trails of fog wreathed the rosebushes and trees as though dragged there by the rain. A wheelbarrow sat tipped over next to stacked bags of fertilizer and soil amendment.

Finn swore as his cane sank into the mud, and Paul laughed.

"Need a hand?"

"How about a new leg?"

Crossing the deserted road, they entered through the gate. They knocked on the front door, and after a few seconds it opened. Miss Minton, dressed in comfortably baggy flannels and jeans, stared at them in surprise.

"Finn Barret. Something wrong at The Birches?"

"Nothing like that," Finn said apologetically. "I was hoping to maybe have a word with you?"

"Well, well." She directed a skeptical look at Paul. "I expect you'd better come in."

They followed her into a large room with a picture window that looked out on the road. The room was comfortably furnished in crisp blue and white. A fire burned cheerfully in the grate. A black cat leisurely groomed itself on the pillow-piled sofa.

"Well, you'd better have a seat," their hostess said. "This isn't weather for fooling around on the roads. It must be something pretty important to bring you down here?"

Finn glanced at Paul, who was watching him, clearly wanting Finn to take charge here. Which was all very well, but it seemed sort of tactless to hint to Miss Minton he thought her longtime friends and neighbors might be murderers.

"This is going to seem like an odd request," he said. "I wanted to put that famous memory of yours to the test."

Miss Minton raised her eyebrows but said nothing.

"August, three years ago…Fitch and I both left the island." He paused, but Miss Minton had nothing to say to that. "I left on the nineteenth. It was a Tuesday, about eleven o'clock in the morning. We always thought Fitch left on the previous Monday afternoon."

"But?"

"But no one ever saw him again," Finn said. "At least, if they did, they're not admitting it."

Miss Minton's brows knitted. "I'm not sure what you're getting at. Are you saying… What *are* you saying?"

"We think Fitch is dead," Paul said as Finn groped for a less shocking way to break the news. "We think someone on this island might have killed him."

Finn turned on him, and meeting that exasperated stare, Paul said, "What? That's what we think!"

To Miss Minton, Finn said, "It does seem like Fitch never left the island, and what we were wondering was whether you remembered anything that might have stood out from the ordinary."

"When?"

"That Monday. The eighteenth of August. I thought you might remember because it was during the time you were still taking art lessons from Uncle Tom."

Miss Minton looked taken aback. "You expect me to remember something that happened three years ago? Such as what?"

"Like who traveled to and from The Birches that day."

She was watching him with a peculiar alertness. "Ah," she said finally. She seemed to look inward. At last she said, "My lessons were Monday and Wednesdays, but I don't remember taking a lesson that week."

"Uncle Tom was supposed to fly to Boston or somewhere for an art show or a lecture. His flight was canceled on Monday, but he spent most of the day in Portland at the airport."

"That's right..." Miss Minton said slowly. "I do remember. Con walked past here about lunchtime right before I came in from the garden to change clothes. I don't remember seeing him walk back, but he wasn't at The Birches when I arrived about half an hour later. No one was there at all, and I came back home."

"Did you see anyone else pass here on their way to The Birches that day?"

"It was a long time ago, Finn. I seem to remember your uncle driving past early in the evening. And you and Con walked by about an hour and a half after that." Her smile was wry. "Con's voice carried. I remember that."

Finn colored.

"I'm surprised I remember that much after all this time," Miss Minton commented, reaching for the cat and cuddling it in her arms.

"Why do you suppose that is?" Paul asked.

Miss Minton gave him a considering stare. "I don't know. I guess the reason it stayed in my mind is because it *was* the summer — the very week, in fact — the Barret Boys left Seal Island."

◊ ◊ ◊ ◊

"She's like something straight out of Stephen King," Paul commented as they got back into the car. "Or possibly, *What Not to Wear.*"

"I don't see that," Finn replied irritably. Sometimes Paul's casual unkindness reminded him of Fitch. "She's had a hard life."

"So had Dolores Claiborne. So had Cujo."

Finn sat unmoving, not really listening. The fog blanketed the car in white, giving them the illusion of complete and utter privacy. "She used to be different when she was younger."

Paul groaned. "*Why* do people always say that? *Everyone* is different when they're younger. Nobody is born a crotchety old fart." Studying Finn's profile, he asked reluctantly, "Different how?"

"Happier. Softer. Pretty."

"I'll take your word for it."

"I didn't know her well, but she and Uncle Tom have been friends for years. She used to babysit Con — I didn't know her *then*, naturally, but she was always crazy about him. They're third or fourth cousins, I think."

"Toto, I have a feeling we're not in Arkansas anymore."

"I don't mean that way. She never married, never had kids of her own. Actually, I always thought those art lessons were more about the way she liked Uncle Tom than her really wanting to become a painter."

"Sacrilege. I thought it was old Barnaby she had a thing for?"

"She did. Well, I mean…I have no idea. What do kids know? She might have been sweet on Barnaby or he might have been sweet on her."

"As fascinating as Miss Minton's love life is, where to now?"

Finn said slowly, "The lighthouse."

"I think so, yeah."

There were a few alarming seconds while the car's tires spun in the mud, but then they gained traction and were on the road once more, proceeding with great caution through the white nothingness.

"For the record, I hate driving in this," Paul said.

Finn nodded absently.

"The fact that she didn't see anyone but Con that day doesn't mean that no one else went up to The Birches," Paul said when Finn's silence persisted. "They could have gone in the back way. We didn't talk to Ezra or whatever his name is."

"Hiram."

"Right. Maybe he saw someone. Or maybe she missed them. Him."

"Maybe."

The car bounced along the uneven track, Paul accelerating as the mist thinned out in patches. "If you think about it," he said, "it's kind of hard to believe that someone would simply walk up and shove Fitch off the tower, and then what? Scrape him off the rocks and hide him under a bush?"

Finn rubbed his forehead, smoothing away the little ache in his temple.

"True. To really hide a body you'd either have to weight it down and dump it in the ocean or dig a grave deep enough that no one would accidentally uncover it."

"If he was dumped in the ocean three years ago, we're wasting our time."

"I know."

"Obviously, if he was killed at the lighthouse, whoever did it couldn't take a chance on moving a body around in broad daylight. That's what we think, right? That he was killed in broad daylight?"

"Yes. No one seems to have seen him after he and Con parted ways."

"Which leads me to wonder — and you won't like this — how could anyone know he'd be up there?"

Finn sighed. "Either it was Con, and he killed Fitch when he hit him — which I don't believe — or it was someone who was maybe following Fitch?" He said slowly, working it out, "*Or* maybe it was someone Fitch had originally planned to meet? Because I remember that night Con was saying to me that it hadn't been planned, that it hadn't been arranged, it had just happened. That he'd actually come up to the lighthouse to find me because I was supposed to be sketching there that day."

Paul's eyes were trained on the road ahead. He grunted. "Not bad."

"Here, you've missed the turn."

Paul braked sharply, reversed, and turned off the road leading up to the lighthouse.

"So...you think Fitch arranged to meet this person, but Con showed up first, and Fitch grabbed the opportunity as it presented itself? Yeah, I can see that. He'd enjoy rubbing someone's nose in it."

Finn shot him a sideways look and said nothing.

"It could have been someone who was there for another reason, though." Paul spoke meditatively, "Someone who hiked up there for the view or to sketch..."

Finn's stomach did an unpleasant flip-flop

Paul rambled cheerfully on. "Maybe this person had an innocent reason for being there but went a little crazy when he saw what was happening. Maybe he pretended to walk away and hid, and when Con left, he came back and killed Fitch. Because it seems to me that whoever killed Fitch must have been someone Fitch wasn't afraid of."

"Fitch wasn't afraid of anyone."

"No. He wasn't."

Finn added, "And I didn't come back and kill him. It happened exactly like I said it did."

Paul chuckled. "I never doubted you. Here we are." The lighthouse swung suddenly into the windshield's view, seeming to loom up out of the mist.

They took their flashlights and jackets, got out of the car, and stood staring up at the white tower. A gull appeared out of the mist, crying eerily and disappearing once more.

Paul said, "Let's put our emotions aside for a sec and look at this logically. If Fitch was killed here, then there's a good chance he's buried here. Somewhere. I can't see anyone taking the risk of moving a body very far."

"I can't either."

"Could he be buried inside? Maybe put into a wall or stuck under the flooring?"

It took Finn a moment to control his voice. "I guess that's what we're going to find out."

Without further discussion, they went into the light keeper's dwelling. In silence that seemed to grow heavier with each passing minute, they moved around the small residence, checking the empty built-in closets and cupboards, pounding against the walls, which all seemed perfectly solid. The wind picked up, whistling mournfully through the boards across the window, moaning down the chimney. Far, far beneath their feet was the slow, distant pound of the surf hitting the cliffs in phantom heartbeat.

"We should have brought shovels," Paul said.

"That would have gone over well. There's no sense upsetting people if we don't need to." Finn moved the flashlight over the broken flooring.

"You mean if we don't find anything?"

Finn studied the moldering earth beneath the broken patches of boards. Yes, Paul was right, they should have brought shovels.

Paul said shortly, "That *is* what you mean, right? If we don't find anything, you're not going to let them cover this up? You're not going to let them get away with murder?"

Finn stared across the room at Paul's weirdly shadowed face. "Them?"

"Yes, *them*. All of them. Are you going to call the police or not? Or do I need to do it?"

"What's the matter with you?"

"If you killed him…then I understand. I can forgive it. But if it wasn't you —"

"I told you I didn't kill Fitch."

Paul lifted a negligent shoulder.

"I'm not lying." Finn's flare of temper caught even him off guard. "And I'm not going to let anyone get away with anything, but you're not making the call on this. And I'm not doing anything until I've thought it through. Until I know what I'm dealing with. And one of the things I don't understand is why the hell you're so hot to see Fitch get justice. You hated him."

"I *loved* him!"

"You loved him? You *sued* him."

The beam of Finn's flashlight caught tears glittering on Paul's cheeks. "So what? I was angry and bitter — and jealous, I admit that. But I never stopped loving him. Even when I hated him."

Finn opened and then closed his mouth. Finally he managed, "Really? Well, you've hid it pretty well all this time."

"What do you know about it? You've been moping over Conway Twitty for three years. Which ought to tell you something right there, since I'm pretty sure you thought you hated *him*."

That struck a little too close to home. Finn said, "In that case, and since you're so quick to scream for justice, where the hell were you on the eighteenth of August three years ago?"

Paul gasped as though mortally struck. Tears gave way to astonishment and then outrage. "What are you saying to me?"

"I'm saying...you're so quick to want to call the cops, fine. Only they're going to ask you where you were three years ago — especially since, according to you, you were still in love with Fitch. It was one thing when you were an interested bystander, but now you're a potential suspect."

"You...*bitch!*"

"Hey" — Finn shrugged — "I'm just pointing out the obvious. You're a suspect here too. So before we go flying off to drag the state police into this, I suggest we figure out exactly what we're dealing with. Because we're both going to be very unpopular if it turns out Fitch isn't dead. And if he is dead, we're going to be even *more* unpopular — not to mention one of us might end up getting arrested for a crime he didn't commit."

Paul stood very still. "You're turning this around on me to protect Carlyle. He's the only one who could have done this and you know it."

"Do you have an alibi or not?"

"I don't know! I don't remember where I was three years ago. I might have an alibi. When I get home, I'll check!"

"Great. In the meantime, let's keep our mouths shut till we know something for sure. Because right now we don't know *anything*. We don't even have a body."

"Well, why don't I go get a couple of shovels?" Paul offered with acid sweetness. He stared challengingly at Finn.

Finn stared back. "All right," he said finally. "Why don't you?"

"Do you mean that?"

"Of course I mean it. I already told you I —" He shook his head wearily. "Just...try not to let anyone see you. They're going to be very upset if they think —"

"Give me credit for some discretion," Paul said. He propped his flashlight on one of the window shelves and picked his way across the broken flooring.

Finn forced himself to stay where he stood as he heard the car engine fade away. Blackness was *not* the absence of color. If you mixed every color together, what did you get? You got black. Close enough. So there was nothing to fear in the darkness. No reason to stand here with his heart in overdrive and sweat breaking out over his body, because nothing in the darkness could hurt him. And even if there was something buried in the soft, wet square of ground next to his foot, it could not be Fitch. It was not big enough for Fitch.

He forced himself to stand there for another wrenching second or two, and then he crossed the broken floor and stepped outside. The fog had mostly dissipated; the rain was coming down in a fine misting. But overhead, the sky was heavy and dark with the promise of worse weather, and the sea looked black.

He took a couple of deep lungfuls of oxygen, and then he forced himself back into the cottage. The cottage door swung restlessly back and forth on its creaking hinges, and he propped it open with a large flat rock.

Fresh air, daylight. What more could he ask? Grimly, he took his cane and began to poke it into the soft dirt near the far corner of the house where he thought he had seen an unnatural indentation in the bare earth. The ground was very soft. The tip of the cane slid in deep and struck something — which then gave.

He straightened up, stood motionless, looked to the doorway. It stood open and empty. The door tugged in the wind, bouncing against the rock anchoring it.

Finn looked down at the square of damp earth.

An old rug?

It hadn't sounded like that. He lowered himself carefully, kneeling awkwardly, scraping at the thing buried in the soft, damp earth.

After a time he stopped, looked around for something else to use as a shovel. He spotted a broken piece of flooring and grabbed that, carving and scraping, digging away as ferociously as a terrier despite the uneasy feeling crawling down his spine. It had to be the cold of the cottage working its way into his bones; he gritted his jaw against the incipient chatter of teeth.

"It's a suitcase," he got out, and the sound of his own voice startled him.

He dug more quickly, the wood making a rough whisper against the cloth of the suitcase, and then the suitcase was free and he used all his strength to drag it out of the hole in the floor. He braced a hand against the wall and pulled himself up again.

Hauling the suitcase out into the soft, rainy mist, he laid it on the patchy grass and brushed away rust and mud, struggling to yank the zipper open. The smell of rotted material and mildew wafted up. Inside were a jumble of clothes and odds and ends. Finn recognized the moldy remains of a black checked shirt, a moss green sweater, red briefs, the cotton discolored, the elastic deteriorated.

He touched the shirt — his own. Fitch had borrowed it one day, and Finn had never thought of it since.

At last he closed the suitcase lid and sat there, shaking a little with cold and exhaustion and nerves. He had not really, entirely believed it until now, but there could be no doubt.

Fitch was dead. Murdered.

He was not sure how much time had passed by the time it occurred to him that Fitch had had two suitcases. That meant the other must still lie in the cottage in another corner of wet, cushioning earth.

He forced himself back on his feet and back into the pitchy interior of the cottage. Was it darker than before or was that his overactive imagination?

Not so overactive as it turned out.

Finding his discarded cane, he began to poke again in the spongy sections of bare earth.

From outside came the rumble of thunder. He ignored it, jabbing the metal tip of the walking stick into the moldering earth. It took a while, but on the opposite side of the room, near the doorway leading to the light tower, again he struck something in the soil.

And as he did, a blast of wind, harder than the previous gusts, slammed shut the door to the cottage.

His heart seemed to stop. And then, after a moment of utter, abject, paralyzed fear, it jump-started, speeding back into life.

Finn began to feel his way across the uneven boards, reminding himself all the while that he had a flashlight — two flashlights, for Paul's still shone from the window shelf — and that his fear was an irrational, foolish thing.

Except that wasn't right. Maybe there wasn't anything in the darkness to fear, but Fitch had been murdered — and that murderer could only be one of a handful of people, and they were all still on this island.

He was still absorbing the full shock of that when the cottage door was dragged open again. Instinctively, Finn turned off his flashlight as a black outline filled the doorway.

"Finn?" Con called out.

Silently, instinctively, Finn moved back, slipping through the doorway that led to the tower. Watery light from the windows high, high above moved in the base of the tower like ghosts.

"Who's in here?" Con called.

Finn didn't move a muscle. Didn't breathe. He could hear Con stepping carefully; hear the crunch of his shoes on broken concrete and splintered wood. Con was coming his way. Soundlessly, he crept behind the stairwell, hiding in the shadows. He knew the impulse telling him to climb was a false one. If he went up the stairs he would be trapped, and yet everything in him was clamoring for light and air and distance from the threat coming steadily toward him.

If he could stay perfectly silent, perfectly still…Con might leave. Might see the tire tracks in the yard and assume that whoever had been at the lamp had come and gone.

But no. The suitcase was still in the yard. He would see it, surely? Would he believe that they had left it behind? Doubtful.

Con was not leaving. Finn could see the golden circle of Paul's flashlight beam coming toward the tower door ahead of Con's footsteps.

Finn's nerve broke and he went for the staircase, trying for silence but needing to move.

"Finn, you're scaring the hell out of me," Con said, and Finn was so startled he misstepped and came down hard on the staircase, which clanged noisily — no concealing that. In any case, for a red wash of an instant he was in too much pain to worry about it. His cane slithered and fell through the railing, hitting the wall of the tower as it dropped to the ground.

Out of the corner of his eye, he saw a shadow move into the tower — caught briefly in the blue light from above.

"Finn?"

"Here," he got out. Dimly, it occurred to him that he had resolved his fear of Con. It had been that disarming *Finn, you're scaring the hell out of me.*

"*Jesus.* What happened?" And Con was at the stairs and bending over him. "How far did you fall?"

"I didn't. Exactly. Just came down wrong."

Con was running hands over him, checking for broken bones. His fingers were cold, his breath warm. He smelled like rain and aftershave.

"I'm okay," Finn said.

"Are you sure? You could have killed yourself."

He opened his mouth to reiterate that he hadn't been far up the staircase, but stopped. He didn't want Con to know he had tried to run from him. He felt stupid for his earlier fear. He had known in his heart Con couldn't be a killer, and yet a part of him had persisted in doubting. Partly it had been the horror of finding Fitch's suitcase, having his worst fears confirmed. Partly, though, he had feared Con.

Grabbing onto the railing, he drew himself up. Con's hand brushed his back, offering support or maybe reassuring himself that Finn was still in one piece. "You're sure?"

Even in that eerie light he could feel Con's gaze. He met it and couldn't look away. "I'm sure." It was mostly embarrassing now. Had he fallen down the stairs it would have been different — fatally different, probably.

"What in the name of Christ were you doing?"

"I needed the light," he said.

"Finn, sugar…" Con said, and there was a wealth of emotion in his voice that Finn couldn't understand. Con's head bent, his mouth covered Finn's, and he kissed him. It was a strange kiss, though. Strangely tender. Strangely restrained. But maybe that wasn't so strange given everything else.

Finn kissed back, tentatively. How long had he waited for this? No, that was wrong. He hadn't waited. Hadn't anticipated or hoped. Hadn't let himself think about it all — because he had believed there was no chance of it ever again. But he had not forgotten. Not forgotten Con's taste or scent or feel. He'd forgotten nothing — and nothing had changed. Finn was no longer tentative — and neither was Con. Suddenly it was hot and sweet and all the colors of the rainbow.

Finn's fingers clenched in Con's wet jacket, and Con was stroking his hair, kissing his face, kissing his hair. "I'm so sorry," he said, and he found Finn's mouth again, his own hungry and insistent. Finn opened to that delving kiss, that firm, deep, hungry kiss that seemed to call forth everything that had been wounded and sleeping deep inside him. He was waking up, all right, the reds and yellows of the color spectrum were alive and well, dancing beneath his eyelids, and his cock was getting hard for the first time in what felt like a very long time.

It was Con who broke the kiss. Finn swayed a little as contact ended, hanging on for support, and Con yielded, softly mouthed the edge of his jaw, his cheekbone, before pulling back again. His voice sounded uneven as he said, "I saw the suitcase."

And it all came crashing back — Fitch was dead, murdered — and Finn was standing here making out. It was…a jolt. He turned, looking blindly for his cane.

Seeing his fumble, Con moved, finding the stick where it had fallen behind the staircase. He grabbed it, then pressed it into Finn's hand, wrapping Finn's fingers around it.

"What are you doing here?"

"I came to check the tower out. After yesterday…" Con didn't finish it, instead taking Finn's arm and guiding him through the darkness of the cottage. There was something unusually protective in the way Con was hanging on to him. Sort of sweet, but sort of quaint too. Not that Finn minded. It was nice to have Con's arm around him, nice to have a little help getting across the obstacle course of the broken floor. But Con had never been overly watchful.

"The other suitcase is in that corner." He nodded to where he had been digging.

Con stopped. "So it's true." His tone was flat but unsurprised. "You should never have come here on your own, Finn. This is... You know what it means."

"I know what it means. I wasn't on my own. Paul came with me. He went back to The Birches to get shovels."

"What the hell was he doing leaving you on your own?"

Con sounded really angry, and Finn looked at him in surprise. "I sent him to get the shovels."

"I don't care. He had no business leaving you on your own." Con was moving forward, still holding Finn's arm as though Finn couldn't be trusted out of his sight. Which was getting a little odd.

Finn freed himself as they reached the door and stepped out into the murky daylight. Con loosed him reluctantly. "I wish you could trust me."

"I do." He realized it was true. He did trust Con. He knew he hadn't killed Fitch, although maybe that was instinct more than logic. He knew that Con regretted the way things had ended between them.

"Do you?" Con's expression was weary. Almost sad. "I know it's my fault. I wasn't there for you the last time, but I will be there for you this time. If you'll let me."

"If I'll let you what?"

Con was giving him the strangest look. "I was hoping you would tell me, but it's not hard to put the pieces together."

"It's...not?"

"I was afraid when no one at The Birches would talk about it — about your accident. I know how hard this is, but you've got to learn to rely on others a little with...this hanging over you."

Finn stopped, staring. His heart was pounding hard as Con's words sunk in. "What do you mean?"

He was afraid he knew only too well what Con meant, so it was a shock when Con said calmly, "I know you're...losing your sight."

Finn blinked. "I'm…"

Con said, "Do you think it makes a difference to me? It doesn't. I still love you. Still want to be with you. Nothing could change that."

Finn felt a crazy desire to burst out laughing — at the same time tears stung his eyes, closed his throat. "*Con*. Jesus. I thought you were going to accuse me of murder — like I did you."

"I know you didn't murder Fitch." Con dismissed the idea as not worth considering. "I didn't kill Fitch. I give you my word. I know you don't have any reason to accept it —"

"Yes, I do. You never lied to me," Finn said. "You weren't always kind, but you never lied."

"I lied to myself," Con said grimly. "I told myself all the time we were seeing each other that it was just sex, a fling. Nothing more. I told myself I didn't want to get involved. That you were too young for me. I couldn't picture myself in a long-term relationship — an open relationship. But the only person I was fooling was me. There isn't any getting over the way I feel about you, Finn. The way I've always felt about you. I've had three years of trying, and when I saw you again, I knew that, for me, nothing had changed." He put a hand up and lightly traced the scar on Finn's temple. "The car accident —"

"I'm not going blind," Finn said.

Con held very still. "You're…not?"

Finn shook his head. Wiped at the tears welling at the corner of his eyes. "No." He gave a watery chuckle. "I can't believe that's what you thought. Were you really prepared to take care of me?"

"Hell yes." Con was staring at him. "I had a speech all ready about how you needed —" He stopped. "Why the hell was everyone so mysterious about your accident?"

"Were they?"

"Yes. No one would tell me anything." Con began to sound incensed. "I could see you were having trouble with your eyes — and all those headaches —"

"Well, yeah, but that was —"

"And what about that comment in the car yesterday about not wearing dark glasses until you had to?"

Finn tried to remember what comment Con meant. He really didn't remember saying anything that should have created such a dramatic impression.

Con said bluntly, "You're terrified of the dark."

Finn's smile faded. "Yes. After the accident...yeah. I couldn't see, and they did think for a time...there was a chance I'd lost my sight." He couldn't meet Con's gaze. There was too much there. He said gruffly, "It...shook me. Not least because of my painting. It's my livelihood, and it's...my passion. My life. I think that was the worst part. Realizing that *all* I had was my painting. And if that was gone —"

"But it's not?"

Finn shook his head. "I'm going to be fine. Even the headaches have gotten better since I've been home. I'm not sure I believed it at first. I think I was afraid to. But...I'm going to be okay." He grimaced. "Now I just have to get the nerve to pick up a paintbrush again."

"Thank God," Con said and pulled him into his arms.

At which point, with cosmic bad timing, the skies opened up. It wasn't quite the effect of being doused with a bucket of cold water, but it wasn't far from it. Con grabbed Finn's arm, and they haltingly ran for the Rover, then slammed inside. Rain ticked noisily down on the metal roof.

Laughing unsteadily with a combination of stress and nerves, they were back in each other's arms and kissing again with a near-frantic hunger, as though they had drawn back in time from some terrifying precipice. Con's mouth was hard and soft, sweet and harsh all at the same time.

The windows began to steam.

"Ow. *Ouch.* This isn't going to work." It wasn't easy, but Finn pulled away, trying to ease his cramping leg despite protests from other frustrated parts of his anatomy.

Con let him go, but his hands lingered. "Let's go to my cottage."

"Paul is going to be here any minute." His body was already aching with thwarted desire. Well, it never rained, but it poured — literally, it seemed.

"Call him and tell him to meet us at the cottage." Con's smile was mostly grimace. "Better yet. Tell him to forget about it." His breath was warm as he leaned forward to nip the side of Finn's throat.

"Con."

"I don't mean that." Con sighed. "It's too late even if I wanted that. But this storm is going to get worse before it gets better."

He was right. The storm was moving in, black clouds sliding across the sky, flashes of lightning flickering over the water.

"Anyway, your part in this is done. We both know what that suitcase means. It's time to call the state police."

"Yes."

It was the lightning that decided Finn. That, and the fact that if he didn't get some kind of sexual release soon, his guts would be in knots.

He pulled Paul's cell phone out and called The Birches.

Martha answered with the news that she had not seen Paul. Finn thanked her and told her to have Paul call his cell if he did turn up. Clicking off, he said to Con, "I told him to make sure no one saw him, so I guess that's not surprising. He's probably on his way back now."

They were silent while the rain beat down on the roof, and the interior of the Rover filled with the peculiarly erotic scent of damp wool and frustrated desire.

"We can't leave the suitcase out there anyway," Con said suddenly. "I'll grab it and leave a note for Paul inside the cottage."

He was out of the vehicle before Finn could object — not that he had a real objection. He was eager to get away from the lighthouse, to get away from the memories — and from what the future must bring.

◊ ◊ ◊

Con was smiling, tracing Finn's collarbone, fingers brushing sensitized skin. He kissed the hollow at the base of Finn's throat.

Finn shivered.

"Cold?"

He shook his head. They were lying on the cushions and rugs before the roaring fireplace in the cottage. The firelight cast heated shadows over their naked bodies as they moved together, exploring with hands and mouths.

Con's mouth nuzzled its way up Finn's throat, and Finn opened his mouth, panting a little beneath that delicate, shuddery pleasure of grazing lips and tongue. When Con's mouth covered his, he moaned softly. Their tongues touched tentatively, withdrew.

Con raised his head, and they smiled at each other.

"Am I rushing you?"

Finn chuckled. "I don't think anyone could accuse you of rushing me."

"You don't know." Con shook his head — apparently at himself. "I've been desperate from the minute I saw you come walking down the path the other day."

"You hid it pretty well."

"No. You didn't want to see it, that's all. I've been wondering if I could keep sane if I had to watch you walk away again."

Finn smiled uncertainly. Con had to be joking, exaggerating, because he had never seemed anything but in control of his feelings.

"I'd given up on you ever coming back." Con's return smile was twisted. "You don't know how much I wanted to go after you, to find you."

Finn shook his head. "It wouldn't have worked then."

"I know. That's what Thomas said."

"You talked to Uncle Tom about...us?" That must have been some conversation.

Con nodded. "He said... Hell, it doesn't matter now. He was right, though, and I'd pretty much accepted that I wasn't going to get a second chance. Then Martha told me that you'd been in an accident...that it was bad."

"Bad enough."

"When I heard you were coming home to recover, I canceled my book tour."

Finn examined the proud, patrician features — the dark, hungry eyes that held his own gaze.

"I love you, Finn."

"Con —"

"Let me say this," Con said, suddenly harsh. "Let me...get it off my chest. I didn't intend for it to happen. The thing with Fitch and me had been over long before you and I met. I mean met as —"

"I know what you mean."

Con's shadowy gaze never wavered from his own. "I came to find you that morning. I was going to...break it off." Finn closed his eyes. But he could hear the undernote of emotion more clearly. "I was going to tell you I was going to Europe for a few months. It had gotten...so intense between us. And I couldn't handle it. I was afraid to feel that much for you, afraid it was getting out of control. So when I came upon Fitch at the lighthouse, and he made his move...I went with it. I swear to Christ I didn't mean for you to see it. I didn't ever intend to hurt you like that. But I was glad to...take that opportunity to distance myself from you. Do you understand?"

"No." He did, of course, but it hurt like hell. Even now.

"But when you walked in on us, when I realized what I'd done and that there wouldn't be any turning back from it, I knew I'd made a mistake."

Finn opened his eyes. Con was still watching him.

"I don't know why it took that to make me see how I really felt. But it's the truth. I'd been so busy feeling…trapped and pressured that I hadn't stopped to consider how much I cared for you. I'd have done anything to erase those goddamned stupid fifteen minutes with Fitch."

Finn opened his mouth, and Con kissed him — a baby's breath of a kiss, a dragonfly wing of a kiss. "Forgive me," he whispered.

The kiss went from soft to seductive to searing. They seemed to kiss forever, seeming to find new ways every few seconds, the press of mouths, the taste of tongues, the slide of skin on skin, rolling and pushing against each other as they grew more fierce for union.

Finn's healing nerves and muscles protested, but he ignored the various twinges and pains, because Con's touch was sending chills of pleasured sensation down his spine and into his groin.

Con's kisses were harder now, demanding and yet coaxing — making his case for him where words might have failed. His cock was like a steel pole, and Finn shuddered in a kind of sensory overload as Con's hand went to that junction of thigh, stroking Finn's slower reactions to stiffness.

Con was breathing hard, like he'd had to fight his way to get to this moment, and in a way he had. "What do you want? Whatever you want —"

Being asked to choose, to think, was more than Finn was prepared to do. He was running with the tide, riding that wave of feeling all the way out. He gasped, while Con did those wicked, wanton things with his hands, eyes closed, listening to the crackle of fire, the rush of rain —

Con shifted abruptly, lifting up. Finn's eyes flew open, and then he arched, bit back a cry at the warm, wet shock of envelopment. So good, so intensely good it was frightening. Physical response pulsing through his body, flashing up and down his bloodstream like a drug, the rush of release like no other.

Con made it last and last, skilled, yes…but more than that. Loving. Loving in a way it had never been before. Or maybe he was just more experienced now. Maybe he knew enough now to recognize what neither of them had recognized three years ago — until it was too late.

Con worked him with expert hands and mouth, and orgasm ripped through Finn, a kind of convulsion of delight that left him sobbing and breathless while his cock shot spumes of white like sea foam that Con swallowed down like it carried some magical properties.

"What about you?" Finn finally managed, when the tilting world settled back into its frame. Con was holding him, nuzzling his cheek. One hard warm arm lay across Finn's belly, hands cupping Finn's genitals.

Con chuckled, bumped his hips against Finn's backside, and Finn realized from the sticky softness there that Con had come too.

They dozed for a time. It was the crack of thunder that brought Finn back to awareness. He opened his eyes, and he could see the rain sluicing down the windows across the room.

"Why hasn't Paul called?" he asked.

Con lifted his head. "Because he's tactful?"

"He's not tactful. It's been well over an hour now. It's been two hours."

Con considered this. "He must not have talked to Martha."

He sounded unconcerned, and he was probably right, but Finn couldn't help the spark of uneasiness he felt. "He should have seen your note when he got back to the lighthouse, in that case."

"Maybe it took longer than either of you expected."

"How long could it take to grab a couple of shovels?"

There was a pause while Con digested the implications of that. "You think Fitch is buried here? At the lighthouse?"

"I don't know."

Con raised his head, studying Finn's profile. "He couldn't be inside the keeper's house, Finn. Most of the flooring is still intact. A suitcase, maybe two, yes. A man? No. And he couldn't be buried on the grounds — someone would have noticed a mound that size and shape."

Finn shivered. "He could be in the woods."

Con kissed Finn's naked shoulder. "That would be taking one hell of a risk — burying him in the woods there."

"But someone did take a hell of a risk."

Neither spoke for a time; then Finn said, "Paul wouldn't give a damn about disturbing us. We argued earlier, and he was set on going to the state police with or without proof."

Con expelled a long breath. "You think he's up there digging on his own?" Finn's gaze found his. "You want to take a run up to the lighthouse and see what's keeping Paul?"

Finn nodded slowly.

"Okay. Let's get it over with." Con got to his feet in a quick move. He grabbed Finn's discarded sweater and jeans, then tossed them to him.

CHAPTER TEN

Paul was not at the lighthouse.

Con's note was still pinned beneath Paul's flashlight inside the doorway to the keeper's cottage.

"He didn't come back." Finn stared at Con.

"Maybe common sense prevailed. Nobody's getting across from the mainland this afternoon. He probably decided to stay warm and dry up at The Birches."

"That isn't the way Paul thinks."

Con considered this. "Of course not. Well, what do you want to do?"

Finn was already dialing The Birches as they made their way back to the Land Rover.

He got Martha again, and after reassuring her that he was perfectly all right — and with Con — he asked about Paul and was told he'd never arrived back at the house.

"Something's wrong," he told Con as he clicked off.

"He probably got stuck in the mud," Con reassured, turning the key in the ignition. "The roads are hell right now."

That was reasonable. Paul wasn't used to driving rural roads, and the wind and rain made for terrible visibility. All the same, Finn was rigid with anxiety as they bumped and slid down the road from the lighthouse.

"He'll be okay, Finn," Con said without taking his eyes from the road.

"I should never have started this."

"Do you mean that?"

Did he? Despite his bitterness and anger at Fitch's behavior, despite everything —

Finn shook his head. "No."

"No." Con's voice was quiet. "Murder will out."

The wind shook the Rover and plastered soggy leaves against the windshield as they made their way beneath the storm-tossed trees. There was no sign of the station wagon along the road.

Finn rubbed his head, which was starting to pound with tension. "Who could plan something like that? If you and Fitch really didn't intend to meet that morning —"

Con did look briefly from the road at that. "You said once I didn't lie to you. I'm not lying about this. I didn't go up there to meet Fitch."

If he and Con were going to try and make a go of this — and if he was honest, he wanted to try at least — Finn was going to have to stop throwing the past in Con's face. He was going to have to let it go. So he said neutrally, "Do you think Fitch was at the lighthouse to meet someone that morning?"

"No. Fitch followed you that morning. He wanted you to go over to the mainland with him. There was some art show he wanted you to see."

Finn closed his eyes and then opened them. "So whoever killed him…it couldn't have been premeditated."

"I guess it could have been an accident." Con sounded unconvinced. "But why didn't this person come forward?"

"I don't know. I guess there could have been a reason."

Con didn't say anything else. He didn't have to.

They were passing Miss Minton's when Finn said, "Wait a minute. Stop. Paul might have come here."

Con was already pulling to the side of the road, searching for a safe place to park in the wet road. "Why would he?"

"I told him to try and get shovels without anyone at The Birches noticing; he might have thought to ask to borrow Miss Minton's. She's got every tool known to man."

Con killed the engine. Finn opened the door, climbing down cautiously before Con could get around to help him. He slammed shut the door against the wind, shrugging into his jacket and glancing down the woody embankment, and froze.

"*Con.*"

Con came around quickly and followed the direction Finn was pointing down the gully. The brown station wagon was at the bottom of the embankment, hood buried in the overhang of trees.

Con swore. Turned to Finn. "I'll go down and check."

"He must have gone off the road."

"Stay right here. I'll be right back."

Con went slipping and sliding down the muddy slope. Gripping his cane, Finn watched tensely as he reached the station wagon, dragging open the driver's-side door. He turned and waved all clear.

"He's not here," he called up.

"Where is he?" Finn demanded, which was about as dumb a question as he'd ever asked.

Con spread his hands and started back up the hillside. Finn looked over the muddy tracks along the side of the road. He found the spot where the station wagon had been parked. Had Paul tried to back out and gone over the side? But the car was nose-first down the gully, so he'd have had to deliberately pull forward over the edge.

It didn't make sense.

Con reached the top of the embankment. "There's no blood inside the car," he reassured. "He can't have been badly hurt. It's not that far down the hillside."

The idea occurred to them at the same time, and they gazed across the road at Miss Minton's wall of rosebushes and the house beyond.

"He must have gone across to Mitty's," Con said.

"But if he had an accident, why wouldn't he call The Birches?"

"Could he have decided to walk back for some reason?" Con had a supportive hand beneath Finn's elbow as they started across the muddy road.

"I think the normal thing would be to —" Finn broke off as Miss Minton's battered pickup came barreling through the gate toward them.

There wasn't time to think, and there was no way he could have moved fast enough with his injured leg. Con grabbed him and shoved him hard to the side. Finn went sprawling as the pickup swerved, just missing Con and taking out a section of white picket fence before tearing up the muddy road, water flying up behind its tires.

Finn barely had time to register what had happened before Con was kneeling beside him.

"*Finn.* Jesus. Are you all right? You're not hurt?" Con's face was white, his hands shaking as he dragged at Finn. "Finn?"

"I'm okay," Finn managed, clutching his injured leg and rocking a little with the pain.

Con was swearing, in between ordering Finn to let him see the damage.

"We've got to go after her," Finn said, pushing him off.

"To hell with her."

"Con. Listen to me. She's not on her way to the fucking hairdresser. She's heading for the lighthouse. We have to go after her." Finn groped for his cane, and Con got up, reaching down and pulling Finn to his feet.

With Con's help, Finn made it across the road, slamming shut the Rover door as Con ran around to the driver side, then slid behind the wheel and started the engine.

"Call The Birches," he ordered. "Tell Martha to call the state police."

Finn spent the remainder of the short, rough drive on the phone with Martha trying to explain what was happening — which wasn't easy given that he wasn't exactly clear himself what was happening.

He clicked off the phone and asked Con, "Could Paul have stolen Miss Minton's truck?"

"Paul wasn't driving."

There went that theory — that Paul had arranged to meet his ex-lover and ended up killing him. It hadn't been much of a theory to start with, but the other possibility seemed even crazier.

"You saw her? Miss Minton was driving?"

"I saw her. She deliberately swerved in order to miss me."

They were tearing back up the slippery road to the lighthouse. As they topped the crest, Finn could see lightning flashing out over the ocean. Miss Minton's pickup was parked near the cliff's edge. The tailgate was down, and she was dragging something across the grass to the verge.

Con sped forward across the green, braking sharply. He was out of the Rover and running toward Miss Minton. Miss Minton, who was dragging an unconscious Paul by his legs across the short space to the ledge, dropped him and turned.

Finn, moving more slowly than Con, dropped down beside Paul, who was unconscious and gray-faced, his blond hair soaked in blood. But Finn was only dimly aware of this, his focus on Con as he struggled with Miss Minton. For one truly horrific moment, he thought Con and Miss Minton were both going over the side, but Con dragged her back.

Miss Minton was shrieking. It was difficult to make out the words through the wind and rain, but Finn thought he heard her scream, "They should have drowned him at birth!"

◊ ◊ ◊ ◊

"I've been thinking…I'd like to paint you."

Con's mouth twitched, but he didn't open his eyes. He murmured, "Oh yes? I think I'd look good in a nice robin's egg blue."

"Funny." Head propped on hand, Finn studied him. Sunlight gilded Con's hair and turned his skin honey brown against the peach-colored sheets. It was late Monday morning, and they were still in bed — they had barely been out of bed since arriving Saturday night at the little bed-and-breakfast they had stayed at in Union three years earlier.

Con reached over, lacing their fingers and bringing Finn's hand to his mouth. He kissed it lightly and opened his eyes.

He smiled, but there was a certain melancholy in those black cherry eyes that Finn understood only too well.

It had been four days since Miss Minton had confessed to the attempted murder of Paul Ryder and the murder of Fitch Barret three years earlier. With true New England reticence, she had declined to discuss her reasons for either crime with the state police, but she had talked to Con on the drive back to The Birches. In fact, she and Con might have been alone in the Rover for the attention she paid to Finn anxiously cradling an unconscious Paul in the backseat.

"He was bad. He was a bad seed, that one. Selfish and cruel from the day he was born. Everything he put his hand to, he spoiled."

Finn couldn't see Miss Minton's face, her hair and clothes were soaked and her voice was a hoarse croak he had to struggle to hear over Paul's stentorian breathing.

"I saw him that day. I saw him laughing as he spoiled your life the way he spoiled mine. Spoiled every chance I had for love and happiness. First with Barnaby Purdon and then with Thomas Barret. He did it deliberately. Nothing made him happier than when he was hurting people, seeing them cry."

Her eyes raised, unexpectedly catching Finn's gaze in the rearview mirror. She said harshly, "You don't know. He was laughing that day. You ran off and Con knocked him down, and he was still laughing. And then he went up in the tower to see where you'd got to. And I followed him up and pushed him off. It was the easiest thing in the world."

Finn had put his head down at that point and stopped listening.

When they had reached The Birches, everything had grown surreal. Martha had fixed tea and provided dry clothes for everyone, and they had waited together in the kitchen while Con phoned the mainland requesting emergency services and the state police. Miss Minton had stopped talking by then. She was silent and eerily docile.

A LifeFlight helicopter made it to the island to transport Paul to the mainland, where he was currently in critical but stable condition. Miss Minton had declined to say why she'd attacked Paul, but from what she'd said during the drive from the lighthouse, Con believed that she had mistakenly thought Paul had showed up at her cottage to accuse her or blackmail her — that her own guilty conscience had fooled her into thinking Paul had somehow figured out the truth.

That evening, after the state police had taken Miss Minton away, Barnaby Purdon came to the house and there was more muted, shocked discussion. The house had the feel of death after long illness...and after all, that was close to the truth of it.

Barnaby Purdon was the one who remembered that Miss Minton had been gathering gravel at the lighthouse all that long-ago week, transporting it by pickup truck to her cottage, traveling sedately back and forth along the road.

She was a strong, vigorous woman used to hauling rocks and bags of fertilizer and mulch, used to taking care of her own property. It wasn't so hard to picture her dumping Fitch into her wheelbarrow, shoving him into her pickup, and driving him away...to bury him beneath the bloodred roses in garden — the roses she'd been planting that August afternoon when Con had traveled the road to The Birches.

As their nearest neighbor, Miss Minton had a key to The Birches, and she'd been in the habit of going up to the house for art lessons. She knew her way around, knew that the house was deserted that day, and she had packed Fitch's things in his suitcases, dumped them at the lighthouse, and driven the station wagon down to the wharf and then walked home.

Once he knew the why of it, Finn had stopped listening. He didn't care about the details of how and where and when. He was grieving for Fitch. Maybe Fitch was all that Miss Minton said and believed, but he had been more than that to Finn, the best loved companion of his childhood — his other half. He had grieved for him three years ago, and he continued to grieve for him now. It was a strange comfort to think that Fitch had climbed up the light tower. He wanted to believe that Fitch had regretted what he'd done, that he'd wanted to find Finn and had gone to look for him. Con had listened to him and kissed him and said nothing, letting him talk late into the night.

The police had questioned them all; then the reporters had descended on the island, and Con had taken Finn away to Union. For two days Finn and Con had been getting to know each other again.

Now Finn admitted, "I've been afraid to try anything since the accident."

"But you've only been out of the hospital a week or so."

"I know but... From the time I left college — not a day went by that I didn't work. Even if it was just to sketch something. Until the day I woke up in the hospital and couldn't see."

Con didn't say anything at first, his brows drawing together as he surveyed Finn's face. "But you're okay, Finn. There's no reason you can't start working again."

Finn nodded.

Con said, "You can paint me." His eyes were bright beneath the soft fall of blond hair. You can do whatever you like to me."

Finn looked interested. "Is that right? Because I've been thinking I might like to experiment with different mediums..."

Con bit his fingers lightly. "This sounds promising. Tell me more."

Finn lowered himself to Con's arms. "I think I'd prefer to show you."

BODY ART

JORDAN CASTILLO PRICE

CHAPTER ONE

Wanted:

Driver, Red Wing Island. Must speak English and have current Michigan chauffeur license. Room, board, and stipend provided. Single gentleman over 35 preferred. Smokers need not apply.

Was it still legal to discriminate against smokers? I wasn't sure, but I thought it might give me an edge. I read the ad through again. I had a brand-spanking-new piece of plastic that entitled me to drive a cab, bus, or limousine. I was also flat broke, in debt up to my eyeballs, and I sorely needed somewhere to stay. Oh, and I spoke English too.

I'd followed the *Guide to Gainful Employment* to a tee. New haircut. New shirt. New slacks. New tie — new to me, anyway. Even polished my shoes for the first time in my life. The final tip, according to the Guide, was to be sure to address the interviewer by name, using a mnemonic device, if necessary, to do it.

It hadn't mentioned what to do if there were two interviewers. Damn.

Two women turned up for the interview in the back office of the employment agency. There was an old one — eighties, I'd guess — and a younger one, a handful of years older than me. Maybe forty or so. A stocky, sturdy forty, with hair cropped short and gray at the temples and no makeup. The daughter? Maybe. She didn't look like an accountant or a lawyer, that's for sure. She glanced down at her paper, and asked me, "If a drawbridge does not have a signal light or attendant, how many feet away must you stop and check if the draw is closed?"

That was just on my test. "Fifty."

I'd been so excited to know the answer to that one that I'd leaned forward and allowed my tie to slide out of place. The missing button midway down the shirt gaped. I hadn't noticed it at the thrift store. I'd just been glad to find a dress shirt for less than three bucks that didn't need to be ironed. I covered the buttonhole with the tie. And then I realized the gesture had caused my sleeve to ride up and show a glimpse of my ink. Damn it. Maybe they hadn't noticed. They were looking me in the face, weren't they? Both of them? I hoped so — the kind of hope where your stomach twists up and squeezes itself 'til you're sick. Because I really, really needed that job.

The old woman, Mrs. White, which was easy to remember — white hair, white pearls, Mrs. White — reached over and tapped the other one on the forearm. My guts twisted against themselves harder. She'd seen. And decided I wasn't the sort of man she wanted living under her roof.

I couldn't dream up a neat mnemonic trick for the younger woman, Ms. Friedman, but I figured I could handle two names. She nodded vaguely and shuffled her questionnaire. "Do you have any family nearby, Mr. Carlucci?"

I itched to tell her to call me Ray, since I was only "Mr. Carlucci" to the legions of bill collectors I'd been picking off my sorry hide over the last year, but I figured it wasn't my place to dictate who was called what during the interview. "Parents in Florida."

Mrs. White spoke up. "Any wife? Children?"

And then I remembered the ad. Single gentleman preferred. Which seemed about as politically incorrect as specifying a nonsmoker. "No. Never married. No kids."

Queer as the day is long, actually. But right now? A single gentleman. It made me sound a lot ritzier than I was, but I supposed I fit the bill.

"On your application," said Friedman, "you wrote down 'business owner' as your last job. What was that?"

An answer I'd prepared for. "Custom art." Because tattoo parlor didn't have quite the same ring.

"And you list the reason for leaving as financial."

"That's right."

I did my best to sound mild, but inwardly, I steeled myself against the possibility that they'd poke at some old wounds that hadn't quite closed yet. And I reminded myself to take it like a man, sit up straight, and make sure that damn buttonhole didn't show.

Friedman said, "I had a catering business before." Her gaze went inward, just for a second. "So much work — sixty-, seventy-hour weeks. And then the check for a wedding bounced..." She spread her fingers in a "poof" gesture. And I looked at her, really looked at her, and nodded again. Because I could tell she understood that sometimes we fail — grandly, spectacularly — through no fault of our own. It gave me hope.

I didn't feel like I could afford to cling to it, though. I nodded.

Friedman's cheeks flushed. "Those are all the questions I have." She turned toward Mrs. White. "You?"

White leaned forward and squinted. Her eyes had the cloudy, watery cast of age. "He looks fit. How tall are you?"

"Six-three," I said. Not one of the interviews I'd sat through in the past several months had asked me if I had kids or how tall I was.

None of them had called me back afterward either. Until this one.

The cab ride to Red Wing Island took every last cent I had. That was good, I told myself. The farther away my new digs were from Traverse City and my gutted shop, or the nearby town where Johnny and I had shared a rented house on a street full of overpriced boutiques, the better. The bill collectors had started to get nasty. One of them had threatened to have the local police show up on my doorstep. I hadn't mentioned that to the guy who'd been putting me up. It was bad enough I'd taken over his TV room.

Red Wing Island was maybe fifteen minutes outside town, but it was out in the middle of so much wilderness that it seemed incredibly far away. And incredibly far away was just what I needed.

Even as I watched the meter click forward, impossibly fast, every now and then a startling shock of red or gold would draw my eyes away from the ever-rising number and up to the spectacular trees. It was autumn, and the coast of Lake Huron bustled with a surge of yachters and tourists who would pack it all in once all the leaves dropped and the snow started to fall.

The car bumped over a precarious one-lane wooden bridge, then tunneled beneath a canopy of maples that obliterated the sky. The road on Red Wing was rippled and cracked where the roots of the trees had heaved up out of the sandy soil beneath the asphalt with each winter freeze and thaw. We passed by a number of bright mailboxes, cutesy folk art things with shingles that hung off the bottom announcing the name of the owners, the Hunt's or the Smith's. I wondered if all sidewalk-fair woodburners had excessive apostrophes they needed to get rid of, or if it was just their way of getting back at people rich enough to own multiple homes and stupid enough not to know how to pluralize their own names.

I scoped out the driveways as best I could but didn't spot anything that would suggest that the summer residents were still there: smoking fireplaces, dogs, cars, trash.

And then one of the dark recesses between the tree trunks shifted, and I saw that there was life on the island after all. A dark-haired guy dressed all in black stared up into the trees, then reached out and chalked a circle on one of the tree trunks just as the cab passed him by. He didn't strike me as a forester checking for emerald ash borers or Dutch elm disease. Foresters wore reflective orange jackets and Carhartt boots. This guy had hair down to his shoulders and was decked out in a duster worthy of The Matrix.

I craned my neck and tried to get a better look at him through the rear window, but we rounded a curve, and the tree line swallowed him. A few more twists and turns, and the cab pulled up in front of a gate a few yards in from the road.

"Is this it?" I checked the number. That was it. I peered through the trees, blood red maples and black locusts with dangling brown pods, and tried to make out the shape of the building. It was white, I saw, and it peeked through the tree trunks in areas absurdly far away from one another, the width of three normal-sized houses stacked side by side.

Well, what else did I expect? People in modestly sized houses didn't hire servants.

The gates were closed. I glanced at the meter yet again as the driver got out to open them, and I nearly had a stroke. I couldn't afford the trip up the quarter-mile driveway.

I hopped out and jogged up to the half-open gate. "Here." I slapped money into his hand. "Leave me off here. It's all I've got."

The cabbie frowned down at the money with suspicion in his eyes as he counted it. "All right," he said. No doubt he was pissed off that he wasn't getting a tip. But he couldn't very well hold my luggage hostage for not tipping. He unloaded the trunk, slammed it shut harder than he had to, and drove off without a word.

I dragged my luggage, two by two, inside the gate. Given the scarcity of traffic on the island, it was unlikely that the guy chalking the trees was now lying in wait to steal my luggage, but old habits died hard. Everything I owned was in those six mismatched suitcases and single garment bag. I wasn't about to leave them out on the road.

I went to the main house and spent a good ten minutes trying to figure out which door to use, finally settled on one with a pair of muddy boots outside it in back. There was no bell. I knocked, and Friedman answered. She wore a long white apron spattered with partially bleached stains, loose paisley pants, and clogs. She stuck her head out the door and looked around. "Where's your car?"

"I cabbed it," I told her. She looked confused. "I assumed I'd be using the company car for Mrs. White."

"Oh…sure. Of course. It's just that it's a heck of a long walk between Red Wing and anywhere else. I don't know if she'll want you borrowing the Town Car."

"It's fine. If I need to go off the island, I'll call a cab." Hopefully the driver who'd just let me off wouldn't complain too thoroughly to the rest of his fleet.

"That's way too expensive. You could always borrow mine, if you know how to drive a stick." She laughed. "Well, of course you do, you're a professional driver."

She didn't make it sound half-bad; the way she put it, you'd think I drove in NASCAR. "My bags are by the gate. If you just show me where to put them…"

"Your apartment's above the garage. Mr. and Mrs. are old-fashioned that way." Not Mr. and Mrs. *White*. Just Mr. and Mrs. "Raymond? I can call you that, can't I?"

"Ray," I said. I was staring over my shoulder because my eyes prickled at the thought of something as simple as having my own place again, after spending months rotating through the couches of each of my remaining friends — in exchange for tattoos, of course. Until I finally had to choose between selling my gear and eating.

"Ray. I'm Marnie."

I nodded but kept my head still turned away.

"Technically, I'm just the cook. But the housekeeper, Melita — she's been here three years longer than me — only wants to get her job done and watch soap operas. So I've been the go-to person ever since Mr.'s Alzheimer's took a nosedive, and Mrs. started spending all her time taking care of him. So if you have any questions…you can come to… Hey, are you all right?"

I turned my back to her and pinched the bridge of my nose. "Yeah. I'll let you know when I've got all my bags upstairs."

"It's a long haul to the gate," she said. "Why don't I bring my car around…?"

I'd already gone a few yards down the path. I gave Marnie a forget-about-it wave without turning around, and she didn't pursue it. She seemed to understand that I needed a few minutes to myself more than I needed a hand with my luggage.

◊ ◊ ◊ ◊

The apartment over the garage smelled slightly of stale bleach and mothballs. It consisted of three rooms: a bathroom, a bedroom, and an everything-else room with a sink, dorm fridge, microwave, and coffeepot on one end, a couch and a TV on the other. I tried to think of them as *my* couch, *my* coffeepot, in the same casual way that I used to think about *my* shop, *my* custom Ford Explorer, *my* boyfriend. And I found I couldn't do it anymore. It felt like a hotel room, with me just passing through.

I changed shirts, since I'd sweated through the first one carrying all that luggage, and hoped there was somewhere I could do a load of laundry, since I only had two dress shirts to my name — one of them now with a button held on by dental floss, a button that almost matched the others, but not quite.

Asking about the laundry would be a good enough lead-in for me to talk to Marnie without having to explain what my silent treatment by the door had been about, anyway…if I could figure out a way to say I'd gotten choked up at the thought of having my own place again, without coming right out and saying it. Maybe I could tell her there'd been something in my eye. I jogged down the stairs two at a time and noticed that they didn't sound hollow like I would've expected. They were as solid and sturdy as interior-grade stairs. Classy.

I was almost at my usual level of confidence and swagger as I stepped out of that garage, or close enough to it that I'd fool a stranger, anyway. I had a roof over my head and a bed to sleep in, and I was miles away from the shop, the gutted hull that was left of it after Johnny's three-card monte and all the repo men that showed up in its wake. Heartless bastards, running their hands over my chairs, my display cases…

My foot hit something slick and shot out from under me. I staggered and hopped and barely caught myself from going down hard. Good thing. The cobblestone was spattered with blood.

"Holy…"

Blood and feathers. A mangled gull was smeared across the path that connected the garage to the house. It stank of bird and blood, but mostly fish. I rubbed my shoe against the grass. Good thing I hadn't fallen on my ass. My other pairs of pants were all holey jeans that were fine for a day at the shop, not so fine for my first day on the job at a sprawling estate.

I walked the rest of the way through the grass, dragging my feet. Bits of gore and a few feathers managed to stick despite my best efforts. Eventually, I took the damn shoe off so I could rinse it down inside, and when Marnie opened the door, I had a much more distracting conversation-starter in my hand than I could ever have hoped for. "A bird exploded outside my front door, and now I need to wash off my shoe."

She looked at me big-eyed for a long, hard second. And then she burst out laughing.

Marnie was less flashy than the old crowd I hung around with in Traverse City, and in fact was dowdy enough that she looked like she could have been "mom" to some of the younger kids. But what good had all those pretty, pretty peacocks been to me when Johnny was funneling my business loan payments into Oxy and Jack? Someone had to know. Me? I put in twelve-hour days more often than not, rolled into bed sore and sandy-eyed. But our friends? Some of them had to have known.

Fuck. He'd probably been supporting their habits too.

And so Marnie, with her graying hair and her conservatively single-pierced ears and her pale, uninked skin and her robust laugh that threatened to burst out of her at the slightest provocation — I liked her. A lot.

"We don't have to sit here and watch the laundry spin," she told me. "It's not going anywhere."

"Good to know." The seagull cleanup had been worse than I'd expected. At least now I knew where the hose was. I figured I could give the Town Car a good scrub to earn my keep if Mrs. White didn't need to go anywhere that night. And I thought that maybe, blood and guts aside, this whole servant gig might not really be all that bad.

And then a bell in the kitchen rang. Tink-a-tink, like someone making a toast with coffee mugs. We barely heard it over the sound of the dryer "That's Mrs.," Marnie said. She pushed a button on an intercom on the countertop. "What's up?"

A jumble of noises came from the other end. Zombie movie, I thought. Moaning, with frantic talking over the top. "He's had an accident."

I imagined some brittle old guy falling and shattering, but the wince Marnie gave seemed more inconvenienced than frightened. "I'll be right up. And Raymond's here, so we'll have some help." She turned off the intercom and looked at me. "It's shower time."

"Oh. That kind of accident."

"You got it. Mr. will be happy to have a man getting him into the tub again — as far gone as he is, he's still shy about strange women seeing him naked, and it takes both of us to clean him up. We have this harness that's supposed to bear his weight, but it's too tight of a squeeze to maneuver him into the tub…"

"Marnie." She'd been speaking quickly and overly bright, and when I stopped her, the silence was pronounced. "I'm not a nurse. I don't know how to handle someone with Alzheimer's."

"When you filled out your application, you said you had no physical limitations. Is that true? Do you have a bum back or trick knee that'll stop you from helping a hundred-and-sixty-pound man in the shower?"

"Well, no, but…"

"Then come upstairs and meet him." She looped her arm through mine. "He was a really fun guy a couple of years ago. That probably won't come through right now, not tonight, but once you've been here a while, I think you'll see it."

We passed a short, dark woman of about fifty in the hallway. She was dark-skinned, maybe Hispanic, maybe Mediterranean. She carried a plastic laundry basket in front of her with her arms stretched as far forward as they could reach. When I caught a whiff of the soiled clothing inside, I guessed why.

"Melita, this is Ray, the new driver."

Melita glanced at me. "Well, I hope you'll stick around longer than the last one."

"She's crabby because they interrupted her TV show," Marnie whispered, once Melita was out of earshot. "She's not exactly a barrel of monkeys the rest of the time either. But she's really sharp, really detailed."

I wouldn't be a barrel of monkeys either if it was my job to clean up other people's shit.

Mr. White was a few inches shorter than me, about ten years older than my father, and as sinewy as a bantamweight boxer. That first time I met him, he was wearing a blue oxford dress shirt, a green and gray striped towel around his waist, and a pair of monogrammed leather slippers. His jaw was clenched shut tight, and he was doing his damnedest to shove Mrs. White away from him.

"Ray is here," said Marnie. I wished she could take it back. I suddenly wanted to be anywhere but there.

"He's had an accident," Mrs. White said. "He's upset."

"Hey, Mr.," Marnie said. "This is Ray — you gave him a job. How about you let him help you get cleaned up?"

Did Marnie possess the uncanny ability to dig straight into my mind and stab my pride? Maybe I hadn't signed up to see octogenarians naked — but it was true, the Whites had given me a shot at picking myself back up again when no one else would.

I tried to smile, but it felt forced. The best expression I could pull off was "brisk," so I aimed for that. "Hello, Mr. White. Thank you for the opportunity. It's my first day here, so I'd appreciate it if you showed me the ropes…"

I don't know if Mr. White understood me, exactly. He didn't speak. But he stopped struggling, and he allowed Mrs. White to place his rigid arm in mine so I could lead him to the bathroom.

A look passed between Marnie and Mrs. White. Like me, neither of them was exactly beaming. All any of us could muster, it seemed, was a sense of grim satisfaction.

I'd be lying if I said that the initial spark of connection between Mr. White and me foreshadowed the relationship to come. Dementia had its hooks too deep in him for that. Still, he did seem calm as I helped his wife unbutton his shirt — a better shirt than either of the ones I currently owned, I noted, with no stains and all its buttons. Mrs. White ran the shower and made sure the water wasn't hot enough to scald him. "You'll get wet," she told me. "I'm sorry."

She stared at me a half a beat longer than I would've expected. I'm guessing the apology was in regard to more than just the soaking I was about to receive.

The room was warm and the water barely more than tepid. "You probably want to take off your shoes and socks," Mrs. White suggested. "Bare feet have a better grip on the tub."

"You want me…in there?"

"To help him onto the seat and back off again. The showerhead is detachable, but…"

I looked at the white plastic bench that spanned the shower. She was right. I would have better control if I got in behind it, especially barefoot. But the top of my right foot was covered by the trailing edge of the barbed wire tat that took up most of my right leg. I kicked off my dress shoes, since they were the only pair I had, but I left my socks on. "Let's do this," I said, and I took Mr. White by the arm while his wife guided his leading foot over the edge of the tub.

Mrs. White did her best to direct the spray only at him, but I was soaked through within the first five minutes. "All right, Edgar," she said. "Stand up. Almost done."

Between the two of us, we stood him up and nudged him around to face me. I didn't want to look him in the eye, but what else could I do? His fate and mine had conspired to bring us together this way, both of us stripped of most of the things by which we'd once defined ourselves, and both of us covered in our own shit.

My shit was metaphorical. It couldn't be washed away so easily.

And so I did look Mr. White in the eye, and I said, "We're almost done." The stream of water hit him as his wife cleaned away the dregs of the "accident," and he reached out to steady himself on my arm. I wasn't prepared for the strength in those thin, wrinkled fingers. They dug into my forearm like a vise. I kept my expression mild despite the pain. Like I'd just said, we were almost done.

Mrs. White cut the water and draped a terrycloth robe around Mr. White's shoulders. "Thank you, Ray," she said. "That was the easiest shower we've had since Gene left." I planted one wet-socked foot on the bath mat outside the tub and steadied Mr. White while she maneuvered his legs over the edge.

"This would be a lot less work in a walk-in shower," I said. And a lot less likely to end with Mr. Smith cracking his head open on the porcelain. Together, we guided him back into the master bedroom.

"It was easier for him just a few weeks ago. I had no idea it would get this..." Mrs. White stopped speaking. She was looking at my arm so strangely, I wondered if her husband had torn my shirt when he grabbed me.

The sleeve of my soaked shirt clung to my arm. I could see straight through the wet fabric to the flaming skull on my forearm. I was so drenched that all the ink on my upper body showed, the Japanese dragon, the tribal shoulder piece, the cheesy flash tiger and eight ball with sentimental value, and the spiderwebs on my elbows. Everything that wasn't covered by my undershirt stood out plain as day.

"So many of the contractors are only seasonal," Mrs. White said, as if the abrupt pause had never happened. "They get more work down south over the winter. I've put in some calls, but I haven't heard back yet."

"Right," I said. When life sideswipes you, it doesn't call ahead and make an appointment. "I'm sure we'll manage 'til they get around to calling you back."

CHAPTER FOUR

By the time I finally crawled into bed, I ached from top to bottom from wrestling with Mr. White. I wondered if, by some perverse twist of logic, my body would be worse off in the morning for having slept in an actual bed, rather than a couch, or a futon, or an air mattress with a slow leak that was impossible to locate.

I stripped down to my boxers and got under the covers. They'd been through the wash prior to my arrival. They smelled like detergent and dryer sheets.

Clean laundry must be one of those scents that triggers the release of a cocktail of feel-good neurotransmitters. Within moments I was drifting off, finger-shaped bruises, wrenched shoulder, strange bed, and all.

A noise startled me from sleep, just as I started to fall hard and fast. I sat up and shook off the sickening lurch of sudden wakefulness at the cusp of dreaming. The house smelled wrong, of someplace that had been vacant — just a couple of weeks, but long enough to develop the sour stink of disuse. It sounded wrong too, surrounded by the continuous drone of cicadas and crickets and the dry friction of leaves on the roof as the wind made the branches scour the shingles.

Another noise rose from the layered background of insects and flora: a sharp crunch, like something breaking.

I flipped on the bedside light, dug out some jeans and a T-shirt that wouldn't look any the worse for wear if I snagged them on the undergrowth, unearthed my leather jacket and biker boots from the heaviest suitcase, and went outside for a look.

The first startling thing was that the moon was bright. Maybe I'd seen it, or something like it, in paintings or in films. But there were no streetlights on Red Wing Island to taint the glow of the stars. The porch light that had lit my way from the main house to the garage was off. And since all the neighbors had migrated back to their winter homes, the houses all around the estate were dark too.

I had never seen the moon so bright.

I stared up at it as if I'd never seen the moon, period. It was so intensely luminous, that maybe I never had, not really.

Another loud crack from the tree line startled me out of my moongazing as effectively as it had pulled me from the oblivion of sleep. I wished I had a flashlight. I could probably find one in the garage or the car, if I knew where to look, but I didn't. Still, I needed to see for myself what was going bump in the night if I ever hoped to get to sleep. I took a few steps toward the trees and listened. Cicadas droned louder than I would've ever thought possible, louder still if you actually tuned in to them and tried to imagine where that wall of noise might actually be coming from.

A few more steps, and I was at the tree line. The wooded area wasn't large, maybe ten yards deep, and beyond that, more moonlight, bright through the black vertical slashes of the tree trunks. I eased forward, feeling for rocks and fallen branches with my boots as I half shuffled, half walked. I was almost through the trees when I heard the sound again.

Crrack.

I squatted and groped. My fingers brushed fallen leaves and points of cool sliminess, probably slugs. I flicked them away, found a branch with the diameter of a Louisville Slugger TPX, and hefted it. Longer than a TPX. Awkward. But better than nothing.

I inched to the clearing with my heart in my throat, dead sure that every shuffle, every tentative step, had sent a telltale crackle broadcasting my presence throughout the island. A twig snapped. I froze. The drone around me continued, unaffected. I took another few steps forward, now moving even slower, and as I came to the edge of a clearing, I saw him.

A man.

More accurately, the guy in black from the side of the road. Or if you wanted to split hairs, his silhouette. He hung from the lowest branch of a tree, maybe seven feet off the ground, arms and legs locked around the tree limb. His long coat, long hair — and now a long scarf that he'd added to his ensemble — dangled beneath him. He inched forward and caught a smaller branch with one hand. Moonlight glinted off metal as he pulled a blade from the grip of his teeth. He clenched hard with his legs and started to saw at the smaller branch. When he'd sawed about halfway through, he bent the branch back upon itself.

Craack.

"What are you doing?" I called.

His silhouette shifted as he faced me. He tucked the knife away, let go with his legs, hung for a second by his hands, and then dropped. The leaves below him gave off a rumpled sigh.

He trailed the branch he'd cut behind him as he crossed the clearing. It dragged through the fallen leaves with a *shish-shish-shish*. He walked like a runway model, all attitude and hips. And when he stopped in front of me and tossed his dark hair over his shoulder so he could get a look at me, I forgot how to breathe. He was breathtaking, in a wasted sort of way. All soulful eyes and long sideburns and five o'clock shadow.

"What are you doing?" I said a second time. Because what else could I say? *Don't tell me you're an overbooked gardener?* Or, *it's late?* Or, *what's it gonna take to get you out of all those clothes?*

"I'd tell you," he said. "But then you'd think I'm crazy."

I was forming a fast opinion of him, all right, but *crazy* wasn't the word that sprang to mind. Hot. That was more like it. Because straight men didn't walk that way, and no matter how much I told myself not to notice, my eyes kept raking him up and down. "Try me."

A full smile then, wide enough that moonlight glinted, bluish, off his teeth. His teeth had character. Not quite straight, a hairline gap between the front two. Very white.

"What am I doing? Trying to make sense of the world. Just like everybody else."

He pivoted on one foot, stepped over the branch, and started walking back the way he'd come. I watched the silhouette of his back and tried to decide if he was real or just a really vivid dream induced by the scent of mothballs and bleach.

He paused halfway across the clearing and looked back at me. "Aren't you curious?" he said.

The thought of waking up in my garage apartment the next morning to a day of cleaning up blood and shit, and if I was lucky, driving Mrs. White to an ophthalmologist's appointment, without ever knowing what the mystery man in the trees was actually doing...that really didn't seem like an option. I followed.

He walked quickly, sure-footed in the dark. I walked right behind him in the path he created by dragging his branch. He strode up to a tripod of tree branches tethered at the top in a crude tepee shape, and he propped the branch he was dragging against the existing structure. "Give me a hand, and I'll show you," he said.

He kicked a couple of the branches apart and centered the new branch between them. "Hold this." He grabbed me by the wrist and guided my hand to the hub where the four branches met, then pulled a ball of twine from his pocket and wrapped the joint. He drew his knife, cut the twine, then tucked the knife away again.

"My mother told me never to talk to strange men with knives," I said.

"Good thing your mother's not here." He stepped back with his hands on his hips and scrutinized his tepee. "Unless you're a White." He cocked his head toward the estate. "Is that where you came from?"

"Yeah. But I'm not family. I just work there."

"Doing what?" he said, skeptical. Which irritated me.

"Driver." My tone of voice said, *Got a problem with that?*

He turned to face me and squinted at me in the moonlight. "But they just got a new driver a couple of months ago — and you're not him. This other guy was blond. Kinda dumpy."

"I don't know why he quit. I guess it was sudden."

"Hmph. You got a name?"

"Ray."

"Hello, Ray. I'm Anton, the family pariah who only has a roof over his head due to the kindness of his sister's heart." He pointed somewhere among the trees. "That's Diane's summer home. She ever so generously lets me stay in the guesthouse. And she locks me in if she's entertaining, so I can't frighten her guests."

"How does one go about becoming an pariah?" I asked. "It sounds like an interesting career move."

"That's true. There's never a dull moment in the we-all-think-you're-crazy profession."

Anton and I stared at the tepee together in silence for a long moment. And then I said, "Are you?"

"What?"

"Crazy. Because last I heard, building wigwams by the light of the full moon didn't rank real high in the 'sane' category."

"That reads as a wigwam to you?" He stepped back a few paces and took in the whole structure with a critical glance. "It's a pyramid. Obviously."

"My mistake."

Anton circled his branch pyramid, then nodded and kicked one of the limbs into position. "You have to get everything right, the position, the angle, or else it won't work."

"It does something?"

He backed up a few steps and stood beside me, appraising his handiwork. "We'll see. It's a test."

"Like the circles you were chalking on the trees by the road."

"Exactly." He wiped his hands on the front of his long coat, then shifted topics as if we'd been talking about something so obvious and mundane it required no explanation at all. "What bothers me is that I didn't know the old driver was gone. Marnie should've told me. How long ago did you say he left?"

"I didn't. I think it was about a week ago. Maybe ten days."

He clucked his tongue. "That means my count was off for a whole week."

He circled his stick pyramid again, and a little voice inside me suggested that I should probably back away. Now. I told my caution to go to hell. Where had it been when Johnny was robbing me blind? It was no wonder my caution was currently in the doghouse. "What's this count?" I said. "Or can't you explain that to me either?"

He turned from his pyramid and looked at me, surprised. "Don't mock me."

"I'm not."

He crossed his arms over his chest, glanced back at the pyramid, took a deep breath, and began. "Me. Marnie. Mr. and Mrs. White — the guy never leaves the house — Gene, the driver — now you, and not Gene, and the housekeeper. I always forget her name."

"Melita."

"Right. Only us. Six. If we're all accounted for, then who's wandering the island at night?"

I felt a chill that wasn't entirely from the cold. "What do you mean? Did you see someone or just hear them? Maybe it's an animal."

"I can tell the difference between an animal's footsteps and a human's. Especially when the leaves are this dry."

"So you're going by sound."

Anton nodded.

"It could be anything. The wind. Or some homeless guy who walked over the bridge looking for a summer home to flop in."

"No bums, not around here. Every property on the island is wired up to a security outfit on the mainland, just over the bridge and fifteen miles down the road. You so much as rap on a window, you've got a deputy on your doorstep in half an hour." He toed some leaves out of the way, dislodged a stone from the ground, and rocked it with the sole of his combat boot. "I should know. Diane's got her main house rigged so I can't even go in to grab a coffee filter."

"She got a reason to worry?" I said. Because it occurred to me that maybe I had a "type," and maybe that type was the sort of guy who'd sell his elderly mother's hearing aid for his next fix.

I'd expected Anton to take offense — and in fact, I had a suspicion that I'd been trying to pinch something off before it even had a chance to grow — but instead I caught the glint of moonlight off his teeth as he cracked a grin. "It's not my fault she's got such atrocious taste. That redecorating jag last April? I am never gonna live that down."

Anton took a few more steps back, planted his hands on his hips, and looked at his pyramid. "Too steep. Proportion's all wrong. I'll need to spread out the base. Here. Hold that side for me."

I held the limb he pointed out while he went around the other side and adjusted the angle. The stick pyramid gave rustling protests each time he repositioned a leg. "So once you've got the angle just so. What then?"

"I have no idea. I told you. It's an experiment." He approached me around the back of the structure and grabbed the branch I'd been steadying. "C'mon, pull it out. Think Great Pyramid of Giza. That's the shape we're aiming for."

I realized I had no idea what sorts of angles the sides of the Pyramid of Giza formed. "Is that the same shape as the pyramid on the back of the dollar bill?"

Anton stopped pulling on the branch and stared.

"The one with the floating eye over it?" I said. Because his silence was a little bit on the creepy side.

"The eye," he said. "What's that. Masonic? Rosicrucian?"

"I have no i…"

Anton sprinted off so fast, I swore someone was chasing him. Twigs snapped and leaves crackled, but he made surprisingly little noise for a guy running through a foot of dried foliage in near darkness. "Wait," I called after him. "Where're you going?"

About thirty yards away from me he stopped and turned, a silhouette in a long black coat. "I've gotta look this up. Don't wait up for me. I'm in the zone."

I'll say. The Twilight Zone. A whirl of his coat and a couple minutes of receding leaf rustles, and he was gone.

CHAPTER FIVE

"Ray? Are you awake yet?"

I had a moment of "where am I?" panic, followed by cascade of images — Mr. White in the shower; the empty apartment that smelled like bleach and felt like abandonment; Anton hanging from the tree branch with long hair, coat and scarf dangling beneath him.

"Yeah. I'm awake." I glanced in the direction of Marnie's canned voice. I had my very own intercom. There was a digital clock next to the speaker. It was after ten. Then I looked at the intercom itself. There was a button to press to talk. "I'm awake," I repeated, once I'd pressed it. "Was I supposed to be there at nine or something?"

"I'll let you know ahead of time if we'll ever need you that early. Breakfast is on. After that, I thought I'd go over the job and then show you around the island."

I showered, dressed in my second shirt and my slightly damp pants, and made my way to the kitchen without skating partway there on an exploded seagull.

Breakfast was fresh honeydew melon, bran muffins, and an egg white frittata. It could've used some bacon, but I wasn't about to complain. "I'm accustomed to putting in long hours," I said as Marnie loaded the dishwasher. "But the live-in thing's new to me. What's the routine?"

"The staff is salaried. Theoretically, that means our salaries are based on a fifty-hour work week minus living expenses." She shrugged. "Then again, last night was a good example of how things can crop up."

Marnie wiped her hands on a towel that hung from the apron tie at her waist, and found a small stack of papers. "Here it is in black and white. I think they'll let you take the Town Car out once they've known you for a while, but like I said, you can borrow mine if you need to. Let me know if you're going off the island, so that I'm available in case Mr. needs anything."

Like a trip to the emergency room. She didn't need to spell it out.

"We can negotiate nights off between us. If you want Friday and Saturday, be my guest. I hate the bar scene, I'm not seeing anyone right now, and I have no plans to put myself on the market."

"Ouch."

Marnie wiped her hands on her towel again, even though they were already clean. "I stopped just short of saying that men are pigs. Did you read my mind?"

"Must have. And I agree — but then one comes along and gives you a look, and it's all downhill from there."

She opened her mouth to reply and then broke into a surprised smile. "You're into guys." She shook her head. "I never would've guessed."

I stood, slid my melon rinds into the trash, and loaded my plate into the dishwasher. "Is that supposed to be a compliment?" I teased.

She'd crossed her arms over her chest and was giving me the once-over. "What about the tattoos?"

"Mrs. White told you about that, huh? Gay guys are allowed to have them too, you know."

"Can I see?"

I gave Marnie a tour of my tats — the ones I could show her by rolling up sleeves and pant legs, anyway. I started, as always, with the tiger behind the eight ball. That had been my first piece, seventeen with a fake ID, and distorted and awkward as it was, it was still my favorite.

In return, Marnie gave me a tour of the island. I drove, to get a feel for the car. I was accustomed to being higher up off the ground, in a pig of an SUV that bragged that the environment could kiss my ass, but that I secretly felt guilty for owning. The Town Car's suspension was impeccable. It floated down the narrow roads like we were drifting along on a two-ton cloud. The radio station was tuned to smooth jazz. Definitely an old-man car.

"That house belongs to the Shapiros," Marnie said. "They use it maybe two weeks out of the year."

"So is everybody…gone for the season?" I wasn't really sure why I wanted to hoard my late-night meeting with Anton, tuck it away, and not show it to anyone, even Marnie.

"Harlan Scott's always the last to go. Take a left. We'll swing by his place."

The Scott house was distinctive among the other island properties. Not only did it lack a decorative shingle that read *Scott's*, but it was completely fenced in by a twelve-foot monstrosity that conveyed in no uncertain terms that its single occupant valued his privacy. The **TRESPASSERS WILL BE PROSECUTED** sign across the gate reinforced this impression.

"Cozy," I said.

"I know it looks bad," said Marnie, "but I've talked to Mr. Scott. He's really not a bad guy, he's just private."

The car idled soundlessly.

"And he's kind of into disaster preparedness."

"What do you mean?"

"Oh, I don't know." We watched a red squirrel dart to the center of the road, tail flicking. It paused, gave us a haughty look, then dashed to the other side and up the tree trunk of a leaning maple. "It wasn't as if he went around passing out pamphlets he'd printed up in his basement or anything, we just got to talking when I ran into him at the grocery store. Sometimes he told me 'the grid' was going to go down. But then sometimes he said a pandemic was long overdue. But really. He's not that weird. Just shy. A good neighbor."

A sprinkling of maple seeds twirled down and tapped on the hood of the car. "So that's it? The Whites are the only ones who stay the winter?"

"And the sculptor, Anton Kopec. I don't know if he'll stay this year. He came pretty early in the spring, so I'm thinking that either the cold doesn't bother him or he's here to get away from the distractions of the city. I'll show you his place. Follow this road to the end, then hang a right."

I followed Marnie's directions, and a house emerged from the woods. It was orange, in a fake-redwood sort of way, and the cutesy mailbox with folk art doves painted on it read *Arnesons*. At least there was no apostrophe. "I thought you said his name was Kopec."

"Right. This is his sister's place. He lives on the property, in one of the outbuildings on the edge of the woods."

I put the car in park, and Marnie opened the passenger door. My heart started racing at the thought of Anton seeing me gawking at his place from the road. And I wondered what he'd look like once I had enough light to actually see him in detail.

Marnie walked across the lawn, and leaves rustled around her feet. "Here," she said, pointing to the mailbox post. "Here's one of his sculptures."

I had to really look hard to pick it out, but when I saw it, finally saw it, a chill raced down my spine. What looked at first like a tangle of dead vines clinging to the mailbox shifted and resolved itself into the withered husk of a creature, as if something had crawled up out of the bowels of hell and then crisped as the sun broke over the horizon and touched it with its rays.

"Whoa," I said.

"Yeah. Tell me about it. They're not all so…what's the word, figurative? But even the abstract ones are still pretty creepy, in a Blair Witch Project kind of way. I don't know how anyone can stand having something like that in their house."

If I had stumbled across art like that, back when I was working twelve-hour days and booking appointments six months out and had more money than I knew what to do with, I would've been all over it, whether I understood it or not. "It's interesting," I said, as noncommittally as I could manage. "He sells them?"

"His sister does. He stays here and does…whatever he does. I make him sound like a slacker, I guess, but that's not it at all. The woods behind his place brush up against the Whites' property." She pointed. "Well, you can see it in the winter, once all the leaves have dropped. Anyway, he's usually up working all night long. Sometimes, if the wind's blowing the right way, you'll pick up the sound of a drill or a staple gun."

I looked at the hellcreature husk and tried to imagine if the wigwam we'd built the night before looked anywhere near as cool.

"You're an artist," Marnie said, "right? Isn't that what you said during the interview? Custom art. I thought you'd meant you did portraits or something."

"Tattoos."

Marnie laughed. "Right. Custom art. That's a good way to describe it. I was going to ask what you thought of this stuff, but I'll bet it's right up your alley." She lowered her voice and leaned toward me, grinning. "Not me. I like a nice landscape. Maybe with a barn on it."

We headed back to the house so that Melita didn't have to hold down the fort by herself. Marnie started lunch, and I sat at the kitchen table with a cup of coffee and read through the description of my duties. I was expected to keep the car detailed and maintained, to be available between ten and seven for errands — earlier and later by prior arrangement. Two nights a week off. "A couple of things, Marnie."

She was grating carrots for a salad. She didn't look up. "Mm?"

"One, there's hardly fifteen hours of work in this schedule, not unless Mrs. White gets her hair done every single day."

"Will you be busy every hour of every day? No. There's a library half an hour from here. They'll give you a card if you show them your license and a letter from Mrs. stating that you live here."

I'm thinking she knew what the second thing was. I waited for her to address it, but she didn't. She kept on grating.

"I don't see anything about showering people either."

Marnie put down the carrot. "Ray, you've been honest with me. So let's keep things that way. You're not just here to drive the car. You're the muscle." When she spoke, she arranged the carrot gratings into a perfectly symmetrical cone, which brought to mind the Great Pyramid of Giza. "I know it sounds old-fashioned to want a man around the house. That used to be Mr., and when he started forgetting how to get home when they were out on their day trips, Mrs. hired her first driver."

"Melita made it sound like there's been a long line of drivers."

"You're the third. Stanley Marsh worked here for nearly six months, but right around the Fourth of July, he left all of a sudden. Mrs. was beside herself. And then she found Gene."

She spread the grated carrot into a patty and then mounded it into a cone shape again. I kept my mouth shut, though it seemed to me there was more to the story than she was letting on, if it was that difficult for her to find the words to say it.

"Mrs. adored Gene," she said finally.

"But he left all of a sudden too. Did he have a run-in with Mr.?"

Marnie's head snapped up. "Don't say that, Ray. Mr.'s sick, he can't help what he does. Sometimes when I look into his eyes, I think I can see his old personality trapped inside this body that doesn't work right anymore." She flattened the carrots again. "And besides, I know why Gene left. It wasn't anything Mr. did."

I finished my coffee and hoped she wasn't going to make me guess. She put the grater in the dishwasher and started plating up the salad, and finally, she said, "It was me. Gene had this crush on me. I had no idea, not until he said something." She weighed her words even more carefully. "He wasn't my type. It was a really awkward conversation. Beyond awkward."

"Well. You won't have to worry about me putting you on the spot."

She laughed. It sounded a little bit nervous and a lot relieved. "Would you believe that was the first thing that popped into my head when you told me you're gay?"

Marnie took lunch upstairs to the Whites, while Melita and I ate in the kitchen. "So," I said. "You work here long?"

"Ten years."

Shit. Ten years seemed like forever to me. Ten years ago I'd been backpacking through Europe.

"Anything to…do around here? Off duty?"

She waved her arm toward the kitchen window. "What, you think maybe there's a nightclub on the island, only nobody told you about it?"

I managed not to spit food, but I did shake a little as I stifled down a laugh. "What do you do in your spare time?"

"What spare time? I clean up after everyone — I dust, I vacuum, I scrub the floors, and the next day, it starts all over again."

"But you get two nights a week off," I said, wondering if maybe she was pissed that Marnie had suggested I take Friday and Saturday. "There's got to be something to break up your week."

"I don't need any nights off. I talked to Mrs. White, she pays me overtime instead. I stay here, send the money to my brother in Mexico City."

I ate my pasta, farfalle in a pesto sauce. It was incredible.

"What do I need money for, anyway?" Melita said, after we'd eaten in silence long enough that I thought she was done with the topic. "I live in a good house, I have food. I have my own television, my own phone. My family, they're using the money to send my nieces to school, make sure they get good jobs. We all make out good.

"Besides, it gets too cold up here to go anywhere. Once it starts snowing out, I'd rather stay inside 'til spring comes."

Mrs. White entered the kitchen with an armload of men's shirts draped over her arm, heavy wood hangers dangling. "I was going through Edgar's closet last night, and I realized he hasn't been able to wear these 17-1/2s in such a long time. Would you be interested in them, Raymond? Otherwise, they'll just go to waste."

My typical MO for buying shirts was to go for the XL with the longest sleeves. I glanced down at my cuffs. My ink was covered. "The sleeves might be a little short."

Mrs. White's eyes went to my cuffs too. "Don't worry about that. It's only us here."

I could tell from where I sat that Mr. White's old shirts were crisper, newer, and better made than the ones I'd picked up at the thrift store. It would save me a lot of grief to own more than two dress shirts. I would've thought Mrs. White's offer would rub me the wrong way, make me feel like a charity case — but instead I was touched, maybe from seeing her as vulnerable as she'd been last night. "All right. Thanks."

She draped the shirts over the back of a chair. "I'll leave you to your lunch."

"Good," said Melita, once she'd left. "I thought she had more laundry for me. You need clothes? Gene left most of his stuff behind when he took off. I got 'em in a bag in the laundry room. I don't know how good it would fit, though. He was a couple inches shorter than you, and he had a big belly."

If he was heavy, he might have some XLs that would fit. Melita's warning about the upcoming winter had me spooked. Winter in Traverse City was never fun for anyone but cross-country skiers, and Red Wing Island probably had sharper gusts and higher drifts. "I'll take a look, if you don't mind."

"Don't matter to me. Only one I can think of who'd care is Mrs. White. She treated Gene like he was her own kid. But since she's giving you her husband's clothes, it's probably okay to give you Gene's."

I went through Gene's old stuff and found some long-sleeved T-shirts and sweats that would fit. He had a couple of ties. I took them and his dress socks. His shoes were two sizes too small.

I walked back to my apartment loaded down with clothes, and I wondered if maybe I could stand to adopt Melita's attitude. Sure, I'd had possessions — mostly toys — and I'd lost them. But what did I really need? I had a job, I had a place to stay, and now I even had clothes. Maybe what was daunting me was the isolation.

I'm not a people person, not like Johnny, who'd had so many friends he couldn't begin to count them all. (Though you have to wonder how many of those were friends and how many were people he got high with.) I was no social butterfly, but I wasn't a loner either. Tattoo art isn't solitary. Once you've inked everything you can reach on your own body, you've got to start working on other people.

Here, I had only the Whites, Melita, and Marnie for company.

And Anton. Assuming he'd want to see more of me, which seemed premature. And exciting.

I was so wrapped up in mentally undressing Anton, scoping out that sexy mouth of his with my tongue, running my fingers down his long, lean body, under the waistband of his jeans, that I barely swerved in time.

Gore splattered the walkway and the threshold of the door to my front stairs, startlingly red. I staggered into the grass, felt something soft and wet give way under the sole of my shoe.

It didn't stink of fish this time. No feathers clinging to the guts. Instead, fur stuck out here and there in little tufts. I recalled the squirrel who'd watched Marnie giving me the tour of the island. I'm sure it couldn't possibly have been the very same squirrel — or what was left of him — here. But I couldn't help but thinking of it that way.

◊ ◊ ◊ ◊

"Foxes," Mrs. White said. She sat in the backseat of the Town Car, speaking to the back of my head. I had my eyes on the narrow, winding road, and half my brain wondering if she saw through my hair to the Celtic knot at the base of my skull. "Mr. Scott — he's very familiar with wildlife — tells me that he has never seen, nor heard, coyotes on the island. But there are foxes."

"Scott. He's the, um…" Crackpot survivalist. How had Marnie put it? "…the guy who's into disaster preparedness."

"Yes, Harlan Scott. He's kept a summer home on the island for almost twenty years now. He usually stays through October, so I'm surprised he's gone already. Although, he really isn't the sort to stop over and say good-bye. He tends to keep to himself."

I guided the car over the bridge, which felt sturdy enough, but sounded hollow beneath the tires. It was a relief to hit the two-lane that led to town.

"Did you sleep well last night?" she asked me.

"Fine, I guess. Strange bed and all. And it sounds different on the island than it does in the city." And maybe I'd been listening to see if I'd hear Anton romping through the woods again. And maybe I wondered if he was busy TP-ing my front door with entrails in some bizarre, postmodern initiation ritual.

"Edgar used to say that, and also that the air was different on the island too. He felt like he slept more deeply here than he ever did in the city."

"So you didn't always live here year-round."

"No, not until Edgar retired. We always looked forward to coming and hated leaving, until finally we decided to sell our condo and stay."

Mrs. White had me escort her to all the pit stops, which was fine by me. I'd rather walk around than just sit there in the car and stare at the windshield. We stopped for a late lunch at a trendy coffee shop with sandwiches that looked a lot better than they tasted.

"I'm spoiled by Marnie's cooking," Mrs. White told me. "She should really be working in a fancy hotel. But she says she wouldn't care for the hours."

I was raising my chicken club for another bite when the door opened and three twentysomethings wandered in, all jeans and leather and crayon-bright hair.

And Johnny. Shit.

It was a small town, and I was bound to see him sooner or later…but I'd really been hoping it would be later. He'd colored his hair cherry red and sprayed it up into a short fin, but even though I'd never seen him as a redhead, the tat on his neck, a thorny vine, was hard to miss. I'd designed that piece myself.

It was almost one thirty. He'd probably just rolled out of bed. Probably someone else's bed. Probably the bed that belonged to the pink-haired girl in the leopard-skin coat, and her boyfriend with a complexion like skim milk. I turned away from them and studied the stand-up display on the table that encouraged us to make dinner special by taking home a whole pie: apple, cherry, or pecan.

I looked at that pie ad so hard I'm surprised I didn't burn a hole through it. The pink-haired girl laughed, and the violent hiss of the espresso machine muted the sound. It occurred to me that I didn't know which overpriced coffee drink Johnny would have ordered. Because I'd seldom just hung out with him; I was too busy working.

The time it took to make three drinks was excruciating. Thank God they took their mocha-whipped-latte-whatevers and hit the road. If they'd opted to stay, no amount of twisting and turning would've kept Johnny from spotting me.

"You didn't want your friends to see you with an old lady," Mrs. White said.

"What?"

She smiled, a bit sadly. "You were trying very hard not to be seen."

"Oh." I hadn't realized it'd been that obvious. "Not because of you. It was…" What *was* my problem, anyway? Was it that I couldn't stand for Johnny to see me in a tie? Fuck that. He thought it was "cool" to drift from bed to bed because he was too lazy to earn his keep, so I'd be damned if I let him look down on me for earning a living. No, it was more that I just couldn't stand the sight of him. "They weren't friends of mine. Just…someone I used to know."

We finished our lunch and hit a couple more stores; then Mrs. White stopped to visit with a friend before we headed back. I read the Town Car's owner's manual from front to back — twice — by the time she was done. "I hear there's a library in town," I said. Because I hoped that maybe she would add it to her list of stops.

"It's just up the road."

I waited for her to suggest we stop. She didn't. "This road?" I prompted.

"Over there. By the pizzeria."

"Did you…need any books?"

"They're closed on Thursdays. Tax cuts, you know. Not enough circulation to hire another staff member."

I sighed.

"You're welcome to borrow any of my books you'd like."

"I don't know that we'd have the same taste in reading material."

I glanced in the rearview and saw Mrs. White smile. "You're probably right. I don't see you as the Jane Austen type. You should pay a visit to Mr. Kopec, in the redwood house on the other side of the woods. You'll probably have more in common with him. He's right around your age, and he's into all those 'artistic' sorts of things."

I assumed she meant my ink. Probably. "You've seen his artwork?"

"I have. Very different. His sister's friend represents him. She has a gallery in Detroit. His work sells better in a big city than it would around here."

"He makes a living at it?" I was surprised; I'd had the impression that he'd be destitute without his sister.

"He does rather well, so I've heard."

"Then how come he lives in his sister's guesthouse?"

"You'll have to ask Mr. Kopec. He's never mentioned it to me."

I'd been fishing for a trip to the library and found myself with an airtight excuse to get another look at Anton instead. After dinner, I mentioned Mrs. White's book-borrowing suggestion to Marnie. It wasn't my night off, but since both Marnie and Melita were home, and since Mrs. White had actually suggested it, I suspected I could get away with abandoning my post.

"Wait a minute," Marnie said. "Before you go." She went into the utility room off the kitchen, and I heard the sound of drawers opening and closing. She came back with a rubber mallet. "I borrowed it from him a couple of months ago. Bring this with you — that way, if he's in a mood, you can just say you were returning it for me, and you can take off again."

"A mood."

"You know." Her hand fluttered, as if it would help her locate the right word. Evidently, it failed. "A mood."

Whatever. "You got a flashlight too? Someone keeps leaving presents on my doorstep."

"I've been thinking about that. Someone must've brought a cat with them this summer and left it behind. Probably the Shapiros — too busy checking their stock portfolios to notice that Fluffy's missing. If you want, I can pick up some cat food when I get groceries tomorrow."

"For what?"

"Put a bowl of food and a bowl of water outside your door. If it likes you enough to leave you presents, maybe you can tame it."

"You think I need a cat."

"Why not? I don't think Mrs. would mind, especially if it was an outdoor cat that just kind of eased its way in. This island's a lonely place when roads drift over and you're waiting for the snowplows to dig you out."

There was one creature on the island I was hoping could ease that loneliness, but he wasn't of the feline variety.

I wished I had something to put in my hair to make it look less Wall Street. I went through the medicine cabinet to see if Gene had left anything behind, but given that no one had made him out to be the type of guy to spike his hair up, I wasn't surprised to find nothing but dental floss and cheap aftershave.

I changed into my real clothes — jeans, T-shirt, biker boots, and leather jacket — and headed through the woods to see a man about some books. The sun was down by the time I'd dressed. I took the flashlight and the mallet and tried to figure out where, exactly, I'd built wigwams by the light of the full moon two nights before. It took me nearly half an hour. I'd tripped over several tree roots and nearly broke my ankle in a gopher hole, but I found the stick pyramid. And three others just like it that had sprung up around it.

The original pyramid had looked kind of artsy in the moonlight.

The four of them together in the flashlight beam looked a little creepy.

I circled around the pyramids and inched through the trees until I saw a pair of windows glowing yellow in the thick, cicada-droning darkness. I tripped over another tree root, staggered, then did my best to stay upright as I made my way toward Anton's house.

It was a tiny thing, maybe twenty by twenty, with five steps leading up to a narrow porch with a dilapidated rocking chair on it, and a wind chime made of dozens of small, fragile white bones. I wondered if he'd shot any photos of the time he'd redecorated his sister's house. I was guessing he and I had similar taste.

Music seeped through the front door, mostly bass, a thudding beat — nothing I recognized right off the bat, but maybe it wasn't something that was meant to be sung along with. Maybe it was more of a trance inducement. I pressed my fingertips to the frame of his storm door and felt a faint vibration. It would be loud inside, but the house was very well insulated. I looked for a doorbell. There was none. So I opened the storm door and knocked on the leaded glass pane of the front door. Hard.

The music cut. The door opened, and there he was — Anton, framed like a vision in bright yellow light. I'd been worried that maybe the light of the full moon had played tricks on me, that maybe once I got a really good look at him, the spell would be broken and I'd see that he was just some guy. A guy with black hair down to his shoulders and finger bones dangling from his porch, but just a guy, nonetheless.

I'd been wrong. Up close and well lit, Anton was a wet dream.

He looked me over and smiled, and that hairline gap between his front teeth was startlingly hot. "Ray of Moonlight, fellow insomniac and pyramid craftsman. I've been wondering if I'd really met you the other night or if I'd just invented you to amuse myself. But here you are." He glanced down at the flashlight and mallet. "And you brought toys."

I stepped inside. He backed up far enough to let me get in the door and no farther. "I hear you're a big-time gallery artist."

"So they say. I have no empirical proof. Diane's worried I might be myself in front of the art scene and blow my reputation, so she's billed me as some kind of socially retarded recluse so she can handle all the deals without me."

"Maybe that's for the best. Dealers would try to steer you toward making things they can sell. Maybe it's easier to be true to your art when you don't have to deal with any of that shit."

He tilted his head back and stared at my lips with sultry-lidded eyes. "Spoken like a true artist."

"You could say that."

"I just did."

"I wasn't always a driver, you know. My license is so new it squeaks when I put it in my wallet."

Anton dropped his gaze to my jacket, my chest, then raked it back up to my eyes again. Either he practiced seductive looks in the mirror, or it just came naturally to him. And he didn't strike me as the type of guy who was able to slap on a false front — if he would even bother to.

"You can tell me what you were before, or not. I like to think we reinvent ourselves each and every day. Even our cells shed and regenerate. We're literally not the same people we were seven years ago."

"That might explain why I do such stupid things," I said. And the way Anton stood right up in my space, the way neither one of us backed off, I suspected I was on the verge of adding one more act of dubious intelligence to my collection. "I was an artist."

"Was? I don't think the artistic temperament is something you can misplace. Once it finds you, you're stuck with it." Anton straightened the lapel of my jacket. Blood surged downward. He hadn't even touched me yet, not any more than my jacket, but my body was giving me the green light already.

"The artistic temperament's a bunch of bullshit. Something trust-fund kids at art school use as an excuse to leech off other people." Or more accurately, a label used by people like Johnny to make a sucker out of people like me. "I had my own business."

"Better you than me. I always thought the more I owned, the more it tied me down. One day I'll probably hike out into the middle of nowhere and live off the land. But those other idiots you're talking about, the self-styled *artistes*? I've got less use for 'em than you do. So even though I like to bitch about it, I'm sure I'm not missing much by letting Diane handle the galleries."

Anton stared me in the eye while he talked, and never broke eye contact. I can stare anybody down, but his unflinching attention had me unsettled. "I didn't come here to psychoanalyze myself," I said. "I'm just returning a hammer."

My lapels were lying flat, but Anton smoothed them again while he watched for my reaction. If I even had one, it was subtle. I stood there, close, and I stared back at him while his hands moved up my chest and over my shoulders. He shifted, and our thighs brushed. I stood my ground. Then he grabbed my head two-handed, cupped my jaw, and pulled himself even closer, excruciatingly close, into an almost-kiss I was just on the verge of feeling. I closed my eyes and breathed. He smelled male. And different from Johnny, which was good.

I slid off my leather jacket, let it drop to the floor with the flashlight and mallet inside the sleeves. I eased my body against his, felt his breath on my lips. His grip on my jaw tightened. He eased forward too, until gradually, finally, his mouth pressed against mine. That first kiss was slow and deliberate. It lingered, as if we both needed to get our bearings. Anton pulled away first, but only to speak. He pressed his forehead to mine. "Did my sister hire you to keep me from going blind?"

I mouthed the word *blind* against his lips.

"Excessive masturbating." He traced my cheekbones with his thumbs and stared into my eyes.

"Nope. Your sister's got zero to do with me."

Anton's eyes narrowed. He cocked his head. "That's probably the hottest thing I've ever heard. Which shows you how pathetic my life is lately."

He leaned in for another kiss, and this time, he eased his tongue into my mouth. I put my hands on his hips. He felt slimmer than Johnny. Taller too, almost as tall as me. And I told myself to quit comparing, but how could I stop? That's just the way it is, when you've been with someone for a couple of years and you're still smarting where they've stung you.

Anton slid one hand around the back of my neck and wove his fingers through my hair. His other hand dropped, made its way underneath my T-shirt. His breath hissed in, cool over my lips. "It's been so long since I touched someone," he said, "it feels like it happened in another life."

Another life? That described the way I'd been feeling lately so well that it made the hair on my forearms prickle.

I ran my hands up and down Anton's sides. He had one of those wiry builds that he either nurtured by jogging and biking, or by fretting away his calories with caffeine and nicotine. Or maybe he was one of those naturally thin people who can live on Yoo-hoo and doughnuts and never gain a pound.

Anton took hold of my T-shirt and pulled it over my head. It was cool in his tiny guesthouse, but the tightly coiled anticipation in my gut made considerations like "hot" and "cold" seem negligible.

"Oh," was all he said, when he saw my ink. Just a syllable. And I'd been waiting for recognition to kick in, for him to tell me that inking tats made me an artist as much as picking a box in the football pool made someone an athlete, but from the sound of his voice — soft and filled with wonder — I could tell he saw what I saw in it. Even if he did sell stuff at some swanky gallery. Or his sister did.

He touched my cloud dragon, my densest, most colorful piece, which covered me from ribs to shoulder to elbow on my left side. He nodded, very grave. "This is good."

"Thanks."

He traced a lightning bolt that wrapped my ribs, and a shiver rippled through my body. "All of it's yours?"

"Not all. Most of the newer pieces. It's slow going, inking yourself." I hadn't been prepared for the experience of meeting people who didn't know me as Ray from Body Art Studio…the now-defunct Body Art Studio. It made my tats feel exotic. Maybe taboo.

The way it'd felt when I got that tiger and eight ball. Several lifetimes ago.

Anton dragged his fingertip along the clouds, over to my right side, where a gargoyle crouched. "No piercings? I'm surprised."

"I hate needles." The sight of them poking through to the opposite side of whatever's being pierced, anyway.

He nodded, lifted up my arm to get a good look at the gargoyle's expression. I'd had the gargoyle's face done by my favorite apprentice, a skinny girl named Alice with more holes in her than I could count. She'd had a good, steady hand.

I held still while Anton moved around me, stroking my body as he read my skin. I stared at the wall straight ahead. Something that looked like a cross between a dried apple-head doll, a pair of mummified testicles, and a souvenir from a fateful trip down the Amazon hung over a filthy microwave splattered with tomato sauce and grease.

It was repulsive, whatever it was — the sculpture, not the microwave. Yet I couldn't stop looking. And I supposed, again, that if I was flush with cash, I'd buy it in a second.

Anton sidled around me in a crouch, passed the cloud dragon, and hitched his fingers into my belt buckle. They were long fingers, stained with dirt or pigment. "Show me the rest." He tugged at my waistband.

"It's your turn to take something off," I said.

"My tribal markings are nowhere near as colorful." He crossed his arms, grabbed the tattered hem of his gray, long-sleeved thermal top, and pulled the shirt over his head.

His body was already winter pale, like someone who can't be bothered with the sun. The dusting of hair on his chest looked stark against his white skin, and it occurred to me that he didn't dye his hair, which was unheard of in my most recent social circles.

He dropped his thermal shirt and pointed to a crescent-shaped scar alongside his stomach. "Age nine. Ruptured appendix." He flipped his arm over and showed me the underside of his wrist. A thick ridge of white scar tissue crossed his forearm, an inch below the base of his palm. "Age eighteen. Suicide attempt. Unsuccessful, obviously." He smirked. "Don't worry, I've been out of that phase for years."

He held out his right arm. "Ditto." The scar on that wrist was thinner, less pronounced. I guessed that he was right-handed, unable to slice himself as decisively with his left hand. Either that, or he'd already cut his left wrist, and the amount of blood that must have been spreading had given him second thoughts.

I glanced at the apple-head testicle thing. Maybe not.

Anton flipped his arm over and pointed to a couple of small puncture mark scars. "Neighbor's Chihuahua. Age eleven. Me, not the dog. I don't know exactly how old the dog was. Maybe he was eleven too."

I wrapped my fingers around his scarred forearm and pulled him against me, skin to skin. Our mouths met. They fit together more readily than they had the first time. That was all it took, I supposed, to get used to somebody. A single kiss. It didn't seem like nearly enough of a prerequisite. But I was glad, and ready to forget whatever traces of Johnny were still left on me, wipe the slate clean for someone new.

Anton rubbed his whole body against mine. His hands raked me, anywhere he could touch, over my ribs, down my back. A quick squeeze of my ass, then greedy between my legs, cupping me, feeling me.

My breath caught. Anton covered my mouth with a deep, bold kiss. My cock stiffened beneath his roaming hands.

I turned my mouth away from his. "I don't have any condoms," I said. Because I didn't have much of anything. Not anymore.

"Good. Then we won't have to fight about who gets to use up his rubbers before they expire." He took me by the waistband of my jeans and towed me into the bathroom. It was incredibly small, just enough to fit a toilet, shower stall, and sink, cramped enough that he probably stepped out into his studio so he could get dressed without banging his elbows on the towel bar. He flipped the toilet seat shut, unbuttoned my jeans, pulled them down around my knees, and gave me a shove. I sat down hard.

He opened a medicine cabinet above my head, and cotton swabs and safety razors rained down on me. "One look at you and I'm dying to suck some minty-good latex."

He dropped a green foil strip into my lap. Mint. Then he knelt down between my knees and looked up at me impatiently. I tore off a condom, checked the date. Still a few months left. I opened the foil, rolled it on. Good thing I'd been cultivating a steady hand for twenty years; otherwise, he would've seen me shaking.

Not that I was nervous. Well, actually, I was. But it felt more like shock. Everything was too new. This room, this man. This island. Me. Seven years to shed my cells and become a new person? Hell, I was a different guy than I'd been seven months ago. I looked down at my tiger and eight ball to reassure myself that I was still me — because lately, when I'd glanced down and seen the buttoned cuff of a white oxford dress shirt instead of the studded bracelet and ink-smeared latex glove, I'd felt like a ghost who was too stubborn to move into the light and had ended up possessing some Mr. Average America who'd been too oblivious to notice the hijacking of his own body.

Anton grabbed the base of my cock and exerted enough pressure to make things interesting. My body responded by flooding my groin. I went from hard to super hard. He bent his head to me and planted a long, wet lick across my balls, and I shuddered from my scalp to the soles of my feet.

I buried my hands in his hair, felt it glide like silk through my fingers, unhampered by spray or gel or paste or wax or whatever the new, hip product might be. Me, not me…I stopped dwelling on it, swept away by the touch of his hair, the heat of his mouth.

Anton seemed as hungry for me as I felt for him. He swallowed me deep and grunted his satisfaction as my cockhead bumped his throat. All the while, his hands roved over my hips and thighs as if they could never manage to touch enough of my skin.

I moaned out loud. I'm not a screamer, but the feel of his mouth closing over me was so incredible, so right, it dredged the noise up from somewhere inside me I hadn't even realized was there.

Anton made a noise in return. An encouragement. And he started stroking my balls in time with his sucking, until finally I couldn't watch anymore, and I tilted my head back and focused on the feeling. The heat. The pressure. The trail of saliva that slipped down past the ring of his finger and thumb, the base of the condom, and rolled, startlingly wet, down my nuts while he stroked them.

I saw the brink coming already — fast, but hell, it'd been so long since I'd been with anyone it was hardly surprising. The strangeness of it all, the unfamiliarity of everything, including myself, clicked into place and dragged me toward the edge.

Anton must have sensed it in the clench of my thighs. He backed off.

He kept his finger and thumb locked around the base of the condom, and he pulled off with a slurp so loud it rang against the tiles. I opened my eyes, just a crack, as he threw his long hair back and gave me a dazzlingly naughty smile.

I probably looked stunned. I sure felt that way.

He stood and ran a hand over the bulge in his jeans, then caught one of my hands and pressed it against him so I could feel his stiff cock through the denim. "Let's go to bed."

I fished the strips of condoms off the floor where they lay among the scattered cotton swabs, a few crumpled tissues, and an empty prescription bottle. Anton grabbed me by the arm and dragged me out into the studio. The farthest corner was hidden by a folding screen that might have been kitschy once, but had been painted, textured, sanded, and repainted so many times, and in the loose, decayed way that Anton handled every medium he touched, that it looked like something that'd been scavenged from an abandoned movie set that was buried by an earthquake.

The screen hid a twin bed with mismatched sheets and pillows, unmade. Nothing else. I shuffled behind Anton with my jeans around my ankles. He spun me and pushed me back onto the bed.

"Take off your pants," I said. "And leave the light on."

"Lights-out never crossed my mind. There's too much of you I haven't seen yet."

We both stripped off our jeans while we kept our eyes glued to each other. Anton's inkless body looked like a blank canvas, no markings other than his battle scars. I couldn't remember the last time I'd been with someone who didn't have any tats — even if it was only an unfortunate cartoon character they'd chosen from a wall of flash on a teenage impulse.

Strangely enough, I didn't itch to fill that canvas with whorls and spikes and gradations of color. I just wanted to enjoy it for what it was, like a blanket of fresh snow that makes the world white and clean, if only for a few hours, before the pollution settles and turns everything a uniform shade of gray.

"You're tattooing me with your eyes," Anton said.

I pried off my boots and sank back onto my elbows. "No. Just the opposite."

"Flaying me?"

"You've got one fucked-up sense of humor."

"I try." He stepped between my feet, leading with his hips in that odd sashay of his — leading with his cock, I realized, now that it was pointing at me, hard and thick, red. He ran his fingertips along the barbed wire piece that snaked down my leg. "It balances the dragon."

Anton straddled my leg and stroked his hard cock. I stared at the fleshy head, appearing and disappearing within the loose grasp of his pigment-stained fingers. He crouched and touched his cockhead to my barbed wire tattoo where it bisected my thigh. He let out a shuddery breath when his bare skin glided over mine, and I realized that I hadn't been breathing either.

His eyes roamed my body — or maybe just my ink — while he stroked himself and petted my thigh with the tip of his cock. I watched him looking at me, and I fixed the line of his cheekbone and jaw, the pattern where his dark stubble came in, the tilt of his head and the shadows his long eyelashes cast.

Anton let go of his cock and brushed his fingertips over my balls. "How do you want to do this?"

"Every way we can."

He caught his lower lip in his teeth, flashing that sexy gap, and twitched his eyebrows. "Good answer."

He rolled on a condom and lay on top of me. More kisses, starting slow, then building in depth, intensity. He ground into me, and my cock found the hollow inside his hip bone. I stroked myself on him while his tongue learned my mouth and left me breathless.

He broke the kiss. Our hips had locked into a rhythm, rubbing our cocks against each other's bodies sure and hard, so good I might come just from rocking against him and kissing his hypnotic mouth.

But Anton reached under the bed, groped for a moment, and came up with a plastic bottle of lube. He flipped the cap up with his teeth and squirted some into his palm as he eased up into a kneeling position.

"Try this on for size," he said. He pulled the mint condom off and grabbed me hard, stroked my cock with his slippery hand.

My back arched up, and I gave a guttural moan.

"Very nice, Ray of Moonlight. Can I bury myself in your colorful ass while I do my best to make you make that noise again?"

I wasn't exactly thinking in words anymore. I nodded.

Anton slicked his condom with lube, then hooked his forearms behind my legs and folded my knees toward my chest. "I'm dying to see the story unfold on your back," he said, "but right now, I'd rather watch your face when you come."

My cock twitched. Johnny had never said anything like that...in fact, he hadn't been able to rub two words together in bed. Tired, high, going through the motions, who knows? I was usually the one on top too — at first because I was more experienced, and eventually, because Johnny realized he preferred to lie there looking pretty, rather than expending any actual effort.

"Second thoughts?" Anton said.

I hadn't realized he could see it in my eyes when I was revisiting Johnny. I shook my head.

"Good."

His cock prodded my hole, big — damn it, I might as well be a virgin again. "Go slow," I said. My voice was sandpapery.

"Yeah, let's make it last," he said. He stopped pushing and swirled lube over my ass with his cockhead. The room was filled with the sound of our breathing and the crinkle of the reservoir tip.

He swiped my ass and retreated, swiped and retreated, until finally I was ready to beg. "Not that slow," I said.

Anton treated me to a very naughty smile. "Just making sure." He lined himself up and pushed, and I let my breath out, did my best to relax. Both of us moaned, him, me, and I rode on the high of my ass so full of cock that it was painful — a delicious sort of pain that would make my balls tingle, days later, from the mere thought of him sinking it in.

Anton turned his head and dragged his tongue over the inside of my knee, then raked my skin with his teeth while he hugged my thigh to his chest. "How's that?" he said. It was a whisper.

"Feels good."

His breath was hot and moist on the crook of my knee as he pushed in deep. My cock was slick with lube. I stroked it gently while the painful pleasure intensified, and every nerve ending in my body seemed to coalesce in my groin. Anton pulled out and pushed in again, slow, but deep. Again, and again.

"I wanna pound you so bad," he said.

My cock throbbed. I was ready. "Do it."

Anton let his body weight drop onto my thighs, and my knees pressed toward my shoulders. My breath whooshed out, and I had a hard time catching it. His face hovered over mine, black hair hanging down, tickling my cheeks, forming a wall that narrowed my world to nothing but his dark eyes.

His thrusts picked up speed, but he never pulled out more than partway, kept his cock half buried. He moved faster. His balls slapped against my ass, softly at first, then louder. Pretty soon he was fucking me hard.

I was so tangled up in my knees and my inability to draw even one single deep breath that my orgasm sideswiped me, and I made a strange, strangled sound, eyes wide open, staring up into Anton's eager face.

He grabbed my shoulders as I shot, and pulled us together so tightly it was as if he was trying to merge us. The breathlessness, the sweet-edged pain — it uncoiled deep in my gut, and I came so hard, it was as if the word *orgasm* could hardly describe the sensation.

And then I realized that Anton was still and just watching me, staring down at my face. My eyes were still open, but it might have been a few seconds since I'd actually seen anything.

"That was beautiful," he whispered.

It was a wonder I emerged from the woods anywhere near the Whites' property. My knees were so rubbery that they couldn't quite carry me in a straight line, and my brain wasn't paying any attention to where I was headed either.

Anton had tried to convince me to stay. He'd very nearly succeeded. But I'd agreed to two nights off each week, and tonight wasn't one of them. I'd gone to Anton's to return a mallet and borrow a book. It was suspicious enough that it'd taken me two hours to do so.

Especially since I'd forgotten to ask him for a book.

I pushed through the undergrowth and found myself at the front of the house, where a gazebo covered in withering vines stood, drifted with leaves.

I lurched past the gazebo toward the house, leaves rustling all around me. I glanced over my shoulder at the structure and staggered back. A silhouette I'd taken for a tree moved in a very untreelike way, and it resolved itself into the shape of a man.

Three steps back, I finally found the button of the flashlight, even though it was right under my thumb the whole time. I swung the beam at the phantom in the gazebo, and the figure turned.

Mr. White.

My relief was so palpable I felt giddy. "Mr. White? What're you doing?" I said, before it occurred to me that he couldn't answer.

And yet, he did. His eyes went wide, and he shielded them from the flashlight beam with an outstretched palm. "Who are you?"

I swung the light from his eyes and aimed it at myself. "It's Ray. The driver." Mr. White looked puzzled. I didn't think he remembered meeting me, and given the circumstances, that was probably for the best. "I'm new."

"Where's Stanley?" he said.

I was pretty sure the previous driver's name was Gene. Stanley must've been the first driver then. "He left," I said, and I decided it was best to keep the explanation simple. "I don't really know the whole story, just that I'm his replacement."

Mr. White nodded and squinted at me. I kept the flashlight on my face and took a few steps forward so he could have a look at me. I'm not sure what I expected. That he'd mix me up with this Stanley guy or lapse into confused silence, or maybe that he'd mingle past and present and take me for some long-dead brother of his, or worse, his father. But instead he surprised me. He laughed. "They must've found him playing with the safe. He did that every time he thought no one was looking. Especially me."

He looked up at the moon, which was waning now, but just shy of full. "It's cold out here. Walk me back to the house, if you don't mind... What did you say your name was?"

"Ray."

"Shine that thing on the ground, Mr. Ray. I don't want to fall and break my neck."

I offered Mr. White my arm, and he took it. We walked together, arm in arm like a couple of old friends, up the porch stairs to the front door. I opened the door. Mrs. White was on her way down the staircase in a robe with her hair wrapped in a towel. "Edgar? Raymond, I almost didn't recognize you." She looked from Mr. White, to me, and back to him again. "Were you outside?"

"I was just checking on the gazebo. I thought I heard something."

"It's pitch dark out there. You could have hurt yourself."

Maybe I'd thought the same thing, but Mrs. White wasn't going to score any points if she impugned her husband's manliness. "We're all in one piece," I told her. "I had a flashlight on me." I kept my tone easy and turned to Mr. White. "You ready to go back upstairs now?"

He considered. "All right. Yes. I'd like to sit down."

"Why don't I walk with you? I was going that way anyway." And even though there couldn't have possibly been anything I needed upstairs — and in fact, I'd never seen more than the route between the bathroom and the bedroom — Mr. White seemed to understand that if I wanted to spin out a little fantasy where we were just a couple of regular guys, it wasn't because I was mocking him. He might forget who I was by morning, and I might have to get into the shower with him again, but for right now, at least, that's what we were. A couple of guys.

I got Mr. White settled in a well-used wingback chair in his bedroom, and turned to go downstairs. Mrs. White approached me in the hall. "He gets restless sometimes and wanders. It's impossible to watch him twenty-four hours a day."

"Maybe you should hire a nurse. There are male nurses, you know."

"Raymond." She slipped her hand through my arm. It rested against the sleeve of my leather jacket, parchment skin and a diamond band that was worth easily as much as the Town Car. "Come with me."

We went down the back stairs together, past Melita's room where a laugh track from some inane comedy swelled through the closed door, and into the kitchen. Mrs. White filled the teapot and put it on the stove. "I promised Edgar, no nurses. So until he can't possibly know the difference, I will keep that promise."

"But you could always say it's just a new maid."

She took two mugs down from the cupboard, added tea bags, and set one in front of me without asking whether I wanted it or not. "This spring, maybe I'll look into it. But, Raymond, you see how it is. He has these moments where he's his old self again, and I couldn't stand to have him realize that I'd done something he specifically asked me not to do."

I nodded and looked at the bright logo on the tea bag tag. It had a little saying on the back. *A wise man's actions speak for themselves.*

The teakettle whistled, and Mrs. White filled both our mugs. "I'm going to go up and be with Edgar until he falls asleep. He seems calmer after he's been with you."

I shrugged and dunked my tea bag.

"Thank you, Raymond."

I couldn't quite meet her eye for some reason. "S'okay," I said.

I steeped my tea, hunted for sugar unsuccessfully, then drank it down black. Marnie had been right — I wished I had met Edgar before the Alzheimer's took him. He seemed like an okay guy.

All the money anyone could ever want, and still his life was shit. I'd thought money, or the lack of it, was to blame for all my problems, so I found the idea that money can't solve every problem hard to wrap my head around.

"I wondered why the light was on."

Marnie. I flinched and wondered how many millions of miles away I'd been when she came in. "Just...thinking."

"Mrs. said you found Mr. outside. I won't lie, it scares the heck out of me that just enough of him comes to the surface to get him in trouble." She pulled a chair out, sat down, and crossed her legs. She had on a pair of backless slippers, and she jiggled one loosely on her foot. "And that's what you were wearing when you caught him?"

I looked down at my leather jacket. "What?"

"You were at Anton's this whole time? And you got dressed up to go there?"

"I'm not 'dressed up.'"

"You think he's gay, don't you?"

I tried to get a read on where Marnie was going with the whole line of questioning, but all I got from her tone of voice was "intense." "Yeah," I told her, "I do. Any particular reason you're busting my balls over it?"

She slumped against the back of the chair. "Just be careful."

"Can you be a little more specific?"

Marnie's leg jiggled harder. The slipper flapped against the sole of her foot. "Don't expect too much. Like I said, he's moody."

"Moody."

"He was probably being all charming with you — that makes sense, if he's 'up,' and he's into guys, like you say. But he stays awake for days at a time, making all that creepy stuff, and then his temper…"

"Marnie," I said. She stopped talking and looked me in the eye. "I'm a big boy."

She sighed. "Yeah, I know. But you haven't seen him freak out over something. Don't say I didn't warn you."

"Consider me warned."

She got up and put my mug in the dishwasher. "Don't forget to turn the lights off when you're done in here."

"I won't."

Silence, then, except the flap of her slippers on the tile. She stopped in the doorway. "Is your hair wet?"

I touched the back of my head, which confirmed it. And I still smelled like his soap, his shampoo.

"You slept with him already? My God."

I stood and walked toward her and didn't hesitate to tower over her as I reached past her shoulder and turned off the light. "I'm an adult, remember? Good night, Marnie."

◊ ◊ ◊ ◊

Marnie seemed cooler to me after that. Nothing overt, just a harder set to her mouth, more abruptness when we talked. I turned over the events of that first night with Anton in my head. I'd walked through the woods, spent a couple of hours, and come home. What went on while I was there? No one else's business.

So, what was she all ticked off about?

She'd told me her relationship with Gene had gone sour, not only to the point of him quitting, but him quitting without a word to anyone and leaving all his stuff and his last paycheck behind. Maybe I'd just read her wrong initially and she was actually the source of all the drama. Lord knows I'd known enough head cases who seemed perfectly normal at first.

The next morning, the gardening crew came from town in an extended-cab pickup and set to work on getting all the leaves corralled into a burnable pile. I washed and waxed the Town Car while Melita and the lawn crew supervisor chewed the fat in Spanish, which I speak maybe five words of, and which makes even the most mundane conversations sound fast paced and gripping to my ears.

The air was filled with the sound of leaf blowers, and the Whites' estate buzzed with activity. And when it was time to come in for lunch, I realized that I hadn't thought about Body Art Studio all day. Not once.

Melita quit lunch early to go outside and gossip with the supervisor some more, which left Marnie and me at the table. "It's Friday," she said.

I nodded and waited for her to go somewhere with that.

"You get six to ten off. Tomorrow night too. Stanley used to go into town a lot, stay over. He had some friends there."

I kept on nodding, eating.

"I imagine you'll stay at Anton's."

"I imagine I will, if he seems agreeable to that."

We were both nodding by that time. It was catchy. Difficult to stop.

"Your apartment is your apartment. You can have visitors up there."

"What are you saying?"

"Nothing. I just thought I'd tell you. You don't have to sneak around."

"Who's sneaking?"

"The main thing is that you're here if we need you. Just in case."

In case an accident went beyond something that could be washed down the drain. "I got it."

Marnie stood up and rifled through a drawer. "Cell phone coverage is spotty here — not that you've ever mentioned owning a cell phone — but two-way radios work great. The range covers the whole island." She pulled something that looked like a cell phone with a black rubber antenna out of the drawer and put it on the table. "Gene had one, but he took it with him when he left. This was Mr.'s. He doesn't know how to use it anymore, so you might as well keep it on you. That way, after work, you can go where you want, and nobody's got to worry. Just keep it turned on and tuned to channel twelve."

I wasn't sure if the phone represented freedom or just the opposite. I figured if the walkie-talkie got intrusive, I'd cross that bridge when I came to it. "Okay."

Since I wasn't being called upon to drive Mrs. White anywhere, and the car was spotless, I went outside to watch the landscapers work. While I was eating lunch they'd piled the leaves at the far corner of the property and set them on fire. Two of the workers were unloading a big piece of heavy equipment from the back of the truck, while the third guy wandered in and out of the trees, blowing out the last few leaves, and the supervisor kept gossiping with Melita.

The machine, some kind of digger, had a gas motor that was loud enough to let you know it meant business. I leaned beside the garage with my arms crossed and watched the landscapers do their thing. And I realized I hadn't lived anywhere with a lawn since I was a kid.

Lunch had ended with prosciutto melon rolls fastened by toothpicks, and I'd kept one of the toothpicks to give my hands something to do. I've never smoked — unhygienic when you're tattooing, if you ask me — but I was beginning to see the appeal of keeping my hands busy.

I'd gotten one end of the round toothpick chewed flat by the time Anton slinked around the side of the garage, head-to-toe black, long coat, wild hair, and five days of stubble. "I had absolutely no idea that a tie and a button-down would do it for me," he murmured. "You look like a thug playing dress-up."

Bullshit. Though I'll admit I got a charge out of the idea that Anton didn't find me laughable in the work getup. "What're you up to today?"

"Seeing what's so frickin' loud." He stood beside me and mirrored my pose, arms crossed. "That's one massive rototiller."

The name of the bucking, droning, loud-as-hell machine gave me no indication of what it was actually supposed to be doing, but I figured the landscapers were the experts.

"It's Friday," I said.

"Is it? I don't keep track."

"I get Friday and Saturday nights off."

The rototiller bucked, and the guy to the side who seemed to be coaxing the motor along yelled in Spanish at the guy who walked behind, steering. Anton and I listened. I didn't understand, but I think I got the gist. Job swearing.

"Come over," Anton said, eventually. "Wear that."

I glanced down at my tie. "My work clothes?"

"Yeah. Don't say anything. Just bust in and nail me, like a total badass."

"Hate to be a buzzkill, but I'm not a ba —"

The motor guy yelled — really yelled. I'd thought at first the rototiller had run him over. The steering guy reached around and cut the engine, and the motor guy's screaming filled the sudden silence.

"*¡El brazo! ¡El brazo!*"

I looked at Anton. He shrugged, then pushed away from the garage and strode over to see what the commotion was all about. I followed and veered over toward Melita to get a better handle on whatever was happening. "What's he saying?"

She hurried toward the rototiller with quick steps, but her legs were short and squat, and she started to fall behind. "An arm?"

The foreman was the first to reach the screaming man, who pointed to the ground and kept on screaming.

"It came up out of the ground," Melita translated, breathing hard.

The three landscapers crowded around the front of the rototiller and spoke frantically, while Anton edged his way into their circle and peered at the soil. I didn't need to squeeze anyone aside. I could see right over the shortest landscaper's head.

The earth had churned up in huge chunks, brown on the surface, black underneath, filled with fibers, rocks and roots, and a few dangling earthworms. And down in the crevasse that the tiller had torn up, dirt crusted and grayish, fingers slightly furled, lay a human arm.

The sheriff and two deputies came to get a look at the arm. It turned out to be attached to a body. There was a lot of commotion. I did my best not to look. Anton looked so hard I think he went for an hour without blinking.

The landscapers were questioned and dismissed, and they looked pretty eager to leave. Anton stuck around. It seemed logical. His house bordered the same woods as the garden plot. He'd been there when we discovered the arm. But trying to talk to him was useless. He was so focused on that trench in the ground that trying to engage him in conversation was like talking to one of his sculptures.

Since I'd only set foot on the island for the first time a few days before, the sheriff talked to me for all of five minutes, mainly to get a sequence on the events in English that had led to the discovery. He moved on to Anton, and I turned toward the house to make sure the Whites were okay.

"Ray?"

I turned. One of the deputies looked at me expectantly.

"Yeah?"

He looked down at the paperwork the Sheriff had just handed him. "Ray Carlucci?"

Fucking-A. I had no idea the bill collectors' reach would extend out to Red Wing Island. "Yeah?"

"Ray from Body Art Studio, right?"

"Yeah." What good would it do to lie? They already had my name on record. "That was my shop."

"I got my first tattoo from you," he said. He was thirty, maybe. He turned and showed me the back of his windbreaker, pointed to his shoulder. "Right here. An eagle."

Cops and soldiers got eagles. A lot. I nodded and tried not let my relief show on my face.

"You probably don't remember… Say, why'd you close the shop? Everyone I ever knew who ended up with an ugly tattoo from one of the other dives said they wished they'd gone to you instead."

"I retired." And because I was really in no mood to talk about Body Art Studio, I turned around and kept on walking, back to the house. Marnie stood by the window that looked out onto the yard. I don't think I had ever seen somebody literally wring their hands. She was doing that.

"Mrs. is upstairs with Mr. She's trying to keep him from getting upset. I think he knows something is going on, though. Go up there, Ray."

"I don't know what good it'll do…"

"Would it kill you to comfort them?"

Way to make me feel like a jerk. I went upstairs.

At the top of the stairs, I heard something fall and break. "Edgar…"

Shuffling. The sound of chair legs scraping on hardwood. I rounded the corner to the master bedroom and saw Mr. White grappling with his wife. He had her by the arms. I remember the feel of his fingers digging into the muscle of my forearm, and I stepped into the room without being asked, without even telling them that I was there.

"Hey, Mr. White. It's Ray. You probably don't remember me — I'm new. Mrs. White needs to go talk to some people. But you and me, we can hang out for a little while. What do you say? We can see what's on the radio. Or catch up on some talk shows."

"Raymond, what's happened?" said Mrs. White. "I don't understand."

I glanced at Mr. White. He didn't look like he was listening to me. But then again, according to him, Stanley never thought he'd been paying attention, and Stanley had been wrong.

"The landscapers found something in the yard. I think the sheriff will have to talk to you."

I encouraged Mr. White to sit in the armchair, turned on the radio, and found a station that wasn't playing news or advertisements. I sat beside him in a matching armchair, found the toothpick in my pocket, and gave the end of it a few good chews.

"You know Anton Kopec? He lives behind you. I wonder what you made of him — what would it have been? A few months ago? Or maybe you mostly knew his sister, before he came to live on the island."

Maybe Mr. White heard me and, in some part of his mind, understood. Or maybe not. We sat together and listened while the radio played smooth jazz.

Nearly an hour later, Marnie came upstairs. "They took him."

I thought I knew what she meant, but I hoped I was wrong. "Who took who?"

"The sheriff. He took Anton."

I looked at Marnie, hard. I wasn't sure what she expected me to say. "Did somebody call his sister?"

"He told me not to."

Mr. White shifted uneasily in his seat.

"Okay, they took him. And what?"

Marnie pulled me out into the hall and spoke in a whisper. "That was Stanley Marsh out there, our first driver. Anton recognized the buckle on a belt that the rototiller tore off the body."

"And because Anton spotted that, they think he put that guy in the ground?"

Marnie went over to the hall window, pushed aside the curtains, and gazed out over the treetops. "I don't know what they think. But what about you? Do you think he could do something like that?"

Actually, I didn't really know, and it unsettled me deep down inside. I'd thought Anton seemed okay — more than okay — but I'd been fooled by a pretty face before. Still. If he had buried Stanley in the yard, he'd been doing a damn good impersonation of someone who was more interested in my after-work plans than in what was going on around the rototiller. "I doubt it."

Once the deputies were through talking to Mrs. White, she asked me not to say anything to Edgar. I promised her I wouldn't. "We'll keep the floodlights on the house from now on after dark," she said. "If you don't mind looking out your window now and then, and making sure you don't see anyone in the yard…"

"You got it," I said. Marnie gave me a hunk of a frozen casserole to take back to the apartment over the garage. I was glad. I wanted some time to think without a bunch of frightened women contaminating me with their suspicions. I positioned my small table in front of the window and stared out over the yard. Anton had said I looked like a thug playing dress-up. I'd thought he was teasing me. But what if there was a grain of truth in that? What if somebody at the White estate had been looking to hire a thug, and I fit the bill?

Marnie had said they wanted a man around the house — that I was supposed to be the muscle. I ate my microwaved leftovers without really tasting them. Maybe my sleeve *had* ridden up during the job interview, or maybe the missing button was more noticeable than I'd imagined. Maybe I really was a thug, albeit one who'd never seen himself that way.

The sheriff, the medical examiner, and the body were all gone by the time I finally turned off my light and crawled into bed. I stared at the ceiling, flinching at every rustle or noise, and it seemed as if I wouldn't sleep at all. Except I must have fallen asleep, because the sound of a phone ringing jolted me out of an uneasy slumber.

I turned on the light and cast around for the phone. I hadn't even known that there was a phone. An answering machine picked up before I found it.

"Hello, this is Gene. I'm not here, so leave a message after the beep." The sound of the second driver's voice gave me a start. I picked up a pile of kitchen towels next to the microwave and found a phone with a built-in answering machine beneath it. A couple of clicks, and then I heard:

"God damn it, Ray, you'd better fucking be there…"

I grabbed the receiver. "Anton?"

"Get me out of this fucking trailer they call a town hall, would you? The coffee fucking sucks."

"Okay. I'll be right there."

And I had no idea what I was really thinking when I promised him that, but I'd spoken before my brain was fully engaged. My work clothes were hung over the back of the chair, and I pulled them on, hoping that if I was wearing a tie, the deputies would be less likely to harass me for the bad loan. Even if I did look like a dressed-up thug.

It was after midnight, but Marnie and Melita were still awake when I rapped, low and urgent, on the kitchen door. "Can I borrow your car?" I whispered to Marnie.

She narrowed her eyes.

"Okay," I said. "I know you don't like him. But Anton needs a ride back to the island."

"I don't dislike him. It's just that he's got so many problems." She sighed and pulled a set of keys off the hook beside the door. "Take it. But hurry back, okay? Every little noise sounds like a murderer."

Marnie's car was a Subaru hatchback with four-wheel drive and a broken radio. I got a feel for the car on the narrow, pitch-dark roads of the island by the time I came to the bridge that led into town. The corrugated metal trailer that housed local utility payments, the local cops, and traffic court every other Tuesday had a squad car and two deputy's sedans in the parking lot. It was probably the most action the place had seen since the last election.

I opened the door and was bombarded by the sound of raised voices.

"…the phone number…"

"You want to talk to Diane so bad? Call her yourself. Or don't they teach you how to find a phone number on the Internet at the police academy?"

My gut sank. I knew that whatever I was walking into, it couldn't be good. I passed the dark window where people paid their utility bills and turned into the main room. Anton was pacing, and the flowing black-on-black that looked so fitting by moonlight was nowhere near as flattering in the green-tinged fluorescent of the town hall. Here, he looked like the type of nut job who'd bring a semiautomatic rifle to a shopping mall and let loose. The agitated pacing didn't help.

"Ray," he snapped, when he saw me. "I need to leave in the worst fucking way."

There were three deputies and two local cops standing around the perimeter of the room, all on high alert, though thank God, none of them had a weapon drawn. The deputy I'd talked to back at the Whites' house, the kid with the eagle tattoo, took a few cautious steps toward us. "Mr., uh, Carlucci? You okay to take him home? 'Cos we're prepared to hold him."

Anton stopped right in front of me, his face maybe a foot away from mine, and stared me in the face like he was trying to communicate with mental telepathy.

"Is he being charged with something?" I said. I kept my eyes on Anton. A sinew pulsed in his jaw where he clenched it.

"No, it's just… I mean, we're trying to track down his sister."

Anton shook his head no so subtly I almost didn't see it.

"Don't bother. I'll drive him home."

Anton shoved past me, kicked open the front door, and burst out into the parking lot. I didn't linger behind and give the cops a reason to detain either of us.

By the time I got to the Subaru, he was on the opposite side of the car, repeatedly snapping the passenger door handle. I beeped the lock open, and he got in and slammed the door.

I got in and started the car. "You all right?" I asked.

"No." He hugged the front of his coat to his chest and bounced his left knee.

I pulled out of the parking lot and onto the street. The closest window filled with deputies and cops, who watched us drive away.

"I take it you don't play well with law enforcement."

"Not when they fucking accuse me of fucking killing my fucking friend."

"You and Stanley were friends?"

Anton shrugged sullenly. "I dunno. We hung out sometimes, when he scored weed."

Practically soul mates. I rolled my eyes, but I told myself to count to ten and not fan the flames. "They actually came out and said they thought you…"

"No, of course not. They can't. But stupid questions. Like whether I was screwing him. Whether maybe we had a lovers' quarrel."

I watched the road very carefully.

Anton pushed the seat all the way back and stretched out. "Whole thing's a fucking joke. You wanna stop at the bar and get me a six-pack? I'll pay you back."

"I don't have any cash on me."

"There's a cash station right inside the door."

I drove past the bar without slowing down. "Yeah. I don't have a debit card either."

I steeled myself for some of the abuse that the cops had been getting, but instead Anton started to laugh. "You mean you have no money? None at all? Zero?"

"Glad you find that so amusing."

He kept on laughing, an edgy sound, wild. "Oh, Ray… Ray of Moonlight. I'm not laughing at you." His head lolled on the headrest. I could see him staring at me in my peripheral vision. "Tell me you don't have a sister who suckered power of attorney out of you, then won't even give you the courtesy of a prepaid Visa card?"

"I don't have a sister," I said.

I saw him watching me as I drove, and I ignored him. They say that when you meet a guy, he'll tell you everything you need to know about him within the first five minutes. Johnny had spent the first five minutes gushing over my tats and my shop, which he eventually leached out from under me. Anton had asked me to build pyramids with him. And I believe he also mentioned that I'd think he was crazy.

"It freaked me out a little when I got Gene on the answering machine," Anton said. He seemed a lot calmer now. Maybe even normal, for him. "I remembered thinking I'd made you up, and for just a second there, back at the town hall, I had myself convinced that's what had really happened."

"I'm real, all right."

Anton put his hand on my thigh. "I'll say." Before I knew it, he'd slipped his fingers deep between my legs, far enough to cup my whole groin and slide his palm up and down.

The car swerved. I righted it. "Not the best time," I said.

He ignored me and manhandled my crotch. "You didn't give me any shit on the phone, you know that? You didn't make me explain or beg, or anything. I told you I needed you, and here you are. I called, you came."

I downshifted to first, then pulled over on the gravel shoulder. "There's probably a deputy tailing us to make sure I get you home." Or maybe to talk to me about a loan. Or both.

My cock was already stiffening. His fingers found the shape of it, glided up and down as it swelled and hardened. "Who said you should stop driving?"

"Anton…"

He launched himself at me, covered my mouth with his. I knew I shouldn't, but I let him suck my lower lip into his mouth, tease it with his tongue and teeth, while his hand stroked me through the dress slacks. His stubble was long enough to feel soft, and it tickled my upper lip. He smelled like turpentine and autumn leaves and coffee. And his hand, my God, his hand…it had me totally hard in a minute flat.

I turned my head to catch my breath, and my panting sounded harsh and close in the interior of the hatchback. "Don't jerk me off in Marnie's car." Because it was dark, and we were in a hurry, and if she saw or smelled or even sensed anything, I was sure I couldn't count on ever borrowing it again.

Anton nipped my jaw with his hot, wet mouth. His stubble whispered over my cheek. "Okay," he said.

He eased my fly down.

"I said…"

"Shh." He slid toward the passenger door, but only to make enough room to bend his head to my lap.

"Shit." I squeezed my eyes shut tight, hit the clutch, and jammed the shift into park under the weight of his upper body. I grabbed his long hair in my other fist. He coaxed my cock free from my slacks, and his mouth closed over it. Hot and wet. It was all I could think. Wet. So wet. So totally and utterly wet. He took me deep, gagged on it a little, then did it again, over and over. My cockhead squelched into the back of his throat. He sucked, hard, while he jacked the base with his fingers.

I held his head as it bobbed in my lap, and my fingers slid through his hair. I shouldn't. I thought those two words, over and over. I shouldn't. I shouldn't. Not in Marnie's car. Not on the side of the road at the edge of town, especially when the cops and the deputies were already looking at us sideways. Not without a condom.

Anton slurped his way up my cock, then licked his hand and polished the knob with his wet palm while he delved down low to slip his tongue into my fly and lick my balls.

I let out a shuddery breath, squeezed my right arm out from underneath his chest, and clutched his hair two-fisted. My hips rose to meet his strokes.

He tongued his way back up again, then swallowed my cock back down and deep-throated me while he toyed with my damp balls.

I thrust my hips — involuntary, almost a spasm — and Anton grunted his encouragement, sucked even more. I grabbed his head hard, and he gave a long, low moan. The noise warbled in his throat, because my cock was sinking in and out of it. I was close, so close I didn't care anymore. I pulled his hair, jammed his head down against my lap, and flicked my hips up to bury myself deep.

Wet, so wet…and I was gagging him, and I didn't give a damn, because all I cared about was coming in that irresistible, hot, wet mouth.

The first spurt was halfway there when I realized I was peaking, and I tried to pull Anton back. He ignored me, sucked me even harder, brutal and demanding. My cock pulsed in his mouth, and he sucked and sucked, until finally my hips stopped moving and I stopped making that strangled, fatalistic sound.

The bobbing of his head slowed and grew still, and he pulled off without any hurry, pausing to kiss the shaft and the glans. The sound of his lips smacking against my cock was wet and loud in the dark interior of the car.

He pushed up, stroked the front of my shirt, my tie, and then pressed his mouth to mine. His mouth was sticky and hot, and his lips felt swollen. I tasted my come on his kiss.

CHAPTER NINE

An overly cheerful doorbell woke me the next morning, and I wondered how many ways there were, in that three-room apartment of mine, that someone could wake me up without my prior consent. "I'm coming," I yelled, though I suspected that it probably didn't carry all the way down to the door on the side of the garage, and in a passive-aggressive sort of way, I didn't care.

I pulled on last night's slacks and dress shirt, left my feet bare and the buttons on the shirt undone, and dragged my ass to the bottom of the stairs. A deputy as big as me filled my doorway, khaki uniform and mirrored cop shades. The sun slanted into my eyes from behind him, just risen and brutal, and the grass and leaves glittered with frost. Here we go, I thought. Here's where I go down for that fucking loan.

"Sorry to wake you, Mr. Carlucci." The deputy didn't sound all that sorry. I waited for whatever words would come before he hauled me off. "We found something in the woods, and we wondered if you might be able to shed some light on it."

Woods. He wasn't there about the loan, after all. "Depends on what that something is."

He turned back toward the tree line. Sunlight glanced off the silver frame of his shades. He grimaced. His teeth were large and very white. "Someone's been monkeying around in the old burial plot."

I stuck my forefinger and thumb into my eyes and pinched out the sandy residue of sleep, and wondered if he could've possibly just said what I'd just heard him say. It seemed as far-out as, "…and developers built the place on an ancient Navajo burial ground." And not much better than, "I'm here to see you about a debt."

"Define *monkeying around.*"

"Branches stacked around the headstones, tied off at the top."

Relief and revulsion flooded me at the same time. Relief, because I'd imagined grave robbing, or worse. But headstones? Jesus. "They're some kind of modern art...thing," I said. "I don't really get it."

The deputy's shoulders relaxed, and he nodded. "So it's Kopec."

"Yeah. An installation piece, I think. Something about pyramids."

"Takes all kinds, I guess. I hear his work sells in Detroit."

"I've heard that too."

"All right then. We'll let you know if we need anything else."

No doubt. I closed the door, went back upstairs, and got dressed. I'd figured I'd be less likely to be singled out by the cops if I did my best to blend in as one of the staff.

I went into the house and walked right into another "accident" of Mr. White's that left me bruised and soaked to the skin. As I held him steady in the shower, his eyes were totally vacant, and I wondered how it was possible that the part of himself that had spoken to me just a few nights ago could just completely and utterly vanish.

I ate my lunch at the kitchen table. Marnie moved around the kitchen a lot more forcefully than she needed to, and she banged things around the cupboards as she emptied the dishwasher.

"What?" I said finally.

She planted her hands on her hips and looked out the window over the sink. "We haven't said anything to Mr.," she told me, "but I swear, it's as if he knows. And he's upset, which is making him worse."

"I think he sees more than we know. Or maybe he picks up on our body language." Or maybe it was just the progression of his Alzheimer's.

Marnie pulled out a chair and sat down hard. "Yeah. Something like that." She planted her elbow on the table and put her face in her hand. "What are we gonna do, Ray?"

"Maybe it's time for them to look into a nursing home."

She sat back and combed her graying hair from her forehead with her fingertips. I did my best not to think about running my fingers through Anton's hair while he sucked me off.

"Mr.'s brother went into a nursing home — a ritzy one too — and he was dead within a month. He'd been spitting out his high blood pressure pills. No one noticed."

I wasn't exactly an authority on elder care, so I wasn't going to argue with her. "Have you met Anton's sister?"

"Sure. Why?"

"He said she had power of attorney over him."

Marnie nodded to herself. It looked like there was a lot she knew, but she was picking and choosing her words carefully. "I guess she didn't want to keep him in a home any more than we want to put Mr. White away."

I steeled myself for something bad. "So what's his deal? Schizophrenic?"

"Bipolar. I've never seen him depressed, though, not in the traditional sense of the word. Usually he cycles between up and really up. Sometimes when I hear him working at night, I wonder if he even sleeps during the day, or he just keeps going."

"Everyone says his artwork sells. Why doesn't he have any money?"

"He spends it, I guess. The second it's in his hand, it's as good as gone. So Diane makes sure he has a place to live, has food and medications delivered every week, and she knows he's okay. As okay as he'll ever be."

We both stared at the table for a minute or two. "You think he killed Stanley?" I asked.

She toyed with her coffee cup. "Last night, when the police were digging in the yard, I had myself convinced that he'd done it. But you seemed so sure he hadn't, and the more I thought about it, the more I realized that even if he had — let's say, by accident, they fought about something and it got out of hand — that I don't think he'd be able to cover it up and just forget about it, act like nothing had happened."

Not exactly a glowing recommendation of Anton's mental state. But probably pretty accurate.

Mrs. White came into the kitchen dressed in a lavender sweater set, low-heeled pumps, and pearls. Her skin looked gray underneath her rouge. I wondered when the last time was she'd slept more than a couple of hours at a stretch. "Your paychecks," she said and handed Marnie and me each an envelope. "I'd meant to give them to you yesterday, but all the excitement…"

"We understand," Marnie said. "Don't worry about it."

I nodded my understanding and had to restrain myself from tearing open the envelope and rubbing the paycheck all over my body in an uninhibited display of relief.

Melita followed with a vase of drooping flowers. She stuffed the flowers into the trash and dumped the water in the sink. "You got a bank account, Ray?"

"Not…currently."

"Drive me into town, and I'll let you sign the check over to me so you can cash it."

"That's a wonderful idea," said Mrs. White. "The bank closes at three on Saturday. I feel terrible that you didn't get your night off. Why don't you take the Town Car?"

Melita and I didn't have anything to say to each other on the way to the bank. We got there right before they closed. The teller informed me that I could open my very own checking account with a deposit of as little as fifty dollars, plus fourteen fifty for checks. Since my three days' salary minus tax had come out to less than two hundred bucks, and especially since I had no desire to leave my new address so that bill collectors could start hounding me again, I declined.

Melita and I made our way back in silence, until she pointed to a tiny strip mall at the edge of town. "Turn in there." The mall contained a car wash, a liquor store, and a tax preparation office, which was closed.

"You went through all this so you could get some booze?" I said.

"What do you mean, 'all this'? I wanted to get out of that house for a few minutes, that's all." Melita went into the liquor store and came back out stuffing a pint into her big vinyl purse.

She pulled the car door shut and clasped her purse on her lap. "Don't say nothing, all right? I had trouble sleeping last night. I kept thinking about that hand in the ground."

The dirt-crusted nails sprang to mind. I shuddered. "Nobody's business but your own," I said. "And thanks for cashing my check."

"Eh, *de nada.*" We drove down the winding tree-lined road, and I squirmed as I passed the shoulder where I'd pulled over the night before.

"I'm glad it was Stanley," Melita said, out of nowhere.

I glanced at her.

"I mean, him and not Gene. Stanley was kind of an asshole. Gene was quiet. Didn't bother me."

That was the opposite of what I'd heard so far about the previous drivers. Stanley had been Anton's friend — friendly enough to smoke pot together, anyway — and Gene had made Marnie uncomfortable by putting the moves on her.

"Last Christmas was the worst," she said. "Mr. White gave me a nice bonus, 'cos I'd been there ten years. I wasn't bragging or nothing. I just thought it was a nice thing for him to do, and Marnie did too. But Stanley, he got all crazy. Jealous. I had Marnie drive me straight to the bank, put the whole check in, all but twenty dollars."

We bumped over the narrow bridge, turned onto the winding road that led to the house.

"After that, Stanley was always nasty to me, made a point of complaining about the way I did this or that." She clucked her tongue. "I thought when he left, he'd come back eventually. Maybe he met some new girl in town, went on a drinking binge with her. Tried to show everyone how bad we needed him by staying away. But Mrs. White must've figured out that he wasn't coming back. She started looking right away, found Gene."

"Seems like it should've been Gene buried in the yard," I said.

Melita looked at me sharply.

"I mean, if Stanley's an asshole, and he takes off to prove how valuable he is, and instead Mrs. White replaces him right away with Gene. And then Gene disappears…"

Melita nodded. "Yeah, and I wouldn't put it past Stanley neither. But Mr. Kopec could tell one from the other. You'd never mix up the two of them, even if they was dead awhile." She sketched a big belly in the air, all the way out to the dashboard. "Gene was fat. And besides, there was that belt buckle."

I dropped Melita off at the house with her secret stash and told her I was going for a walk, and that I had my two-way radio on me.

A pair of crime scene techs were still processing the spot where they'd dug up Stanley Marsh. I went around to the front of the house to get some distance between them and me, and then I slipped into the tree line that divided the Whites' property and Anton's place.

I was chilled within minutes and wished I'd helped myself to one of Gene's sport coats, whether it fit me or not. The woods seemed larger during the day, as if by seeing the depth and breadth of the rows of trees, I couldn't fool myself into thinking that it would just be a few more steps before I emerged into a clearing.

I wove through trees, decided that I was well and truly lost, then reassured myself that the island just wasn't that big and that eventually I was bound to come out on either the road or some wealthy snowbird's backyard.

Once I finally broke through, I found myself in the hollow where I'd first met Anton. Four branch-pyramids stood at the opposite end of the long, narrow clearing. They were only heaps of sticks and twine, I told myself. Nothing more. But the way they hulked together, like a herd of lumbering beasts, filled me with a vague revulsion. My dress shirt pulled across my shoulders and throat like it would suffocate me. I loosened my tie, rolled my shoulders, and approached the pyramids.

Sticks and twine. So why did they feel so ominous?

I parted the dried leaves that still clung to the branches and looked inside. There, in the center, was a stone slab that I would've taken for a cast-off cinder block, especially in the dark. Except now the deputy's words rang in my head: old burial plot.

Headstones.

Pyramids, Rosicrucians, and graves. I probably didn't want to know what Anton's "experiment" was all about — but I was hoping there was some thread of logic in it that a person might be able to follow, even if he was just marginally sane.

I thought about banging on Anton's door, demanding to know what he was trying to prove by lurking around the woods at night and building tepees on people's graves, but I decided not to. Either I'd end up having to admit to myself just how screwed up he really was, or he'd manage to sidetrack me with his hands and mouth and cock so that I'd forget what explanation I'd gone there for to begin with.

I ducked into the woods again and made my way back toward the Whites' property. The phone in my apartment had a caller ID readout. Nobody ever cleared those things. I'd look back on that, see if there was a call left over from Stanley's days. Anton had known the number by heart, so obviously he'd called it before, frequently. I could get him on the phone and see what he had to say for himself, without the distraction of his mouth on mine and his hand down my pants.

I pushed aside a thick tangle of branches and shrubs and stepped out into what I thought would be the Whites' expansive front yard. Except a tall chain-link fence stretched in front of me. A metal sign was riveted about five and a half feet off the ground, and it repeated every few yards. **PRIVATE PROPERTY - PROTECTED BY HURON SECURITY.**

Great. The survivalist's house.

I tried to picture the lay of the roads and orient myself. I'd veered around in an arc, somehow. I followed the chain link until it ended at the back corner of the property, then abutted the spike-topped wrought iron that encircled the rest of the house. I adjusted my course, and made my way, eventually, back to the Whites' property.

At that point, the nip in the air had gone way beyond the point where I could call it that. I saw my breath, strikingly white, with every exhalation. And I was so cold that by the time I finally did wander out into the right clearing, I'd been chewing on stories about people who get lost in the snow and lie down in a drift and simply fall asleep as hypothermia takes them.

The kitchen door was locked. I banged on it, and Marnie let me in. "Look at you — you're all red. How long have you been outside without a coat on?"

"I got a little turned around in the woods."

"Go sit down. I'll get you something hot. Coffee? Tea?"

"Coffee, black, one sugar."

The top of the kitchen table was clear, save for a single key and a blurred digital photo printed on plain white paper. The photo had been taken right there in the kitchen, a shot of a guy who needed a haircut, in a shirt and tie. "Stanley?" I guessed, because he didn't look portly enough to be Gene.

Marnie nodded. "There's his key. You should take it. We'd feel better knowing you can come in even if we're locked down for the night."

"Or the day," I said.

She put a cup of coffee in front of me, pulled out a chair, and sat down. "I know that they don't have enough police to keep anyone on the island, especially since Stan's probably been dead for a while and whoever killed him is long gone. But I wish they could leave someone here anyway."

I pulled out my keys and tried to pry open the ring and slide the house key on. My fingers were bright red, and they stung like a bitch.

"Here, you have frostnip." Marnie took my keys and slid the new key onto the ring.

I nodded. I should've worn my leather jacket, on duty or not. I'd misestimated the depth and breadth of the woods. "When did it get to be winter all of a sudden?"

"Gets worse every year, doesn't it? They're saying record lows tonight, in the single digits. You'll need to dig out the area between the house and the garage if it snows. A plow comes from town to do the driveway…and you usually have to dig out the garage door again once they're done. Snowblower, rock salt, and shovels are on the right side of the garage."

I hadn't shoveled snow in ages, but I suspected it didn't take a PhD to clear a driveway. I hoped it did snow. At least shoveling it would help me take my mind off Stanley's body in the rototiller trench.

I holed myself up in the apartment above the garage, layered on Gene's old sweatshirts, and drank cup after cup of instant decaf thick with sugar until finally I felt warm again, though my stomach didn't care much for the faux joe. I listened to the clock radio for a while, but the severe weather warnings started to outnumber the songs, which all sucked, and also made me miss the CD collection I'd sold to pay off a creditor who never appreciated it anyway. Digging through the recycle bin yielded some relatively fresh newspapers. I caught up on the state of world affairs; then I tore out every crossword puzzle I could find. I turned in somewhere around an eight-letter word for apex.

The bed still smelled strange, like the apartment. Not lived-in enough to smell like me, yet. I pulled the covers up to my chin and listened to the wind howl while hail pelted the roof, and tree branches scritched across my bathroom windowpane.

And I wondered what the storm sounded like from Anton's house.

I slept and was woken by Marnie's voice on the intercom. "Ray? Are you there?"

Where else would I be? That was the first reply that sprang to mind. Though since I hadn't mentioned how edgy Anton had been acting when I picked him up at the town hall, I could see her thinking that maybe I'd decided to wait out the storm in his sister's guesthouse. After all, it had technically been my night off.

I pressed the button. "Yeah."

"It's a sheet of ice outside. I need you to spread salt to the end of the driveway."

It was still dark out. I looked at the clock. Six thirty — practically the middle of the night. But I didn't complain about it. I'd been itching for something to do.

I layered hand-me-down sweatshirts under my leather jacket, then went out and started spreading salt. Marnie hadn't been exaggerating when she said it was a sheet of ice out there. I could have played hockey on the driveway.

Not only that, but the whole world was glazed with at least a half inch of ice — the grass, the rooftops, and weirdest of all, the trees. The autumn leaves that hadn't gotten a chance to fall looked candy-coated, and the branches drooped low under the weight of all the ice.

It was beautiful, in an eerie, surreal kind of way. Anton was probably loving it. Unless he thought it was the work of aliens. Or Rosicrucians.

The first overburdened tree went down as I was looking in the general direction of Anton's place and trying to figure out what sorts of things went on inside his head. It was loud. Leaves that had once rustled together now made a weird, dull clatter, and the roots snapped as they tore from the sandy soil. It left an indentation in the tree line of the woods that separated the two properties.

Once the tree was on its side, everything was quiet again except the constant patter of hail.

I took a few steps toward the kitchen door and slid. I decided it might be better to stay put and try out my two-way radio instead. It was tuned to channel twelve already. "Marnie?" I called. No answer. I headed carefully for the house and let myself in with the key.

"Marnie?"

She was elbow-deep in dough. "What was that noise?"

"A tree fell. It was so full of ice it just tore up out of the ground. I tried to call you on the two-way."

"Oh. Right. It helps to turn it on and have it near you, doesn't it? Gene was the only one who ever seemed to remember it. I'll dig it out, just as soon as…"

"No big deal." I poured some coffee, looked out the window at the gray of the gradually lightening sky against the silhouette of the glassy treetops. The wind howled, and hail clattered on the windowpane. And then I heard the clattery rustle turn into a series of ominous snaps. A gap appeared in the tree line. "Damn. Another one."

I craned my neck as if I could see Anton's house from there. Which, of course, I couldn't.

"Call him," Marnie said — and maybe she sounded a little resigned, like she knew I was a goner when it came to him, and there was nothing she could say that would change it. But I was glad she'd suggested checking on him to make sure he hadn't been flattened by an ice-covered tree. I turned and looked at her. She was forming the dough into rows of tiny crescents. She indicated the phone with her head. "He's on memory dial. I forget which. Just look at the list."

I picked up the phone. "Do I have to hit nine to dial out?"

"No, just memory dial, then the number."

There was no dial tone. I followed her instructions anyway. The phone dialed a Mr. Kopec, memory dial six, but nothing happened other than the quick series of seven touch tones.

"I don't have an outside line."

"What do you mean? It's automatic." She put down her dough, took the phone from me with a kitchen towel–covered hand, and wedged the handset between her shoulder and cheek. "Damn. The phone's out."

I glanced at the window. A gust of wind peppered the glass with hail, and the trees gave off their clattery rustle. "Maybe I should check."

"Anything happens to Mr., I'd need you to drive."

"The roads are beyond slick. Your Subaru's gonna handle the ice better than the Town Car ever could." And who else would check on Anton, if not me? His sister, wherever she was?

Marnie thought for several long seconds. "Make it fast," she said, finally. "Get him to come back here if you can. It'll be safer here than in that dinky house of his."

We tested the two-way radios, then I set off for Anton's. Even the grass was slippery, and it was slow moving until I got to the woods, where the tree canopy had caught the ice before it hit the ground.

I hadn't been prepared for the sound of the creaking. It surrounded me. And the thought that once of those monster maples could uproot and flatten me scared me shitless.

I hurried through the clearing, overcompensated, and ended up in the backyard of Anton's next-door neighbor. A tall row of privacy shrubs separated the properties. Who knows what I expected to see when I rounded the bushes. Anton, surrounded by a hundred glasses, bowls, and jars? Not that.

But there he was, catching hail with the delight of a child gathering fireflies. His hair was plastered to his forehead and cheeks, and his long black coat caught the wind like a sail as he moved from one container to the next, adjusting them as if their position made any difference one way or the other.

"Anton," I said. I could've asked him what he was doing, but really, did I need to know? He was in his zone, and whatever it might be, it undoubtedly made perfect sense to him.

And, I realized with no small amount of envy, maybe I'd rather be catching hailstones than salting a driveway, myself.

"Ray!" He straightened up, beaming. Ice glinted off the ends of his hair. He'd shaved. His smooth, pale cheeks looked gaunt and vulnerable, and his disarming smile seemed wider. He held his arms out as if to encompass the newly glazed world. "Look."

I approached him through the obstacle course of glasses and jars.

"It's really you, Ray, isn't it?"

"As opposed to…?"

"I don't know, I had a wild night. Talked to Stanley for a while. I asked him if he wanted me to build a pyramid over his grave. He said I'd better wait until the cops are done poking around."

"Real Stanley or metaphorical Stanley?"

"Reality is relative, isn't it?" He poked at a large hailstone inside the glass he held. "But since he's dead, it must have been the Stanley in my mind."

At least he knew the difference. Kind of. "Phones are out."

He looked at me oddly, as if he couldn't imagine why it would matter. When I got close enough, he dropped the glass, took my face two-handed, pulled me up against him, and kissed me. He smelled like winter.

I turned away reluctantly. "It's not safe outside," I said. "Trees are falling left and right; they can't take the weight of all the ice."

"I've never known anyone to succumb to death by hardwood, have you?"

"And I don't want you to be the first. Come back with me."

Anton looked up at the sky. Hail, and now a bit of snow, dusted his cheeks, caught in his black eyebrows and lashes. "Nothing will happen to me."

"Come on, I haven't got time to argue. I came and got you last night, right? So you owe me one. Come back with me, so I don't have to worry."

He cupped my cheek with his palm and cocked his head. "You'd worry about me? You don't strike me as the type, all tattoos and macho." He looked down, gazed longingly at his glasses and jars, then shrugged. "Okay. I suppose I can hang out at the Whites' for a while."

He took me by the hand and started toward the tree line. He didn't bother to lock his door, and I decided I was better off not compromising whatever momentum we had by suggesting that he should. He slid on an iced-over patch of leaves, and I hauled him up by the arm. He laughed and went even faster. And I realized I felt alive when I was with him. Maybe not always in a good way. Sometimes I was spooked, and sometimes I could smack him. But whatever was going on inside me, when we were together, good or bad — it was always vivid.

An ominous cracking sounded to one side of us, and a massive, ice-laden branch came crashing down. Anton yanked my arm and dragged me into the woods.

"Maybe we should've taken the road."

He answered me breathlessly, not with fear, but excitement. "It's ten times longer — and besides, the trees are just as thick."

Anton knew the woods. We came upon the clearing in minutes and found ourselves surrounded by seven-foot-tall branch pyramids. The forest floor was wet but not icy, so we technically didn't need to keep holding on to each other, but I didn't let go of Anton's hand, and he didn't let go of mine.

"Could you imagine how they would've looked with ice?" he said as we passed them.

I could. Creepier still.

"This way," he told me, and although I didn't have the firmest grasp of direction in that clearing, I did recognize the gap that had led me to the survivalist's house the last time I'd been there.

"That's the wrong way."

"I'm not lost — I just want to see something quick."

"Seriously, I gotta get back. They're all spooked about the weather...and about Stanley."

"Trust me, Ray. It'll take two minutes."

Anton ducked through the gap first, then hauled me after, but instead of taking the obvious path that I'd taken the time I got lost, he sidestepped into a smaller gap and dragged me along behind him.

I was so busy waving annoying branches away from my face that I didn't see the smaller clearing until we were in the middle of it. This one was bright with diffuse gray light, as the canopy above didn't quite cover it. "I was hoping there'd be more ice," Anton said, looking up.

I followed his gaze. The entire clearing was surrounded by a giant web. Its strands were thick and utilitarian — a web of twine. Sections of the twine glittered with ice and frost, and in those spots, it was magical. "I did this last night," Anton said, "when I heard the storm was coming."

We ducked under a hub of crossed twine. He led me over to an area where the ice had coated everything thickly. "Wouldn't it be cool if it all looked like this?"

"You got a camera?"

Anton petted my cheek. "You fail to see the point, although I'm not really surprised. After all, everything you do is permanent. As permanent as frail mortality, anyway." He let go of my hand, opened his arms, and spun around. "We've seen it. That's enough."

I'll bet his sister would have a great time trying to sell that to a gallery. I followed one of the glittering lines, saw it cross another spoke of the web, head over to a branch, wrap it, then go off in another direction. I couldn't imagine how much twine he'd gone through. It must've taken him hours.

Everything was crooked, intriguingly asymmetrical. I decided that I liked the way the frost had hit portions of the web but not others. I found myself rotating in circles too, so I could take in the whole thing.

And then I spotted the part where something had broken free, and dangling tails of snapped twine swayed in the wind.

"Whatever you were trying to catch? I think it escaped." I pointed at the hole.

Anton darted over to the ruined section. He didn't seem angry at all. Actually, I'd say he was fascinated. "Now, what on earth would be tall enough to snap these lines?"

I felt a chill that had nothing to do with the cold wind blowing down the back of my neck. "Okay, I saw your web. Let's go back to the house."

"This is five and a half feet off the ground. What do you think, are there bears on the island?"

"That's not funny."

"Depends on your sense of humor — take yours, for instance. I thought it was a little sicker. But don't worry, I'll bring you around to my point of view, eventually. Okay, it probably wasn't a bear. A bear would be walking on all fours, and he would've gone right underneath. So it must've been a human."

"You said there wasn't anyone on the island but us."

"Did I? No, what I said was that security was tight and that my count was off. And what good's the security, anyway? You need electricity to run the burglar alarms."

"The phones are out, not the electricity."

"Really? I haven't had power since midnight."

God damn. "Come on. I need to get back."

I imagine he heard me, but he felt no need to pay attention. He stepped through the gap in the trees that was surrounded by dangling twine. I followed. Not eagerly, but I followed.

I came through the trees yet again on the survivalist's property, this time at the opposite corner from the one I'd visited before. Anton was busy squeezing through a gap between the chain link and the wrought-iron fence. "What are you doing?" I said.

"This fence used to be tight. Somebody's been here before. Don't you want to take a look?"

Not particularly. I hadn't signed on for that. "I need to get back to the Whites. Are you coming or not?"

"Go." He made a shooing motion with his hand. "I'll be right behind you... Hey, I see a footprint." He crouched and ran his fingers along the ground.

Right, as if I could turn around and not look. I tried to slip through the gap in the fence. I was too big to just cram myself through. I bent the chain link back, and it took a lot of squeezing and swearing, but finally, I made it.

"Someone must have walked through right before the ground froze." Anton pointed at a very distinct footprint. "See?"

"Hey." I caught his hand, held it between mine. "We shouldn't be messing around here. We should tell the police."

Anton raised my hand to his mouth and kissed each of my knuckles. The feel of his mouth tugged at my memory, and I imagined it closing around my cock. "The police?" he said. "I'm tempted to do just the opposite. I hate those pricks. But for you? Maybe...for you."

I turned back toward the gap in the fence, meaning to leave. But then I took one last look at the footprint, except then I saw another footprint, and another, and then I saw an old-fashioned tornado door where the footprints obviously led. I pointed. "There. That's where they go."

"Seriously, Ray, how can you want to leave now?"

"Easy. I want to keep myself in one piece."

"You know how Stanley died? He was strangled. That's what those dumbfucks at the town hall told me. Actually, they suggested that maybe I strangled him when that supposed lovers' quarrel of ours went a little too far. Do you think the murderer's going to pop out and instantaneously strangle you? I think between the two of us we can overpower a single unarmed guy."

Just because the killer strangled Stanley didn't mean he didn't have a gun. Maybe he'd just been trying to be quiet. "No, no way."

I went into my own pocket and pulled out the two-way radio. I figured I would call Marnie, see if there was a channel the police monitored, if the range was long enough to reach town — or at least see if our phone was working again. Mainly I wanted the opinion of someone who wasn't gung-ho to follow a set of frozen footprints.

By the time I wrestled it out of my pocket, Anton had the cellar doors open. "You think I'm kidding around?" I said. I grabbed a handful of his coat, pulled him back. I spoke into his ear. "This is real, Anton. This is dangerous."

He turned his head, and the frozen tips of his hair brushed my jaw. "Life is dangerous." He was so eager to press on, I felt like I was straining to hold back a greyhound at the starting gate.

"Before you go in there, tell me. If Stanley left the Whites' suddenly, how come Marnie just gave me his key? Shouldn't it have been in his pocket?"

Anton stopped straining against my grip. "He always had his keys. He always locked his door. And I learned fast to call before I dropped over, since he'd blow a fuse if I just swung by and rang the doorbell."

"So where'd they get his keys?"

Anton turned away from the slanted doors that led beneath the survivalist's home, and he grabbed my leather jacket by both lapels so he could talk right in my face. "You saying one of them killed him? It would make for a titillating story around the bonfire, but come on. Whodunit — Mrs. White, in the conservatory, with a figurine?"

"Remember the finger marks on my arm?"

"The spider web–cloud dragon arm, or the tiger–eight ball arm?"

"Never mind. How about this? What if Mr. White finds Stanley poking around, doing something he isn't supposed to be doing, and goes after him. Mr. White's still strong. Stanley wouldn't have expected it; he would've never known what hit him. Afterward, Mr. White forgets all about what he did, but Mrs. White needs to cover it up, or else it's institution time for her husband. So she hires Gene to get rid of the body, then pays him off so he leaves and never tells anyone."

"Hey, that really would make a much cooler campfire tale than I thought, especially if you work on the delivery, build up the suspense, tell it in a creepier voice." Anton pressed his forehead to mine. The icy tips of his hair tickled my cheek. "So if Mr. White's the killer, then we've got nothing to worry about, and you don't have to keep trying to stop me from having a look at whatever Harlan Scott keeps underneath his house. 'Cos it's bound to be good."

He broke away from me, black overcoat billowing as he spun, and disappeared down the cellar door — and no amount of tugging, coaxing, or threatening to leave had even the slightest effect on his trajectory.

My idea did make sense. But it didn't explain who'd been in Scott's basement when the ice storm hit. I took a few steps down, then crouched to see what I could. The cellar was black, with a single flashlight beam flickering around. "Anton," I whispered.

"Grab a flashlight." He sounded disturbingly nonchalant. "There's like five of them on a charging station at the foot of the stairs."

I held on for dear life as I crept the rest of the way down. Who knew that navigating a narrow staircase in the dark would feel like walking a tightrope? A motor chugged a few yards away from me, hard to tell exactly what kind, in the dark. I found the table, groped, and pulled one of the flashlights from it. I turned it on, and afterimages danced in front of my eyes, which had already adjusted to the suffocating darkness. I swung the beam toward the noise. It landed on a generator — a generator inside a padlocked metal cage. "Anton?"

"There's a bed down here." His voice wasn't far from me, but I couldn't find him with my flashlight beam. Too much black. "You should throw me down on it, show me who's boss."

"We just broke into your neighbor's house."

"The door was open. No harm, no foul. C'mon, Ray, you know you wanna. You said no back in the car too…then you jammed your cock in my mouth and held my head down while you came."

"I wasn't thinking."

"Thinking's overrated. I've jerked off three, four times remembering the way your hands felt on my head when you shot your load and forced me to swallow it."

I've never forced anyone to do anything…although I had been holding his head awfully hard, and I damn well knew it. I closed my eyes and tried to imagine something that would get me out of the cellar, and out of the conversation too. "What if the police come back and check this place out? Now it's full of your fingerprints, my fingerprints. Come on, let's go. Come back to the Whites' house for now and then spend the night with me."

Anton was already done talking. His flashlight beam flickered over a bank of supplies, cans and bottles and cartons. "Jackpot." I saw the red-labeled vodka bottles spotlighted by his flashlight beam as clearly as if they'd been on display at the liquor store. He tucked a single bottle into his coat. "Okay, now we can go."

"You came here looking for booze? Jesus Christ, Anton. Who knows what could've been down here."

"A bed…"

"And you're stealing. Have you thought of that?"

"Oh, please, don't be so melodramatic — it doesn't fit with your whole thug image. I'll totally pay him for it. I'm sure Diane will let some cash trickle down before he comes back next spring."

"Okay, that's it." I groped around the buttons on my two-way radio with my thumb until I pressed the key that lit them all up, and then I made sure I was on channel twelve. "Hello, Marnie?"

A crackle sounded on the far end of the cellar, and my own voice echoed back, a fraction of a second after I spoke. It was strange and indistinct, nearly drowned out by the chug of the generator. But I'd heard it.

I froze. I could feel my heart beating in my throat. Even Anton was still.

I put the radio to my mouth. "Hello?"

The word repeated, overlapping itself slightly. *Hell-hello.*

"Now, this," Anton whispered, "this is a much cooler story than Mrs. White in the conservatory."

"Shine your flashlight over there," I snapped. I aimed my beam with one hand, held the radio to my mouth with the other.

"Hell-hello. Hell-hello."

A couple of burlap sacks were pushed against the corner. Flour, potatoes…who knows? But something leaned among them that obviously didn't belong — a seated figure, covered by an old army blanket. A man, judging by the feet sticking out from the edge of the blanket. Or maybe, more accurately, a body, because it seemed too still to call it a man.

I talked into the radio.

Hell-hello.

Anton covered the distance to the body in a few long strides.

"Don't touch it…"

I spoke too late, not that anything I said would have stopped him. He whisked the blanket off, then gave a low whistle. "You should ask for a raise. Your job is a lot more dangerous than it's cracked up to be."

Marnie'd said that Gene always kept his radio on him. "I'm wearing his clothes," I said, because my brain seemed to be stuck on that single, seemingly insignificant point. Not how he'd gotten there, or worse, how he'd died. Just the clothes. Some kind of coping mechanism on my part, I guess.

"I went my whole life without ever seeing a corpse," Anton said, fascinated. "Outside of a funeral home, of course, which doesn't count because it's such an artificial construct — ritualized and sanitized. Now it's two in the same week. Maybe I *should* have brought my camera."

"We're getting out of here." I grabbed Anton by the arm, and he let me haul him back to the narrow stairs. "Go." I shoved him ahead of me, because I didn't trust him not to wander back while I climbed out.

Stanley, Gene, and now me. That would be the logical progression, wouldn't it? The blood and guts outside my front door hadn't been left there by a stray cat. They'd been a warning. Get out — while you still can.

And now I was stuck on the island until the plows made it over the bridge with their salt spreaders, or the weather turned — and judging by the sound of hail pinging off the cellar door, that wasn't happening anytime soon.

Anton cleared the top stair. "Stanley," he said.

"What about him?"

Anton hadn't been speaking to me, however, because another voice answered him. "Go home. You don't need to see this."

"Come back when I'm not with Ray, okay? I'm trying to make a good impression here — and talking to dead people in front of him won't help."

I climbed out of the tornado cellar and found Anton having a conversation with a guy who definitely wasn't dead — particularly in the way he was holding a shotgun. His hair was longer than it had been in Marnie's photo, he'd grown a patchy beard, and his clothes looked ragged and disheveled — like he'd been living in someone's basement for God-knows-how-long. But he was far from dead.

I'd never met Harlan Scott, but I was guessing he wouldn't have taken kindly to a stranger living in his basement. I also suspected he hadn't left the island early for winter after all, and that he'd been napping under the Whites' garden plot for quite a while, with Stanley's belt, the thing that had strangled him, alongside his body, waiting to catch on the rototiller blade. Once the medical examiner ran dental records or fingerprints, we'd know for sure.

No doubt the man we were facing would've loved to have stayed upstairs in Scott's house, with a shower and a satellite TV. But he probably hadn't counted on the locked generator keeping the alarm system running. "So," I said, doing my best to sound casual. "You're Stanley."

Stanley pumped the shotgun. The sound rang through the iced-over yard like a snapping tree branch. He aimed at me. "And you're living in my house."

Anton had gone his whole life without ever seeing a corpse? I'd gone mine without ever having a shotgun pointed at my head. My hands rose of their own accord, as if to say, *You wouldn't shoot an unarmed man, would you?* "Hey, look, it's just a job, okay? You want it back, you got it."

"Just a job." He laughed, an ugly little bark. "Edgar have one of his 'accidents' yet? How'd you like cleaning that up?"

Anton grabbed Stanley's elbow. "Don't point that thing at Ray."

Stanley yanked his arm free. I watched the shotgun barrel leap, and I wondered just how sensitive the trigger was. "You know how long I give Edgar?" he said. "A year, if that. Once old guys start losing it, they slide, fast. And his wife never had kids, never had a job. All she had was him. So my guess is, once he's gone, she's not far behind."

Was there some way to un-pump a shotgun? I didn't know. I'd never touched one, myself. "Why don't you just put that thing down...?"

"That property, that car, all that fucking money. And no kids. Think about it. No kids."

"Put the gun down," I repeated. I sounded a lot calmer than I felt.

Anton made another grab for it, and the barrel swung wildly as Stanley pulled free. "Seriously, Anton, I *will* pistol-whip your crazy ass with this thing if you don't back off."

Anton did back up a few steps, but Stanley couldn't see the look on his face and keep an eye on me at the same time. If he had seen Anton's eyes go hard, I'm betting that I'm not the one he'd currently be aiming at. "You know who gets it all when they croak? Marnie." Stanley's voice shook. "I saw the will. They left everything to their fucking cook."

Anton reached into his overcoat.

I shook my head slowly, hoping that he would understand I meant for him not to do anything stupid. I think he got it. He paused.

"Maybe she'd been there longer than me, but so what? Who was the one covered in the old man's shit? Me. I deserved to be on that will, not her. So finally one day I'd had enough, and I told the old lady, right to her face — and what does she do? She fires me. And then that fat tub Gene came along, and within a month they'd called the lawyer, written him into the will."

"I'm not in anyone's will," I said. "I'm just the driver."

Stanley hefted the shotgun and peered through the sight. "I saw you walking in the yard with Edgar. You're already in tight with them. It's only a matter of time…" His finger squeezed the trigger, but Anton was quicker than he was. A long blade flashed as Stanley fired, and the shot went wide.

Most of the pellets that would've knocked a hole in my skull blew past my shoulder, but a few of them clipped me, and between the force of the shot and the ice beneath my shoes, I went down. My ears rang, and my whole arm was numb, but I pried myself off the ground.

Anton and Stanley were down too. They grappled. A dark red trail of blood marked the frosted grass where they rolled. They struggled, and brighter red appeared — the vodka label, nested in a spray of glass shards that were nearly impossible to distinguish among the ice. I hoped the blood was all Stanley's.

Anton landed on top, probably because Stanley stopped struggling when the bowie knife was pressed into his throat. "I always thought you could be a real prick sometimes," said Anton, "but there was no one else around here to hang out with."

Stanley moved to sit up.

"I wouldn't, if I were you," said Anton. "Don't think my 'crazy ass' wouldn't love to cut you again."

"You wouldn't."

"You so sure about that?"

"Come on, man... I think you really hurt me."

He sounded hurt, but I watched his hands tense and scrabble on the ground for a shard of glass he could use as a weapon. Anton was more difficult to read, but there was something in the set of his shoulders that made me think Stanley had appealed to his sympathy, and he was just about to cave in.

I crawled toward them and grabbed the shotgun. It was heavy, and it stank like a roll of caps that had just gotten a brick dropped on it. I knelt, held the stock, and pulled the pump. A spent casing popped out — the thing was huge — and another clunked into place. I staggered to my feet just as Stanley pulled an arm free and raised a shard of glass.

"Don't move." I leveled the muzzle at Stanley's eyes. The shotgun was a lot heavier than I thought it would be, but I didn't waver. My hands were steady...twenty-years-of-training steady. "Anton might not want to hurt you," I said, my voice low and cold, "but just give me a reason."

I held that damn gun until my arms ached, while Anton wrapped Stanley's arms together, then cut the twine from the ball with his bloody knife. The knife had glanced off Stanley's shoulder blade. The wound wasn't life threatening, but it bled a lot and probably hurt like a bitch.

"Is it going to hurt?" Anton asked me.

"I think you'll be able to handle it." I ran my fingers down the length of his bare thigh. I wanted to follow with my tongue, but it wouldn't be sanitary, nor would it be very professional of me. Not while the other artists and their customers were around, anyway.

The design he'd drawn on himself was strange, not exactly geometric, but not curvilinear either. "Are these supposed to be feathers?"

"Inspired by feathers. Or maybe ferns."

The proportion and flow were perfect. "How do you want them — solid? Shaded?"

"You're the pro. Collaborate with me."

I was the pro. Being with Anton, seeing him shift into his "zone" where nothing mattered but the things he created, made me realize that I might not miss owning a business, but I sorely missed doing tattoos. By the next time Mrs. White and I squared off again about hiring a nurse, I'd heard that Mad Dog Martin had an empty chair in his shop, and the choice seemed obvious.

I imagined Anton's design in delicate shades of gray, ephemeral, disappearing and reappearing as his quads flexed. I ran my hand down his leg again and pictured the design in vivid color, reds and yellows with intricate black outlines.

I glanced at his face. He lay on his stomach, hair spilling over his forearms, watching me, smiling. Pale skin, dark hair, dark eyes. I decided to go with black lines. Bold, like him.

I picked up the gauze in my left hand and the gun in my right and brushed the side of my hand over his thigh one more time. So smooth, even through the latex glove. "You only needed to shave the part I'm inking."

"Just being thorough."

I wondered how far up he'd shaved. His legs? His pubes? His whole body? It would itch like hell when it came back in, but for the next few days it would feel incredibly silky. I had no doubt that had been his intention. He was forever finding new ways to blow my mind. "You got any plans later?"

"Maybe."

I glanced at him. He was still watching me. Still smiling.

"Am I included in these plans?" I asked.

"Stop acting like you don't know what day it is."

"Sunday?"

Anton rolled his eyes and settled his head on his arm.

"I thought you didn't keep track of what day it was," I said.

"You've got a schedule. So it behooves me to know when I might have a shot at keeping you up all night."

"Maybe now you'll have some sympathy for my customers," I said. I spread my gloved fingers over his thigh. "Here goes." I inked a short line first, in case Anton turned out to be a flincher. He made a small noise in his throat, but he held still. A few drops of bloody ink oozed from the line. I dabbed it and inked another line.

"You really don't know?" he said. His voice was muffled by his sleeve.

"Hm?"

"Today. We've been together for six months. Half a year. An entire lifetime, to a dragonfly."

I inked a longer line, a graceful arc. I dabbed. "No — six months ago, we met. You didn't even touch me until two days later."

Anton considered that idea while the tattoo gun buzzed. I inked and blotted, inked and blotted, and a design began to take shape along the side of his thigh.

"Physically," he said, finally. "But mentally? I'd had you at least a hundred times by then."

"That's not a relationship. That's masturbation."

"I guess we'll have to agree to disagree."

We agreed to disagree a lot, usually over things much more serious than the official date of the start of our relationship. I was fine with it. I'd been with enough guys who were happy to lie to my face, then go behind my back and do the exact opposite of what they'd promised. I felt a lot safer with someone who had the balls to say what he meant. I ran my hand down Anton's leg again. He was pretty easy on the eyes too.

"And besides," he said, once he'd thought about it for a while. "If you're willing to shift some of your appointments around, we can celebrate through Wednesday, and then we'll both be right."

"Think so?" There were no appointments to shift. I hadn't set any, since I'd been hoping we could spend some time together, just the two of us. I didn't book myself solid anymore like I used to, and I'd grown accustomed to having some free time in my schedule, especially since I now had someone interesting to spend it with. Even if he sometimes stretched the boundaries of the word *interesting*. "You'll probably be climbing the walls by Wednesday."

"If we stay at your place, yeah. I was thinking something like...road trip."

"Like the time you called me from the U-P with no money and an empty gas tank?"

"Um...not exactly. You can ration the gas money." Diane had seen fit to entrust Anton with a car, most likely to shut me up, because I can be a world-class nag when I set my mind to it. When I also cross my arms and give the "thug glare," as Anton calls it, I tend to get my way. Since I'd engineered Project Mobile Anton, I figured it was my responsibility to answer the occasional SOS. It was better than having him rely on me to get him off that island when he felt like stretching his legs. But that didn't mean I wouldn't tease him about it relentlessly.

I finished Anton's outline and stepped back for a look. I saw where the lines needed to be heavier and where I should shade. It was a sweet piece; we collaborated well.

"You want to see it so far?" I asked him.

"How close are we?"

"Another three, four hours of shading; then touch-ups once it's healed."

Anton settled his head on his crossed forearms. His glossy black hair trailed on the tabletop, and he watched me with one eye, its corner creased from him smiling. "Go for it, Ray of Moonlight. I don't need to see it. I trust you."

About the Authors

Over the past decade, multi-award-winning author JOSH LANYON has written numerous novels, novellas and short stories as well as the definitive M/M writing guide *Man, Oh Man: Writing M/M Fiction for Kinks and Ca$h*. He is the author of the Adrien English mystery novels, including *The Hell You Say*, winner of the 2006 USABookNews awards for GLBT fiction, and co-writer of the Crime and Cocktails series with Laura Baumbach. Josh is a Lambda Literary Award finalist.

You can find Josh on the internet at:
http://www.joshlanyon.com/
http://jgraeme2007.livejournal.com/
http://groups.yahoo.com/group/JoshLanyon

JORDAN CASTILLO PRICE grew up in the steel mill warrens of Buffalo NY, spent some formative drinking years in Chicago, and migrated north to small-town rural Wisconsin once she realized she was going to kill the next person who bumped into her with a shopping cart. She did a six-year stint in art school and played bass in a punk band that crashed and burned just before their first CD was pressed.

Links to Jordan's newsletters, freebies, snippets, and peeks into the writing process can be found at:
http://www.jordancastilloprice.com/

THE TREVOR PROJECT

The Trevor Project operates the only nationwide, around-the-clock crisis and suicide prevention helpline for lesbian, gay, bisexual, transgender and questioning youth. Every day, The Trevor Project saves lives though its free and confidential helpline, its website and its educational services. If you or a friend are feeling lost or alone call The Trevor Helpline. If you or a friend are feeling lost, alone, confused or in crisis, please call The Trevor Helpline. You'll be able to speak confidentially with a trained counselor 24/7.

The Trevor Helpline: 866-488-7386
On the Web: http://www.thetrevorproject.org/

THE GAY MEN'S DOMESTIC VIOLENCE PROJECT

Founded in 1994, The Gay Men's Domestic Violence Project is a grassroots, non-profit organization founded by a gay male survivor of domestic violence and developed through the strength, contributions and participation of the community. The Gay Men's Domestic Violence Project supports victims and survivors through education, advocacy and direct services. Understanding that the serious public health issue of domestic violence is not gender specific, we serve men in relationships with men, regardless of how they identify, and stand ready to assist them in navigating through abusive relationships.

GMDVP Helpline: 800.832.1901
On the Web: http://gmdvp.org/

THE GAY & LESBIAN ALLIANCE AGAINST DEFAMATION/GLAAD EN ESPAÑOL

The Gay & Lesbian Alliance Against Defamation (GLAAD) is dedicated to promoting and ensuring fair, accurate and inclusive representation of people and events in the media as a means of eliminating homophobia and discrimination based on gender identity and sexual orientation.

On the Web: http://www.glaad.org/
GLAAD en español:
           http://www.glaad.org/espanol/bienvenido.php

Printed in the United States
217125BV00001B/2/P